Somebody's Knockin'

Catherine Boyd

Copyright 2018 by Catherine Boyd

Chapter 1

The room was darkened, at her request. She was tired now, the ordeal of giving birth much more taxing than she had supposed. Oh, she had heard it wasn't fun, but the reality of the process was nothing like she had imagined. She had promised herself she was not going to scream when the birth pains hit, but in the end she couldn't control herself, and she joined the innumerable women over the centuries who had cried out in the pain of childbirth.

It was all over now—the birth, the pain, and the guilt. She had done it. She had delivered a healthy baby and her parents would never learn of her deception. They would never suspect they were the grandparents of a beautiful blonde-haired granddaughter, and she wouldn't have to suffer the despair of seeing the disappointment in their eyes when they looked at their daughter. She turned over onto her side, surrendering to her emotional and physical fatigue, and settled quickly, dreamlessly, into sleep, a soft smile playing at the corners of her full lips.

Two hours later, Allison Rose Morgan awoke to her new reality, totally unprepared for the emotions bombarding her. Expecting to feel relieved and contented, Allie found herself crying silent tears. Deep in her soul, a despair she had never known before for some reason had taken up residence. It surprised her.

She rested quietly in the bed, in the dark, quiet room, listening to the sounds of soft footsteps and laughter that echoed in the hallway just outside of her door. She heard the occasional light knock as relatives arrived to lavish affection on new members of their families. Babies. Everyone on the floor was a new mother. Every room welcomed a new infant; every room but hers.

This was what she had wanted, though, wasn't it? This was the whole reason she had moved to Bozeman and started a new job. She was happy she had pulled it off, wasn't she? No one would ever know of her shame. She was not going to be one of those single mothers people whispered about. She was not going to have to work two jobs just to feed her child. She was free to lead her life the way she wanted from now on, without having to consider anyone else. She was free! She had chosen not to see her baby, nor to hold her for even a second. It was better that way, she knew. Better not to risk any possibility of bonding with her. Keep the separation sharp, clean, final.

She was empty, unbelievably empty. That seemed to be the only word for it. It was as if she had lost a special part of herself that she hadn't even known existed. What was wrong with her? She had secured a wonderful home for her daughter, and even knew who the new parents were. She had met them months ago in Billings. They were really nice people who would give her baby everything she couldn't, or wouldn't. Raven and Gus Whittacker could never have children of their own due to Raven's accident two years ago, and they were thrilled at the chance to adopt her baby. She smiled to herself. *Yes, Allie girl, you did the right thing, you know you did. So why the long face now?*

She purposefully shoved that empty feeling to the back of her mind, determined to be happy. She would be getting her life back once more. Everything was going to be just fine.

Her milk began to come in several hours later, and she was uncomfortable. The nurse brought her some medication to help dry her up, but it did nothing to stop the emotional roller coaster she now found herself riding. What on earth was wrong with her? She should be happy, darn it.

Dave had stayed with her throughout the night, and she was thankful for that, but it was Sunday now, and he had a sermon to preach at the church so he couldn't stay any longer. He had been very attentive during the worst of her labor, but as soon as it was over and the baby given to the new parents, Dave had left her. It would have been nice if he had stayed, but he was only a good friend. He was not family and not the father of her baby. She found herself wishing that he would come back. She wanted him, well, someone, to just hold her hand for a while and tell her it was all going to be okay. Someone. Anyone. She wanted to be alone. She wanted to not be alone. She was unbelievably, monumentally, sad.

It wasn't long before self-pity permeated her entire being. She could still hear joyous laughter coming from the hallway just outside of her door. Around five-thirty she heard the cart carrying the dinner trays rattling its way down the tile floor outside her room. She was ravenous, but to her surprise she found herself refusing her tray when the kitchen staff offered it to her. Suddenly the aroma of food sickened her. As the sun set, her room became even darker, and she began to wallow in the blackness. She was alone. No one was coming to see Allie Morgan. She imagined the nurses talking about the girl down the hall who had callously given her baby away that morning. What kind of woman gave her baby away? How could she do that, anyway? And it did not go unnoticed that she had no visitors since giving birth. Unwanted. Unloved. Unworthy.

Tears seeped, warm and unnoticed, from beneath her lids. What on earth was wrong with her? She had, in fact, done the right thing, the correct thing. Her life was now exactly the way she wanted, wasn't it? But no one came to see her. No one brought her flowers or receiving blankets or diapers. No one came at all.

Pastor Dave Benson returned to the hospital around eight-thirty that evening, after the evening service concluded. She heard the tentative knock on her door and turned toward the sound. It wasn't a nurse; by now she could identify them all by their unique individual knocks. She waited, not calling out an invitation to enter. Hopefully it wasn't some "do- gooder" wanting to lecture her about what she had done. A social worker had already stopped by earlier. Allie had promptly asked her to leave.

Dave Benson pushed the door open and poked his head into the dark room. "Allie, are you awake?" The words were soft, nearly a whisper.

"Dave? Is that you?" A smile instantly lit up her face. Someone had come to see her after all. Her friend Dave had not given up on her.

"In the flesh. You were expecting someone else?"

"No, I just didn't expect you'd come back today. After you left this morning, I just, well, I figured you were busy with church stuff and that I wouldn't see you again for a few days."

"Want me to leave and come back tomorrow then?"

"No, silly, don't go. I'm glad you're here."

"OK if I turn on the light? It's pretty dark in here, isn't it? Depressing!" He didn't wait for her to answer and switched the overhead light on even as he spoke.

"Well, since it's on now, I guess it's OK."

"Why were you just lying here in the dark? Are you that tired? It's a little early for sleep, don't you think?" He walked over to her bed, one hand behind his back.

"I just prefer being in the dark, that's all. But now that you're here, the light's okay. Thanks for coming."

Without warning, Dave bent over Allie and planted a soft kiss on her forehead. "A small reward for the new mother who was courageous enough to give her baby the chance for a bright future. And here, for you." His hand came out from behind his back, and he held a small plant out to her.

Allie had always been a popular girl with men, and she was seldom without a man in her life. Kisses were plentiful and always welcome, but she couldn't remember anyone kissing her as Dave had just done, gently, on her forehead. Fresh tears shimmered in her lovely blue eyes. Her friend Dave had surprised her with his unexpected kindness.

"Oh! I don't know, well, thank you. I wasn't expecting . . ."

"The plant or the kiss?" He smiled at her.

"Neither the plant nor the kiss."

"I didn't do something out of line, did I? You just looked like you needed that, and I figured it was something even I could handle. And everyone on this floor has a plant or a bouquet or something, so I thought you shouldn't be the only one that didn't."

"No, you didn't do anything you shouldn't. You just surprised me, that's all." She lowered her eyes. "It was nice. Thanks."

"Think nothing of it." He stood awkwardly at her bedside, seeming unsure just what to do next. "Shall I put the plant over by the window?" He reached out to take it from her.

"That would be fine. What kind of plant is it, anyway? It looks almost like a Christmas cactus, but it sure isn't Christmas! It's spring now."

He smiled sheepishly at her, and then turned to put the plant on the windowsill. "Actually, it is a Christmas cactus. They were on sale, and I confess I'm kind of cheap. But it's the thought that counts, isn't it? It's still a plant!"

She laughed, a light-hearted, clear laugh, her misery forgotten for the moment with her friend's arrival. She patted the bed at her side.

"Come sit with me for a moment, will you? You always seem to know just how to brighten my day." Her smile remained.

"I can't stay long. Sorry. It's been a long day, you know?" He sat next to her on the bed, taking her hands in his, gently stroking the backs of them with his thumbs.

"We did it, didn't we, Dave? We pulled it off."

"You pulled it off, not 'we.' You're the one that did all the work, remember?"

"You're the one that stood by me through this whole thing. You suggested that I move to Bozeman where no one knew me. You found parents for my baby. Most importantly, you remained my friend. Whenever I called, you came. I can't thank you enough for all of that." She sighed heavily, and then smiled warmly once more.

"You know, if someone had told me years ago that my best friend would be a preacher I would have called them a liar! Do you know how nuts this is? Me, friends with a preacher?"

Dave threw his head back and laughed out loud.

"You think that's funny, don't you? Well, it's not. Not really. I haven't met many pastors in my life, and I can assure you I never made friends with any before you. It still amazes me that you've been so kind to me. I think most pastors would have tried to make me keep my baby and marry the father. They definitely would have judged me, I know, but you never have. Well, at least as far as I know, you haven't. You sure never said anything negative, and you have most definitely been very supportive. So, thank you, my friend. How will I ever pay you back?"

"Seeing you smile is all the payment I need, Allie. If you're happy, I'm happy." He turned his head away from her. "You are happy, right? You're not regretting your decision, are you?"

She was quiet for a moment. "No. I can't say that I'm ecstatically happy, like bouncing off the walls with joy happy, but I don't regret what I've done. If I had kept her, my parents would have disowned me. I know that. And as a single mother I could never give her what Raven and Gus can. But...."

"But what?"

"I don't know. It's hard, Dave. It's a lot harder than I thought it would be. I can't explain it, can't put it into words for you. But I'm different. Like something is a little off somehow."

"That's because something is a little off, as you say. You just had a baby, Allie. It would be weird if you were totally unaffected by the whole thing. But you do understand it is all over and done with, right? It's too late now to change your mind."

"Oh, I know, and I really don't want to change my mind. I know it was the right thing to do, and I know I would do the same thing if I had it all to do over again." She grinned up at him. "Except maybe I'd be a little more careful and not get pregnant in the first place."

"There is only one sure way to avoid the occurrence and we both know what that is."

"Total abstinence? Right. Well, I won't be taking any chances anytime soon, you can rest assured of that. Besides, the only man in my life right now is you, so go figure. I'm pretty sure you're not interested in being my boyfriend, so there's not much to worry about."

She failed to notice the pained expression that appeared on Dave's face with these words. He made no audible reply.

"Dave?" She finally noticed the silence.

"Let's talk about something else, shall we? I think we've pretty well covered this subject. When are you getting out of here? Have they told you?"

"Tomorrow morning, the way I understand it." "Are you going back to Joe's then?"

"Yes, I'll go back to my room there, but the other caregiver the family hired will continue working for another week. Then it's back to the grind for me."

"Okay then. Need a ride in the morning?"

"Do you mind? Do you have time?"

"Anything for you, my girl. I'll make time. When should I come?"

"How about I call you as soon as I'm set free? That way you won't have to wait on me."

"Sounds good. See you tomorrow morning then." He rose to leave. "Take care, Allie.

See you."

"Yeah, see you." She turned her face toward the window as Dave walked out, closing the door softly behind him.

He made it three whole steps down the hall before stopping to lean against the wall for support. His head in his hands, he sank slowly to his haunches, his breaths coming deep and labored.

A nurse saw him in this position and stopped to see if he was all right. She put her hand gently on the man's shoulder and squatted next to him.

"Were you here to see Allie?"

"Yes."

"Are you by any chance the fa . . . ?"

He looked up at that, and then rose quickly, smoothly, to his feet. "Thank you for your concern, but I'm fine, really. And no, I'm not the father. I'm her pastor." He turned and walked away.

The nurse stared after him, still concerned at the look she had seen on his face, and then took the few steps to Allie's room. It was time for her hourly uterine massage again. She didn't mention the man she had seen in the hall.

Chapter 2

Pastor Dave Benson was shaken by the nurse's assumption that he was the father of Allie's baby, but he supposed it was natural that someone might ascribe that role to him. He was wearing regular street clothes: leather jacket, jeans, and boots. He certainly didn't look like a pastor; with dark wavy hair, bright blue eyes, and clean features he could have been a model. He was her sole emotional support at the moment, and had been for the past several months. It was a role he was all too happy to fill. It was also a role he knew he shouldn't fill. He was a pastor, and he was in love with Allie Morgan. God help him, he was hopelessly in love with the woman.

He had fallen for the girl after meeting her for the second time in Billings when she had come to see his good friend and recovering addict, Aspen Windchase. Allie had been pregnant and had done her best to convince Pen the baby was his, trying hard to corner him into marrying her. Pen had refused, positive the baby was not his despite what looked like strong evidence to the contrary. Dave had been staying with Pen during his withdrawal period, and Allie had been a total but very pleasant surprise. It had essentially been the proverbial "love at first sight" for him, and he had found himself creating opportunities to be with her ever since.

He was well aware that she thought of him only as a very good friend. Right now he supposed he was her only friend. He understood how she felt all too well. He was nearly twenty years her senior, and he was a pastor. One of those "men of God" people that often made others uncomfortable to be around. Allie hadn't seemed to care one way or the other, and had seen him only as a friend. When he helped her find a good home for her expected baby, her gratitude had sealed the deal, and she accepted all the help he was only too willing to give.

And now, here he was, still making any excuse he could think of to be around her. It seemed that even after all these months she still had no idea how he really felt about her. Was he happy or relieved about that? He had no idea. It was probably safer this way, but that didn't ease his pain. He felt trapped and hopeless. He could see no positive ending for this relationship, and yet, he couldn't leave her.

On the other hand, he reasoned, why should he have to leave her? They were both single adults, and neither of them had ever been married, so what was really the problem here? Why couldn't he love Allie? Why wouldn't it be okay? Why indeed . . . He could reason with himself and with God from now until doomsday but it wouldn't change the facts, and the facts were that she was the wrong woman for him. An unwed mother who had given her baby away and was not a Christian was definitely not an appropriate candidate for a pastor's wife. On top of that, he was old enough to be her father! Those were the facts, and those facts could not be changed any more than he could walk away from her. He clung stubbornly to the one thing that could be changed—she could become a Christian.

There was a country song made popular several years ago by Terri Gibbs entitled "Somebody's Knockin." He found himself often humming the words in his head:

*"Somebody's knockin'
Should I let him in?
Lord it's the devil
Would you look at him?
I've heard about him
But I never dreamed
He'd have blue eyes and blue jeans . . ."*

Allie was the female counterpart to the man in the song. He knew it. He never dreamed the devil would have blue eyes and be wearing blue jeans. He never dreamed the devil could be a woman. He loved her.

Oh, he had prayed long and hard about the whole thing, but it was no use. The Bible said that God always provided a way of escape from overwhelming temptation, but he guessed that in his case he simply was not strong enough to look for that way out. Not strong enough or just not willing? He couldn't imagine his life without her in it anymore. Just the thought of that possibility terrified him.

And yet, what was he going to do? What plans did he have? What did he see happening between them? He really had no idea. He only knew that it was all impossible. He was a Christian. She was not.

Well, she could become one. Anyone could. That was his "out." In the meantime, he needed some sleep. He would keep the phone close, waiting for her call; it couldn't come soon enough.

The phone rang at ten forty-three the next morning. He had been counting the minutes as he always did when he was expecting a call from her. The smile that lit his face disappeared when he heard the voice on the other end. It wasn't Allie.

"Dave?"

"Yes?"

"Dave, it's Gus. I just wanted you to know, again, how much Raven and I appreciate all you've done for us. Catherine is a true gift from God, and we love her so much already. Remember we love you as a brother, and we thank you." Gus's joy echoed in his voice.

"Well, you're most welcome. I know we couldn't have found a better home for that little girl than you and Raven." He meant it.

"Do me a favor, will you?"

"Sure, anything. How can I help you?"

"Well, we thought about writing a note to Allie, thanking her, but on second thought, we decided that was probably not a wise thing to do. Would you please let her know, somehow, however you think is best to do it, that we do truly thank her, we will be praying daily that better days are ahead for her, and that she will have total peace about this whole thing. I think you know what I'm trying to say here. You don't mind, do you? I'm assuming you'll be seeing her again, won't you?"

"I'm heading out shortly to bring her home from the hospital. I'm just waiting for her call to let me know she's ready. So yes, I'll be sure to let her know you called."

"Thanks, Dave. We both appreciate it."

"No problem. You and Raven have a great week and I'll see you next Sunday. Take care." He hung up the phone and began slowly pacing the floor, waiting for the phone to ring again. It was nearly thirty minutes before Allie called to say she was ready. He was out of the door in seconds.

He arrived at the hospital in less than half an hour. Clean-shaven, fresh from a morning shower, he felt like a teenager picking up his date for the prom. His heart began to pound as it always did when he knew he was going to see her. Taking a deep breath, he walked in the front door and up to her room.

Knocking softly, he waited for her to invite him in before entering.

"Hi."

"Hi yourself."

"Ready?"

"As ready as I'll ever be, I guess. Thanks for coming, Dave. I really don't know anyone else I could call besides you. I could have called a taxi, I guess."

"Then let's get you out of here, what do you say? And I don't ever want to hear you talk about calling a cab again. You just call me, got it?"

"Got it." She smiled broadly at him, pleasure written all over her face. He was, after all, a very handsome man in spite of the fact that he was a preacher and so much older. She pushed the call button for the nurse.

"Rules. They have to take me out in a wheelchair, so we need to wait for the nurse to come with my ride. Have a seat while we wait. I already went over the discharge papers and instructions, so we just need the escort. Shouldn't be long." She patted the bed beside her. "Sit with me while we wait?"

He didn't need to be asked twice. Staying as professional as he could, he sat next to her, maintaining a respectable distance between them.

A volunteer arrived within minutes pushing an empty wheelchair. "Your chariot has arrived, my dear. Ready?"

"Ready. Let's go!" She settled herself in the chair, her belongings on her lap.

Dave carried the Christmas cactus he had brought her the day before and followed them down to the main desk. Leaving the plant with Allie, he went to get his pickup.

After settling Allie safely in the passenger seat, they left the hospital. Dave drove slowly, unconsciously lengthening the time he would get to spend with her, taking the longest route he could come up with to her house. Pulling up to a stop sign, he looked over at her.

"Hey Allie, are you hungry? I sure am. How about some lunch before you go home? You up for it?" He held his breath, hoping.

15

"You know, that actually sounds good to me. You know what they say about hospital food, and, frankly, I haven't had much of an appetite since, well, anyway, yeah, lunch. Thanks for asking."

He exhaled softly, and began to breathe normally once more. Good. He could buy at least another hour with her. *Thank you, Lord. Right or wrong, thank you.* He wasn't sure God really had anything to do with her agreeing to have lunch with him, but he was thankful anyway.

"You know, if you're not in a big hurry to get back, it's a beautiful day. How do you feel about driving to Livingston? We could eat at the Stockman? Or if you prefer we could just go down to the Bacchus. What's your pleasure, woman?" He suspected she liked it when he called her "woman."

"You know, I actually don't want to go home anytime soon. If you really don't mind, I think I'd like to go to Livingston. You're right, it is a beautiful day and you're pretty fair company."

"Livingston it is, then." He headed out of town on the Interstate, driving well under the speed limit.

They chatted companionably all the way to the Stockman. By the time they got there, the lunch crowd had pretty much dissipated, and they had the restaurant mostly to themselves. They sat in a corner, ordered lunch, and enjoyed the afternoon, talking about everything and nothing. The fact that she had just given birth was never mentioned, nor was the baby.

Finally, Dave felt he could no longer put off telling her about Gus's call that morning.

He would have preferred not to mention it at all, but he had told Gus he would pass on his message, and he would keep his word.

Allie's face paled as he relayed the conversation and Gus's wishes for her. To her credit her eyes did not tear up, but it was obvious the topic had upset her. He was sorry about that, although he supposed it would be abnormal if she didn't react in some way. But the baby was the proverbial "elephant in the room," and not talking about her didn't render her nonexistent. Looking at Allie's pale face and her obvious effort to control her emotions, his heart clenched in empathy.

"I'm sorry to bring the subject up, Allie, but they really want you to know how thankful they are for the wonderful gift you have given them." He reached over to clasp one of her hands in his large grip in an attempt to comfort her in some small way, and gave it a light squeeze, then abruptly changed the subject.

"Ready to head back?"

She nodded silently. Withdrawing her hand from his grasp, she stood up slowly and headed for the exit. She didn't look back.

Dave followed close behind her, slowing only long enough to pay the check. He had obviously upset her by bringing up the baby, but he hadn't had much choice in the matter. Besides, in all fairness, she had just given birth, and she had, in fact, given her baby away. Life was full of difficult choices for everyone. She had made the right choice.

She seemed to have recovered by the time they got to the pickup. Dave smiled as he opened the door for her.

"Okay?"

"Yeah, I'm fine." She smiled back at him.

"Ready to head back then?"

"I suppose, but . . ."

"But what?"

"Well, do you have time to drive up to Clyde Park and take the drive through the Bridger's back to Bozeman instead of going back on the Interstate? It's such a beautiful day and that's a pretty drive."

He could have hugged her for that suggestion! It would take nearly an hour longer to get her back to Bozeman if they went that route. He tried to keep his voice calm and under control.

"Sounds like a great idea, Allie. I've got plenty of time and the sun is shining. Let's go."

"Thanks."

They pulled out of Livingston and headed north on Highway 89 toward Clyde Park. Conversation flowed easily and the time seemed to pass all too quickly for both of them. The smile never left his face until he dropped Allie off at her client's house where she was living, and even then his mood remained elevated. Driving away from the house he felt as if he was leaving a part of himself behind with her, and that really scared him, but it wasn't until he arrived home that his "withdrawal symptoms" set in.

He knew in his heart that Christ should be enough to satisfy him at all times, and He had been until he met Allie. It was okay to love a woman, but it was not okay to be obsessed with one, and Pastor Dave Benson was nothing if not obsessed with Allie Morgan.

Somehow, some way, he knew he had to overcome this obsession, but he had absolutely no idea how he was going to accomplish that. He had not yet totally succumbed to his feelings, and still held out a small ray of hope for himself; it got smaller every time he saw her.

Relaxing in his favorite easy chair that evening, he found himself replaying every moment of the time spent with Allie that day. He remembered the kiss he had planted ever so gently on her forehead the day before, and kicked himself for his stupidity. Thankfully, Allie had not mentioned it today, and he hoped she had forgotten about it. He had done it on the spur of the moment, and had regretted it immediately, but of course the act could not be undone, not that he really wanted it undone. He had done it because he wanted to. He wanted to do so much more than that! But he realized that he should have more control over himself. Tomorrow. Tomorrow he would do better.

But in the morning his thoughts were consumed with ways to see her again. He usually started preparing his sermons on Monday mornings, but yesterday he had spent all day with Allie. Instead of starting a day late on his next sermon, he found himself going over all sorts of scenarios that would allow him to legitimately spend time with her. What pretense could he come up with? What excuses could be made to see her that wouldn't sound too obvious? At least as long as she wasn't aware of his feelings and it remained one-sided, there was a chance that he would eventually come to his senses, realize there was no hope for a relationship with her, and his life could get back to normal. *Fat chance!*

On Wednesday he finally began working on that sermon he should have started on Monday. While Allie was never far from his thoughts, he refrained from calling her on any pretense. He was dismayed to realize that the old adage "absence makes the heart grow fonder" seemed all too true in his case. He was miserable.

On Friday Allie called him. He was out doing visitations and missed the call. When he saw the blinking light on his answering machine, he waited until he had fixed himself a cup of coffee before checking his messages. His heart literally skipped a beat when he heard her voice on the recording.

"Hi, Dave. Nothing important on this end, so you don't need to call me back. I just wanted to say hi and thanks again for making time for me Monday. It turned out to be a nice day. Have a good weekend. Bye."

He very nearly cursed to himself. She had called him and he had missed it! And she left no opening for him to return her call. Of course, he could call her anyway with some lame excuse, but he mustered all his willpower and held out. Maybe it was a first step in removing her from his life. One could hope.

He made it through the weekend, but caved on Tuesday morning. He called her.

"Allie?"

"Yes? Oh, hi Dave."

"Sorry I missed your call the other day. You said it wasn't important so I didn't call you back. It wasn't, right? Important, I mean."

She laughed. "No, it wasn't important. I was feeling a little lonely and you're always so easy to talk to, I was just hoping to kill a little time chatting."

They fell into their normal relaxed, easy conversation and then Dave, unable to help himself, broke his own rule. He asked her out.

"Say, Allie, if you're free, how about lunch again sometime this week?" He had no idea he was holding his breath as he waited for her answer.

"Sorry, I'm kind of busy this week, but thanks for the invite." His hands began shaking uncontrollably at her rejection.

"Oh, well, that's fine. Just thought you might be wanting a little company."

"Well, I'm tied up this week with appointments, but if you have time one day next week, I'd love to have lunch with you."

Relief surged through him, making him weak. He had to sit down before he fell down.

"Sure, that would be fine. I'll call you Monday and we can set the day and time if that's all right with you?"

"I'll wait for you to call me then. Thanks for asking. I always have a good time with you, even if you are a little old and a preacher besides."

He could hear the smile in her voice, but he was personally devastated. She obviously had no idea how he felt about her, or how deeply her comments pierced. Well, at least she had agreed to have lunch with him one more time.

He caught up with her on Monday, and they planned lunch together on Wednesday. He had church service at six that evening, so it would not be a long lunch, but he was happy; he was going to see her.

She met him at the designated café with her strawberry blonde hair loose, swirling around her face, her complexion glowing, wearing tight blue jeans and a light blue shirt. Every man in the café was staring.

> *"I've heard about her But I never dreamed –*
> *She'd have blue eyes and blue jeans . . ."*

Chapter 3

Allie felt back on top of the world once again, finally. It had been a month since she had given birth, and now it all seemed like some sort of dream. It was spring and the weather was beautiful, she had her figure back, she had a job, and her friend Dave was never more than a phone call away if she needed anything. Her hair shone and her face glowed with her youth and health. What she didn't have was a plan.

Dave had helped her find a job when she moved to Bozeman from Billings. One of his parishioners was looking for live-in help to stay with his elderly father. Joe Manning was ninety-two years young and basically independent, but needed help with meals, cleaning, etc. Allie was perfect for the position, and gratefully accepted the job. She made a decent wage and there was ample room in Joe's house for her to live comfortably. She soon became close friends with her client who was not at all senile; he loved good conversation and clean jokes. A strong Christian, he spent many of his waking hours in Bible reading and study. The family had hired part-time day help for three weeks after Allie's hospital stay, but now she was back taking full care of her client, so she had money in her pocket and a bright future ahead of her.

She had absolutely no idea what she wanted to do with her life. Working as a private duty nursing assistant, she wasn't meeting new people, and her loneliness was alleviated only when she spent time with Dave Benson. Thus she found herself calling him more frequently than she might otherwise have done if she had been working in a facility where there was more opportunity for socialization. He didn't seem to mind, however, so it never occurred to her that it was perhaps unfair of her to call him so often. He was old, and he was a preacher. It was all totally safe, as far as she was concerned.

It wasn't long before she was calling him nearly every other day, just to have another grown-up to talk to. They had lunch together at least once a week, and it was always an enjoyable time for them both. She rarely thought about her little girl, and when she did, it was for only a fleeting moment. That whole experience had happened to someone else, not her. It was as if it had all been a dream, unreal. She was awake now, full of energy, and lonely. She was ready to go back out into the world and meet people. She missed steady male companionship, and while Dave was definitely a man, and a good-looking one at that, she wanted to meet someone closer to her own age, and definitely not a preacher! But where do you go in Bozeman, Montana to meet men? You go to church or to a bar.

She could have gone to a bar on her own, but she was actually uncomfortable with that. It would have been a good way to meet men, but she also realized that it could be a risky venture. She understood very well that men were attracted to her, and sometimes it was way too easy to get mixed up with the wrong type of person. Going to bars alone was simply not very safe, so she didn't. But she was lonely. She missed having dates and having a steady boyfriend. She missed going out to dinner, movies, acting silly at times, and enjoying the freedom her looks and youth afforded her.

So one day she called her good friend yet again and asked him to take her out for dinner. She had absolutely no idea what she was doing to Dave; she only knew that he was a safe date and a fun companion. Maybe she would meet someone while she was out with him.

She greeted him at the door with her hair still damp, wearing new indigo jeans and a lacy top. She looked fabulous, and she knew it. If she had any doubt, it was dispelled when she saw the way Dave looked at her as she opened the door for him. His eyes became piercing, shining, and riveting. She smiled broadly at him, secretly pleased with herself. She still had "it."

He took her to the Black Angus on a Thursday evening. Even though Allie had been the one to ask him out, he avowed that it would be his treat, and encouraged her to order anything she wanted on the menu. His eyes seldom left her, devouring her with an obvious hunger.

Allie was more than pleased. Even if it was just Dave, he was still a man, and she relished his obvious pleasure at spending time with a beautiful woman. Her self-confidence fully restored, she began flirting with him, forgetting for the time being that he was a pastor. She had to admit that he wore his years very well. His bright blue eyes and winning smile could charm any woman, whether he knew it or not, and tonight she was just as charmed by him as he seemed to be by her. She was having a very good time.

"Dave, would you mind too much if I had a glass of wine?"

"Whatever you want, Allie. Go ahead, I don't mind."

"Will you have one with me?"

"Allie, I don't know . . . I . . ."

"Oh come on, one glass won't hurt you. You aren't an alcoholic or anything are you?"

"No, it's not that, but I am a pastor, remember? It might not look too good if someone from church sees me with a glass of wine, you know?"

"Oh for heaven's sake, Dave. It's just a glass of wine. Besides, do you see anyone you recognize from church here?"

He looked closely around the room. "No, I don't."

"Then go ahead and have a glass with me. Please? Wine is much more enjoyable when it's shared."

He hesitated only a moment longer, and then nodded his head in assent. "Okay, one glass won't hurt, I guess."

When the wine came, they raised their glasses together in a silent toast, smiling at each other as they began to sip the scarlet beverage. It was so very good to be out in the world again, babies and pregnancies forgotten. She was with a delightful companion who was also very easy on the eyes. It was a good night.

One glass of wine turned into several, and when the evening finally ended they were both feeling very relaxed, Allie quite a bit more so than Dave. As they walked through the parking lot back to his pickup, she found herself leaning into him. He put his arm around her waist for support, and she leaned into him even more. He felt good. Strong. Masculine. Dave was a really good friend.

As he reached around her to open the passenger door, she gave in to the moment and pulled him to her, kissing him soundly on his mouth. He froze instantly in her embrace.

"Allie, I . . ."

"Oh, loosen up, will you, Dave? I'm not hurting you, am I?"

"Well, no, not in the way you think, but . . ."

"But nothing. You taste good, Dave, like the wine we had. It's been so long since I kissed anyone, I guess I wanted to see if I remembered how." She laughed.

"Well, you're doing a fine job, but I'm not sure . . It's been years for me. But Allie, we . . ."

"We what? We aren't doing anything wrong, are we? You're not married and I'm certainly not. Who are we hurting with a simple kiss? A kiss between friends." She put her hand behind his neck and pulled his face down to hers once more. "Let's try it one more time. See if you can put a little feeling into it this time, okay? Try to remember how it's done."

She kissed him once more, putting more of herself into it this time. His response was swift and obvious as he kissed her back, pulling her close to him as he did so.

A kiss between friends? Who was she trying to kid? If that's how friends kissed she figured she had forgotten how lovers kissed. Dave was good, really good. She didn't want to stop!

He finally came up for air, and taking her forearms in his big hands, he pushed her firmly away.

"I think that's probably good enough, don't you?" He had pushed her away but he hadn't let her go.

"Oh, I don't know, I was having a pretty good time there, friend. Want to try it one more time?"

"No, well, yes, I guess I really would, but I don't think it's a very good idea, Allie.

Let's just stop here. I think the wine has gotten to us a little."

"Spoilsport!" She pouted, her lips pursed.

"Yeah, that's me. In you go, girl." He helped her into the pickup, then walked around to the driver's side, started the engine, and headed for Joe's house.

He drove in silence, which finally made Allie a little uncomfortable. She wanted to have fun, darn it, not be escorted home by a silent man old enough to be her father.

"Dave?"

"Yeah?"

"Do you have to take me home right now? Is there some special reason you have to get back right away?"

"Well, I guess nothing demanding. What did you have in mind?"

"Take me dancing?"

"What? Dancing? Are you nuts?"

"I don't see anything crazy about wanting to go dancing, sorry. Oh, maybe preachers don't dance or something. Is that it? You're not supposed to dance?"

"Well, it's not high on our preacher's list of things we should be doing." Dave was not smiling.

"Dave, I haven't been dancing in well over a year and I miss it. I don't know anyone else that will take me, so how about it? Will you?" The wine was causing her speech to slur and her cheeks to flush a delicate pink; Allie was looking very tempting indeed.

Dave was silent for a moment, and then answered, "No, Allie, I don't think so. It's not a good idea, you know? I'm a pastor, remember, and that means I have an image to maintain, so no, I think I'll just be taking you home for now."

Allie glared at him, pouting. Preachers could sometimes be absolutely no fun at all. But this one sure could kiss like a pro!

"Okay, go ahead and take me home. I'll call a cab and go by myself."

"Allie, don't, okay? It's not a good idea, you know?"

"Look Preacher, you do your thing and I'll do mine. Fair enough? You don't want to take me, that's fine. I'll respect your decision, but don't impose your hang-ups on me. Keep them to yourself."

Dave clenched the steering wheel so tightly his knuckles turned white, and driving faster than usual he had her at her front door in minutes.

"Can you see yourself in? I think I should go home and work on my sermon, if that's all right with you."

"Fine with me. Go do your preacher thing." She unbuckled her seat belt, opened the door and got out. She shut the door and then wrenched it open again.

"You sure don't kiss like a preacher, though. Bet you don't dance like one either, do you." It was a statement, not a question.

Dave kept his face averted, looking straight ahead. "Good night, Allie. Maybe I'll see you sometime next week." He drove off into the night.

Dave's emotions were all over the place. What on earth was wrong with him, anyway? He had actually kissed that woman! Worst of all, he had enjoyed it so much he hadn't wanted to stop—ever. If he hadn't needed so desperately to breathe he might still be kissing her. Shaking his head in despair, he pulled over to the side of the street less than a block from where he had dropped her off. He was shaking, as memories of the evening with Allie washed over him. *Lord, help me! I'm sinking deeper and deeper here, and I don't see any way out of this mess.* He buried his face in his hands as his thoughts raced through his brain.

He had no idea how long he sat there, staring at nothing, trying to slow his thinking down so he could get control of himself and go home. He finally reached down to start the pickup again when a flash of light behind him caught his eye. It was the headlights of a vehicle pulling over to the curb a block behind him. The light on top revealed it to be a taxi. Allie must have decided to go dancing after all and had actually called a cab since he had refused to take her.

Not thinking, Dave put the pickup in gear and followed the cab at a discreet distance. He had to know where she was going and what she was going to do. Watching her go without following was not an option.

He followed her to the Mixer's Club on West Aspen, staying carefully out of sight, well behind the cab. His jaw set, he watched as Allie exited the cab, and swinging her strawberry blonde hair behind her, sauntered slowly into the bar. He felt sick to his stomach.

Dave had spent a good share of his younger days in bars just like this one. They were always dark, smoke-filled, and full of lonely people, as he himself used to be. Closing his eyes, memories of hundreds of other bars like this one flooded his brain. When he had been frequenting them, they were his favorite places to hang out with his friends, and with his good looks, winning smile, and outgoing personality, he had no dearth of friends to spend his time with. Late nights filled with whiskey, cigarettes, and women gave meaning to his life then. Eventually, he found heroin when the other vices were no longer enough.

He shook his head slowly from side to side. All of that was another life. After he had been born-again, his new life in Christ had taken him away from all of that, and, committing his life to his Lord, he had become a pastor. He was reformed and renewed, saved by grace. Yet now he was sitting right outside a bar again, a woman driving all thoughts of Jesus out of his mind. He saw only Allie.

Lowering his head so filled now with conflicting emotions, he tried to pray. *Lord, you have to help me! What do I do? I know I need to turn this truck around and drive away, but God, there's Allie! I don't think I have the strength to leave her there alone. What if . . . ?*

He pounded the steering wheel with both fists, fighting with himself. In the end, he turned the key to start the engine, and then slowly drove away toward home. He would leave Allie where she was; there was nothing he could do if this was how she wanted to live her life.

Arriving back at his house, he seated himself at his desk, intending to get some work done. A pastor was never done with studying and there were always sermons to be working on, calls to make, visits to parishioners; a pastor's life was a demanding one indeed. Dave doubted that most people understood how full and busy his life really was.

He had a commentary open, studying the connotation of a particular Bible verse, when he suddenly came to the realization that he had absolutely no idea what the passage was saying. His mind was full of Allie, and only Allie. Where was she right now? Was she still at that bar? Was she dancing and having fun? Were men hitting on her?

He pounded his fist on the desk, then rose from his chair and began pacing the floor. He couldn't concentrate on anything but Allie and the fact that he had let her go by herself to a bar. Had he done the right thing? Should he have gone with her, if for no other reason than to be sure she would be okay? Was she his responsibility? Or was he already so in love with the woman that he was willing to rationalize every one of his excuses to take care of her? He wondered if he should go back to the bar just to be sure she wasn't being annoyed by some drunk. Or should he go by her house first to see if she had gone home already? Surely it wasn't wrong or sinful to just reassure himself that she was fine? What could be wrong with just going to check on her?

Grabbing his jacket off the hook near the back door, he reached for his keys and nearly ran to his pickup. Jerking the cab door open, he picked up his leg to slide in, when suddenly he came to his senses. Slamming the door shut again with as much force as he could command, he then leaned his head against the window. A dry sob caught in his throat. His fist pounded the doorframe in his agony of emotion. *Why, Lord? Why is it so wrong of me to want to be with her? Is it really wrong or is that just all in my stupid head? It's not like we would be hurting anyone else if we were together. I'm not a priest so that celibacy thing doesn't apply to me. There's no rule anywhere that says I can't be married. And God, you know how much I want to be with her. So why not?*

The thoughts tumbled through his head; pros and cons, yes's and no's, rationalizations and excuses one after another.

Because she's not a believer, Dave. That's why.

Well, she could become a Christian! Then what would be the problem?

She will never be the right woman for you. Never. There's too much, too many differences. Everything about her is wrong for you and you know it. Stop now before it's too late.

He straightened up and then turned and walked slowly back into the house. He would stay home, sleepless, wondering and worrying most of the night.

He called the next day to ask her out to dinner the following Tuesday, and she accepted his invitation with a light laugh over the phone. "I'd love to Dave. See you then. Take me dancing afterward? You don't have any services on Tuesday evenings."

"No, Allie, no dancing. Just dinner. No wine, no kissing, and no dancing. Still want to go with me?"

"I don't know. You're sounding an awful lot like a preacher and not a whole lot of fun. Oh, what the heck, I'll go anyway. I can go dancing Wednesday night when you're busy at church."

Dave sucked in his breath. "See you Tuesday then. I'll pick you up around six."

This time he took her to a truck stop on the east side of town. He wanted a place that was well lit with no hint of intimacy. They sold beer there but no wine. Nothing romantic or suggestive, just friendly. He regretted it the moment they sat down. Right or wrong he wanted that intimacy, a romantic dinner for two in a more private setting, but he was trying very hard to control his feelings and where they wanted to take him.

Allie didn't seem to care one way or the other. She ordered a hamburger and a malt, and appeared quite happy. She acted as if she would feel the same no matter who she was eating with, smiling and chatting easily all evening.

Sometime during the meal the subject of dancing came up again.

"Dave, are you absolutely, positively sure you won't take me dancing tonight?"

"Absolutely and positively sure, Allie. No dancing. It just wouldn't be right for me to do that. I shouldn't be hanging around bars of any kind." He smiled broadly at her. "Have to watch my image, remember?"

"Well, I guess that leaves me on my own then, doesn't it? If you're sure you won't take me, I'll continue to go by myself."

He acted as if he had no idea that she had already gone last week. "You sound as if you already went?"

"I did, since you wouldn't take me."

"When?"

"Last week after we went out to dinner. You wouldn't go so I called a cab after you took me home."

"Where did you go?"

"The Mixer's Club on West Aspen street. Ever hear of it?"

"Yes, I know where it is. Did you have fun?"

"Yup, I sure did. You really should have come with me, Dave. You might have had a good time yourself!"

He hated to ask the next question, but he couldn't help himself. He had to know. "Meet anyone interesting?" He looked down at his plate, holding his breath. *Please tell me you met no one. Please.*

"Well, I met several nice men, actually. I had a great time. I'm going to start going most Wednesdays when I can. It really was a lot of fun! I only had a couple of drinks and it was good to be out and about again. I didn't realize how much I missed socializing." She looked coyly at him. "Not to say you aren't a great friend to hang out with, but that preacher part of you gets a little boring sometimes." She laughed, her perfect white teeth glistening in the light.

Dave's gut clenched, and he changed the subject.

There was no wine, and without the wine and low lights, there was no intimacy. He wanted very badly to kiss Allie again, but he had set this evening up so he had no one to blame but himself. He had done the right thing, hadn't he? Why didn't he feel better then?

The next evening after the Wednesday service, Dave found himself cruising Bozeman, checking out any of the bars that offered music and dancing, hoping to see her— hoping not to see her. He didn't know where she went since he couldn't look for her until the service was over, and she was already gone. Short of going into every bar, the only thing he could do was park a discreet distance away from the house and wait for her to come home. It was well after midnight before he saw the cab deliver her.

Three weeks later he asked an associate pastor to take over for him on Wednesday.

He was parked and waiting when the cab came to pick her up; he followed her to the Mixer's Club. Waiting for two hours in the parking lot, unable to go in and unable to leave, he became a prisoner of his own mind and emotions. He wanted a cigarette, and he wanted one badly. He had quit smoking years ago, but the old craving was now back in full force. He wanted that cigarette, but even more, he wanted Allie.

Finally he shoved all thoughts of right and wrong out of his mind and got out of his pickup. Walking up to the front door of the bar, he leaned heavily against it, his head lowered, before he finally jerked the door open. He had to know.

Smoke assailed him as he entered, stimulating that nicotine craving once more. Familiar odors resurrected old memories, and he was once again back where he had spent so many of his younger years. Shaking his head as if to shake off the present, he sauntered into a corner, and, leaning against the wall, peered through the darkness and smoke intently, looking for the reason he had come.

It didn't take long to find her. She was dancing slowly with a good-looking young cowboy, her body and that strawberry blonde hair swinging in time to the music. She was smiling broadly, obviously enjoying herself immensely. Every now and then she threw her head back and laughed, her eyes sparkling. His stomach churned violently.

He waited until two more dances were finished before he approached her, his jaw set. "Allie? Ready to go home yet? I'll give you a ride."

She smiled up at him, genuinely glad to see her friend. "Dave! You came! Changed your mind about dancing?"

"No, I just came to give you a ride home. What do you say? Coming with me?"

"Dance one time with me and it's a deal. I'll leave with you if you give me just one dance." She winked slyly at him.

He melted under that gaze, all thoughts of appearances gone. "I don't know if I remember how, honestly. I don't want to embarrass you." He was serious; he really didn't know if could remember how to dance.

"It's like riding a bike, Dave, as soon as the music starts it will all come back to you, I'm sure." She laughed up at him once more, and then reached out to take his big hand in hers. She guided him into place on the small dance floor, and waited for the music to start.

The band began to play a slow, seductive barroom song, and Allie deftly positioned Dave's hands on either side of her waist, then placed her arms around his neck, drawing him to her as she started to sway in time with the music.

It was indeed like riding a bike; his feet began to move and it wasn't long before he was totally lost in the dance. He closed his eyes, allowing himself to just "be." He had been a very good dancer in his youth, and age hadn't changed that, apparently.

He felt her warm breath on his ear as she whispered softly, "And I thought maybe preachers couldn't dance. You're pretty good, Preach!"

He went rigid for a moment with her reminder that he was a minister, but her words registered only fleetingly. He was lost in the music and the moment in Allie's arms, which only seemed to hold him tighter with each step. He was enjoying himself way too much.

Church and God were forgotten; there was only Allie and the music, and the combination was as potent as any heroin he had ever used. He closed his eyes, letting himself feel her in his arms, inhaling her clean scent as she rested her head on his shoulder.

Too soon! The music ended too soon! He came back to the present with a start, looking dazed as though he hadn't realized until that moment where he was. He gently removed Allie's hands from around his neck and pushed her slowly away from him.

"Ready to go home now?"

Allie was positively glowing. "Yup, I am. Lead the way, Preacher."

He took her hand and silently led her to the door and out into the soft Montana night, holding her hand tightly until they arrived at his pickup, when he finally released her. Taking a deep breath, he confessed, "I can't believe I just did that! I don't know what came over me! Hope I didn't embarrass you, Allie."

She stood on tiptoe and planted a swift, soft kiss on his cheek. "Embarrass me? Far from it, Preacher! You're pretty good. Better than I expected. Thanks for coming."

"Let's get you home, girl, before I go and do something really stupid." He opened the door for her and waited while she slid into the seat, pretending not to notice her kiss. His pulse was racing.

He drove slowly, in no hurry to end the evening in her company. He had no idea he was smiling the whole time. When they finally arrived at Joe's house, he remained in the vehicle while she got out.

"I'd ask you in for a cup of coffee or something but as you know I don't live here alone. Joe is here, and while I'm sure he's sound asleep now I really shouldn't be having guests over. I know you understand."

"Sure. I have to get home anyway. By the way, how's your patient doing? The family gives you a fair amount of time off, it seems, so I assume he's getting along well?"

"Yes, he's basically independent and only needs help with a few things. I think the family just feels better having someone here with him. He's a very nice old man, a real dear."

"Glad to hear that. Well, good night, Allie."

"Next week, Dave? Take me dancing, please? I'd rather go with an escort than alone, you know? And you're the best escort I can think of. How about it?"

"I don't know . . . I . . ." He stumbled, torn between what he knew to be right and what he really wanted to do.

"See you next week, then. Wednesday around 7? You can get that other pastor fellow to run the service again, can't you?"

"Let me think about it, okay? I'll call you later this week."

Allie blew him a kiss before she turned and skipped up the sidewalk to her front door.

He hadn't thought his emotions could be more in turmoil than they had been up to this point. Had he ever been wrong! He was actually considering taking a woman to a bar on a Wednesday night when he should be leading a prayer service at church. How low was he going to allow himself to sink? He had no idea.

Chapter 4

Dave usually fell asleep instantly when his head hit the pillow, but that was not the case tonight. Tossing and turning, he was unable to sleep and unable to pray. What had he done? What was he doing? What was he going to do? How far was he going to go with this addiction he had to Allie?

Which sin was the worst? Kissing Allie, drinking wine with her, dancing with her, or wanting her? Or were any of these really sins? Was deserting the prayer service in favor of Allie the biggest sin?

So what was it, exactly, with Allie? Was he infatuated, obsessed, or was he actually totally in love with the woman? He would almost have preferred obsession or infatuation, but the reality hit him full force: he was desperately in love with Allie Morgan, a woman young enough to be his daughter. What on earth was he going to do?

Lord, is it really wrong for me to love this woman? Is dancing really that terrible for a pastor? Is it truly a sin to want to be with her? To hold her? To love her? It doesn't mean I don't love you, Lord. But while you fill my heart and my mind, and I really do love you beyond everything else, Lord I miss having someone in my life. I'm lonely, and with Allie, I, well, you know what I'm trying to say here, Lord. God help me! Help me sort this out—tell me what I'm supposed to do, please!

Silence saturated his room. He remained alone. He supposed he didn't need God to answer him; he knew that what he was doing and the direction he was heading was not God's plan for his life. *But loving a woman is not a sin! And there's no reason I can't marry Allie as long as she becomes a Christian. That's the answer to all of this.* He was reassuring himself, rationalizing his thoughts and actions, reasoning as much as he was able. He would simply have to work on converting Allie. Surely she would be open to that, wouldn't she?

Well, she might if she felt about him the way he felt about her. But how could he become more than a friend to the woman? He knew that someone closer to her own age was better for her. She would probably want children later on, and at his age he had to confess he really didn't want to start a family. But maybe she would be okay with not having kids.

Maybe she . . .

Well, he decided, first things first. If he were truly serious about pursuing Allie, he would have to make some sort of a plan. He would have to get his priorities straight and sort out just how far he was willing to go with her. There was no way he could keep missing the Wednesday service and take her dancing instead. He just couldn't do that. No way. Priorities. God. Church. Allie.

On Tuesday he asked Allie to meet him for dinner; he picked her up at seven and they went to the Black Angus steak house again. No mention was made about Allie's request for him to escort her dancing until they were nearly finished with their dessert. He had hoped she had forgotten, but he wasn't that lucky

"So, friend, have you thought about taking me dancing?"

"Allie, you know I shouldn't . . ."

"Oh, come on, Dave. You took me before, so what's the big deal? You're a good dancer, and besides, I know you'll keep me out of trouble." She smiled her best winning, persuasive smile.

"I . . ."

"Good. That's settled then. I'll see you tomorrow. Maybe I'll dress up a little for you, how's that?"

"No, don't do that." He sighed deeply. He had lost once again, agreeing without really saying a word. He had no will power where Allison Morgan was concerned.

He picked her up at eight the next evening, church entirely forgotten, and took her to the Mixer's Club. Placing his hand over the small of her back, he escorted Allie into the bar, all caution vanished from his mind. Allie looked beautiful, as always, radiant and smiling. Young. Energetic. He was both terrified and energized.

Once inside Allie started off with a beer. While she wasn't really a drinker, she did enjoy the relaxed feeling she got with a little alcohol. She felt freer after a drink or two. She smiled more, flirted more, and loved every minute of the attention she garnered from nearly every man in the room. And it seemed her good friend Dave was just as enchanted as the other men, even if he was a preacher.

She was pleased to be escorted by Dave. He had a commanding presence, drop-dead good looks, and perfect manners. Tall and straight, with a dark tan and an easy smile, he was a date any woman would be proud to be seen with. She might even have fallen for him if he was younger and not a pastor, but those two things were insurmountable obstacles for a permanent relationship with him, as far as she was concerned. He was a great companion and the perfect casual date, but that was all.

Occasionally she was concerned that perhaps he was more interested in her than she was in him. The way he stared at her sometimes when his eyes shone with admiration was flattering, and yes, he was nearly always charming. And he could sure kiss! My, where had he learned to do that? He was also a great dancer, and it made her feel safe in the bar when he was with her. But she wanted to meet someone she could have a permanent relationship with, and Dave just didn't fill the bill.

She finished her first beer, and then danced two numbers with Dave. They found a table and Dave went to get her another beer. When he returned to their table, he found Allie talking animatedly with a good-looking young cowboy. He set her beer down and then took his seat. Allie barely glanced at him, engrossed in the conversation with her new admirer.

The music soon started up again, and when the young man held out his hand, Allie took it and shyly followed him onto the dance floor. Dave stared as they left.

Allie began to really enjoy herself. Her new escort was very handsome, attentive, and definitely a good dancer. She felt alive and wanted. It was heady and she wanted more and more of that feeling. Dave was forgotten at their table as she immersed herself in her new companion.

Her new friend's name was Doug, and he seemed totally smitten with Allie. After three more dances he asked permission to take her home when she was ready to leave; she accepted at once. Taking his hand, she led him back to the table she had been sharing with Dave.

"Dave, this is my new friend Doug, and he has asked to take me home tonight when we're done enjoying ourselves here. I knew you wouldn't mind and are probably ready to head home about now anyway, so I told him that would be fine." She smiled widely up at her new escort, beaming at his response. "You can go ahead and leave since Doug will see me safely home later."

"Allie, are you sure? You just met this man, and you don't . . . ."

"It's fine, Dave. You go on ahead and I'll give you a call sometime tomorrow, okay?" Keeping hold of Doug's hand, she turned and led him back onto the dance floor. A few more beers and a few more dances beckoned to her. She never noticed Dave watching her for the next twenty minutes before finally walking slowly out of the bar, leaving her alone with her new friend.

Several hours later Doug carefully guided Allie out of the bar to his car. She had consumed several more beers and a couple of stiff drinks and was feeling very relaxed indeed. Doug didn't even need to ask; Allie directed him to a nice motel on the outskirts of Bozeman where he checked them into a room.

Allie was drunk, but not so drunk that she didn't know what she was doing. On the contrary, she knew exactly what was going to happen and she wanted it to happen, the sooner the better. She wanted the closeness and the exquisite emotions that good sex could give her. While she wanted something more permanent than a one-night stand, this would do for now. But she wasn't a fool and protection was foremost on her mind. There would be no more unwanted pregnancies for her.

Doug took her home to Joe's house two hours later, asking if he could see her again. She readily agreed, having had a very pleasant evening. He kissed her goodnight at her door, and then drove off into the night. Allie smiled to herself, happy with the evening's events.

She was back!

Doug VanCamp now took Dave's place in her thoughts. He was shorter than Dave, and very blonde where Dave was dark. His teeth were just a little crooked, which Allie thought only added to his charm, and he wasn't quite the dancer Dave was, but he was fun nonetheless, and she had to admit he was pretty good in bed. Dave still kissed better than any man she had ever known, but Doug was closer to her age and definitely not a preacher! She had fun with him, and he soon became her constant companion.

Allie had forgotten to call Dave, and it never occurred to her that he might be missing her, or concerned about her activities. She had simply forgotten Dave, period. He had been there for her when she needed him, but she had Doug now. She no longer needed Dave. So she didn't call, and she soon neglected to return his calls to her.

She was meeting up with Doug whenever she had some free time. They became regulars at the motel and several of the bars in town. Doug was fun and available. While she knew she wasn't in love with him, she was certainly enjoying the time they spent together. What she didn't know was that her friend Dave was following her whenever he could.

Dave Benson was beside himself. He had left the bar shortly after Allie told him he could go, but he hadn't gone home. Instead he had waited in the parking lot until he saw Allie leave with her new friend. While the young man had seemed nice, Dave was wise enough to know that appearances could be deceiving. He couldn't leave until he was sure Allie would be safe.

Following them to the motel, he watched, stunned, as Allie excitedly led the way to the room. She was obviously more than willing to be escorted by Doug. As he sat there, he barely noticed the tears that soon slid down his cheeks. His chest muscles constricted until at one point he thought he might actually pass out. Finally he opened the pickup door and was physically sick on the pavement. Sometime later he drove himself home, devastated and sick at heart. How could she?

He called her two days later, but she was somewhat distant with him, no longer chatting freely. He never hinted that he knew what was going on. Conversation was slightly strained, with Allie volunteering nothing. They didn't talk for long, and when he hung up he promised himself that it was over with her. He was "cured"— for good! There was no other option for him. There was no way he could remain a pastor and go out with a woman who slept around so casually. He could now forget about her and get back to his pastoral life. He tried. He really tried.

Three weeks went by, and he managed to keep himself from calling her. But he went out on the nights he knew she had free time, and knew firsthand about the motel visits and their frequency. He was disgusted with both her and himself, yet he followed her. And still, he yearned for her.

About two months after that final date with her at Mixer's, he was startled when the phone rang in the middle of the night. It was Allie, distraught, suddenly needing her old friend.

"Allie? Are you all right? What's wrong?" He was terrified of the unknown.

"I'm okay, but Dave, they just took Joe to the hospital. I think he's had a stroke, a bad one. Dave, I don't think he'll be coming home again. I'm so worried! Can you possibly come with me to the hospital? I don't want do go alone. I'm scared, Dave."

He didn't need to think twice about it. There was no question. Even if it wasn't Allie asking for his help, he was a pastor, and this was part of his job. Of course he would come.

"Deaconess Hospital?"

"Yes. You'll come then?"

"Of course. Are you at home? Should I pick you up?"

"Please, if you don't mind."

"I'll be there shortly. Wait for me." He hung up, and racing to get dressed, was on the way to her house in minutes. Those calls in the middle of the night were the worst, he knew from years of experience. But Allie had called him, and his heart was racing. He was about to see her again.

She met him at the front door, her face tear stained and make-up free. Her hair was uncombed, and she looked a mess. She looked beautiful.

Appearing devastated, Allie literally ran into Dave's arms. Surprised, he held her warmly, concerned, but nearly overwhelmed at the emotions she aroused in him. He didn't want to let her go, but, with an effort, he took up the pastor's role, and did his level best to act professionally. Slowly releasing her from his grasp, he pushed her gently away.

"Tell me what happened, Allie. Tell me everything."

"I was sleeping, when suddenly I woke up. I don't know why, I just woke up." Her sobs punctuated her speech. "And I knew. I knew right away it was Joe. Oh Dave, I think he's going to die!"

Allie reached for him again, resting her head once more on his shoulder, as she sobbed in her distress. He patted her back in sympathy, trying to reassure her and calm her down.

"You want me to take you to the hospital, don't you? I know you won't rest easy until you see how he's doing."

Allie nodded her head silently in assent. Turning her, he put an arm around her shoulder and escorted her to his vehicle; she leaned heavily on him all the way.

"It's going to be okay, Allie. Whatever happens, however this goes, it's going to be okay. I'm here."

At the hospital, they went immediately to the emergency room waiting area to ask about Joe. Several minutes later, Joe's son, Matt, came out to talk to her. He didn't need to say a word; one look at his face told the story. Joe was gone. His family was devastated.

Allie no longer had a job.

She began crying loudly, chastising herself. "I should have . . . I . . . oh . . ."

Matt put his arm around Allie's shoulder. "Allie, don't blame yourself. The doctor said there was nothing that could have been done. It was just his time, Allie. It was his time."

"But . . ."

"No 'buts,' Allie. There was nothing you could have done, do you hear me? No one is blaming you for anything. The whole family is just very grateful to you for making his last days so pleasant. He really liked you and enjoyed having you around. Thank you for being there for him. I mean that, Allie. I really do." He gave her shoulder a squeeze. "Why don't you go on home? There's nothing for you to do here, unless you think you want to see him one last time?"

"No, I want to remember him as he was. He was a dear old man. I loved him, Matt. I really did."

Dave stepped up and introduced himself as a pastor and Allie's friend, asking if he could be of any help to the family at this time, but was informed that Joe's former pastor was on his way. Matt thanked him for his concern and offer, and then suggested he take care of Allie as it seemed she needed someone with her tonight.

Offering his condolences once more, he shook Matt's hand, and then gathering Allie close to him, escorted her out of the building and back out to his pickup. They drove in silence to the empty house where she and Joe had spent so many hours together.

"Do you want me to stay with you, Allie? I can sit with you for a while or leave you in peace, what's your pleasure?"

"Stay, please? If you don't mind?"

He couldn't help himself. He had to ask, "Would you rather call Doug and have him come over?"

"I really don't think he's who I need with me right now. Thanks for asking, but I just need my best friend tonight."

His relief showed on his face, but thankfully Allie was too distressed to notice. "Shall I make us some coffee? Sometimes it helps to keep your hands busy at times like this. What do you say?"

Her blotchy face with reddened, glistening eyes fastened on his as she thanked him. "I think that's a great idea. I can make it; you don't have to do that."

"Just point me to the kitchen. I think I can handle making some coffee. You go sit and rest a bit."

"Okay. You got it." She led him to the kitchen, showed him where the coffee and the coffeepot were, then left him alone with his task.

She was sitting on the couch in the small living room, her feet tucked neatly beneath her, when he returned with two steaming mugs.

"Black, if I remember, right?"

"Yes. Thanks."

He handed her a mug and then turned to sit on one of the chairs in the room.

"Sit here, with me? Please? If you don't mind, that is."

"I don't mind." *If she only knew.* He settled himself on the couch next to her, sitting as close as he dared and while still remaining "proper."

They sat quietly for some time, sipping coffee, minutes passing unnoticed. Dave broke the silence at last.

"Allie, can I ask you some questions about Joe? Do you mind talking about him a little?"

"No, that's fine. I don't mind. What do you want to know?"

He started with some general questions, such as his age, where he was from, some history. Allie was talking freely, seeming to relax as they conversed. Finally, he got to the most important question.

"Do you know if he was a Christian? Death is so much easier for all concerned if he was. Did he ever talk about his faith?"

"Oh, sure, he was a strong Christian. He read his Bible nearly every day. I don't think he ever put it away. He didn't talk about it much. There were a few occasions when he asked me what I believed, but he never pressed me about anything."

It was the opening he had been seeking for months.

"What do you believe, Allie? Have you ever put your faith in Jesus, as Joe apparently did?"

"Oh, I'm a Christian, Dave. You don't have to worry about that for me. My parents took me to Sunday School pretty regularly until I was about ten years old, and they made sure I was baptized when I was a baby, so I'm fine."

"I'd like to talk about this some more, do you mind?"

"No, I don't mind as long as you don't get too 'preachy' on me."

He leaned back, gathered his thoughts, and proceeded to present the Gospel to her in the clearest, least-threatening way he knew. He asked questions, many of them leading, and she answered. In the end, he lost; she failed to recognize that salvation wasn't about what she had done, but about her relationship with Jesus. Allie was trusting in her church attendance and baptism to save her, and was sure there was nothing more she needed. She was spiritually lost, and was content to remain that way.

"I'm fine, Dave. I really am. I'm sure I'm going to heaven when I die and I don't need anything else. I don't want to get fanatical or anything like some of those 'Jesus freaks' you run into now and then."

"Like me, you mean?"

She smiled warmly at her friend. "No, not like you. You might be a preacher, but you're easy to be around. You're more like 'regular people,' you know?" She looped her free arm through his and leaned into him. "You've been a really good friend this past year. I can't thank you enough."

He smiled back at her, but it was a forced smile. That one "out" he had given himself had just vanished. She had no intention of becoming a true, born-again Christian. Given everything he knew, he realized with finality that he must leave her, yet he couldn't imagine taking that first step away from this woman.

Two hours later he finally got up to leave. "I think it's probably time I went home, don't you think? It's after two in the morning."

Allie grabbed his arm once more. "Don't go. Stay with me, please?"

She had no idea how badly he wanted to stay. "It doesn't look too good for me to stay here all night with you, Allie. I think I should go."

"Well, you said it didn't look too good for you to go dancing with me at the bar or drink wine with me at the restaurant either, but you did it anyway. So stay. Who cares what people think? Besides, who's going to know? And it's not like I'm asking you to take me to bed or anything. Just stay here with me on the couch, okay?"

"Okay. I'll stay, but just until sun-up." He sat down next to her once more, confused, depressed, sad, and defeated. He would do as she asked. He would stay. He had absolutely no will power when it came to Allison Morgan.

It wasn't long before Allie managed to move into a more comfortable position on the couch, and soon fell asleep with her head on Dave's lap. He pulled the afghan down from the back of the couch and covered her carefully, then leaned his head back and dozed himself.

Dawn came all too soon, and he left.

Chapter 5

Allie woke late the next morning to find herself alone on the couch, covered neatly with the afghan. Sometime during the early morning hours Dave had apparently left her alone. "Alone" didn't begin to describe how she felt. Her whole world had collapsed in the last few months, and she hadn't really understood that until now.

She had felt bereft in the hospital after delivering her daughter, but Dave had helped that feeling to pass. He was such good company, so easy to be around. But now Joe was gone. The paycheck had been more than generous and the hours easy. She was going to sorely miss Joe as well as that paycheck. She wondered how soon she would have to move out of the house, since the family would probably want to put it on the market. What on earth was she going to do?

For a moment she thought about calling Dave but then decided against that idea. She needed more than a platonic friend today. She picked up the phone and called Doug, who agreed to meet her at their regular motel in a few hours after he got off work. She needed to be held and loved. She needed something, someone, to help her feel wanted and useful, to ease the dull ache that had begun to take over her body. Time with Doug would fix her right up, she was sure.

Doug had indeed made her feel loved and wanted for the couple of hours she had spent with him. He was a good lover with a quick sense of humor, and he was fun to be around. They both knew it was never going to be a permanent relationship, but Doug satisfied her physical needs very well, leaving her feeling satiated and warm. Content. But for some reason that wasn't the case today. Sex had been good, as it always was with him, but she felt empty and lost. Very, very empty and very, very lost. She guessed that was the best way to describe her feelings.

That evening, alone in Joe's house, hard, stark reality began to drape itself around Allie Morgan like a hair cloak, abrasive and harsh. She didn't like her new wardrobe. Was she feeling this way just because Joe had passed away? While she had loved the dear man, he wasn't her father or anything. She had cared for countless other patients over the years who had died, and while she had mourned for each one, she had never felt this alone before. What was the difference? When would life get back to normal, whatever that was?

Allie had never been a girl to sit quietly while the world went on without her. Now she spent a lot of time in introspection, trying to come up with a plan to get herself back on track. Her mind spun for two days before she finally came up with a plan. She hadn't seen her parents in over a year, and maybe it was time for a visit home to North Dakota. She could take a couple of weeks to catch up with her mom and dad, then come back to Bozeman and find another job. She had enough money saved to tide her over for several months, having saved most of her checks from Joe's family. Yes, that was a good plan. She would go home for a few weeks and let her parents dote on her as they had always done. It was summer and the weather was warm. No winter storms to worry about. Good plan.

Matt called her later that afternoon and Allie told him of her plans to go home for a while. The family could empty the house while she was away, and she offered to move out when she returned. The conversation went well, and almost as an afterthought, Matt asked her if she would like to stay in the home and rent it from them. The family would think about selling it perhaps at a later date, but they didn't want to do anything in a hurry that they might regret later. If she was willing to stay, they would negotiate a more than fair rental agreement for her. She was thrilled, and said she would be in contact when she returned to Bozeman.

Her living arrangements settled for the time being, she had one less worry on her mind. The next morning she dragged her two worn suitcases out of the closet and began packing for her trip home. It took her only an hour to pack; she was ready and anxious to leave.

Catching a cab to the Bozeman airport, she rented a small car, then drove back to the house and loaded the suitcases into the trunk. Settling herself onto the driver's seat, a smile suddenly lit her face. It would be good to be home again for a while.

Suddenly she thought of Dave. *I guess I should at least let him know I'm leaving town. He has been pretty good to me, after all.* She sighed, and, exiting the car, went back into the house to call her friend. She owed him that much.

"Hello?"

"Hi, Dave? It's Allie. I thought I should let you know I'm leaving town for a while. I didn't want you to worry if you tried to call me and got no answer, you know?"

"You're leaving? Where are you going, not that it's any of my business, but . . ." She thought her friend's voice sounded a little weak.

"I've decided to go home to North Dakota for a couple of weeks. Maybe longer. I don't know for sure how long I'll be gone, but I want to see my parents and be babied a little for a change. I haven't seen my folks in over a year, so it's time. And with Joe gone, well, it's a good time for me. "

"Will you call me when you get there so I know you've arrived safely?"

She laughed at this. "Dave, I'm a grown-up, remember. I'll be fine. Really. You don't have to worry about me. I can make it home easily in a day. I'll call you when I get back, okay?"

"I'd feel better if you called me when you got there. Please?" She heard the anxiety in his voice.

"Dave, no news is good news. I'll see you in a few weeks or so, and I'll call you when I get back to Bozeman."

"Allie—"

"Dave, take care of yourself. See you soon." Laughing at his seriousness, she hung up. She was on the road in three minutes.

The weather remained warm and clear for the entire drive. She listened to the radio off and on, singing along with some old songs she found on an "oldies" station. It was good to be out of the house, away from everything. Everything? What exactly was she getting away from? She liked her house, she liked her friend Dave, and she had fun with Doug. Why was she so happy to be leaving?

The baby. It came back to Catherine. The thought hit her with an unexpected, nearly physical force so strong she had to pull over to the side of the road. Resting her head on the steering wheel, the emotions she thought she had dealt with rushed into her head, enveloping her entire being. She hadn't thought about her little girl for weeks, having put the whole ordeal out of her mind as much as possible after leaving the hospital. Dancing, drinking, sex—they all helped her to forget. She had her old figure and her life back, filled with everything she wanted. She was single and unencumbered, and she was attractive. Why on earth was she thinking about her baby now? *Get out of my head. I gave you away. You have no hold on me now! You have great parents and a wonderful future. I did the right thing. I did, didn't I?*

But Catherine wouldn't leave. She was there, a part of her, just as firmly as if she was resting on the seat next to her. Allie wanted to escape, but there was no escaping.

Finally the tears came, warm and unstoppable. The tears she had never shed, not really, at the loss of that very real part of her. She sobbed her heart out, unable to even put into words exactly why she was crying. All she really comprehended was that any loneliness she had ever felt in the past was nothing compared to what she was feeling now. Empty? Barren? Forsaken? Lost? There were no words to describe the depth of her despair. *God, I did the right thing, giving her away. You know I did! My parents would have disowned me forever. The shame would have been too great for any of us to bear. And God, you know Raven and Gus, how badly they wanted a baby, how they couldn't have any children of their own. They will give her the home I never could. So why, God? Why in heaven's name am I feeling this way? How do I get past this?*

No answer came. No thunder, no lightning, no still, small voice in her head. She remained lost and alone with her thoughts.

In time—she had no idea how long—she cried herself out. She had no more tears to shed. There were no answers for her, no resolution. Wiping her eyes, she forced all thoughts of her baby along with the emotions associated with her, out of her head. Life would be good again soon enough. She would take her secret to her grave rather than have her parents find out. It was all going to be okay. But she missed her friend, Dave. She missed him a lot.

Later that evening she pulled into her parents' driveway. Allie had not called ahead to let them know she was coming, and their obvious joy at seeing her was all the confirmation she needed to reassure herself that she had indeed made the correct decisions. She had done the right thing by keeping her pregnancy a secret and giving the baby away, the right thing by coming home again. She was still the "good girl" her parents believed her to be.

Allie stayed longer than she had planned, enjoying being with her parents once more. They ate out, visited parks, walked along the river, laughed and settled into being a close-knit family unit again.

Her parents were a very nice, conservative, middle-class American couple, the kind of people often referred to as "the salt of the earth."

Finally it was time for her to return to Bozeman and get on with her life. Good-byes were tearfully exchanged along with tight hugs and well-wishes, and Allie was finally on her way. She felt much more settled and secure within herself and the decisions she had made that year. Yes, giving her daughter away had definitely been the right thing to do. Now it was time to find a new job and hopefully some new friends. Maybe the next time she came home to visit she would be engaged, and she could confidently bring her intended home with her.

Filled with optimism and new hope for her future, the drive back to Bozeman passed quickly, and she was actually surprised to find herself pulling up to the house in what seemed like record time.

She unpacked her things quickly, and then returned the car to the airport, after which she caught a cab back to the house. Settling herself on the couch, she sipped a cup of hot chocolate before heading off to bed. Pulling the covers up and snuggling into a comfortable position, she was smiling softly as she drifted off to sleep. She did not call Dave for two days after her arrival; she had simply forgotten about her friend.

Dave answered the phone on the second ring, sounding breathless as she heard, "Hello?"

"Dave? It's me, Allie. Thought I'd let you know I'm back. I told you I would call when I got here, so I'm keeping my word." She may have forgotten about him for a time, but she smiled broadly as she heard his voice again. She found herself wishing he wasn't a pastor. Old or not, she could have easily fallen in love with him. He was that kind of man; easy to look at and easy to love. But age difference aside, he was still a preacher, a profession she could never permanently live with. Allie, a preacher's wife? Not a chance! Of course if he were to leave his preacher job, now that might be something else again.

"When did you get back? Are you unpacked already? How was your visit?" Words tumbled out of him as he nervously queried her.

"Well, I actually got back a couple of days ago."

"Why didn't you call me? You promised you would!"

"Sorry, I guess I just forgot. Forgive me?" Her laughter carried through her voice.

"You forgot? Allie, I was getting pretty worried about you. I figured you would take a couple of weeks, but three? I wish you had let me know what you were doing. I was nearly frantic." There was no laughter to be heard in his voice.

"I'm fine, Dave, I really am."

"Well how on earth was I supposed to know that? What if you had been in an accident or something? Hit a deer and totaled your car? What if you were in the hospital? How was I supposed to know?"

She laughed out loud at his tirade.

"It's not funny, Allie. I really was concerned. I care about you, you know."

"I know we're good friends, and I guess I should have let you know what was going on, but really, Dave, I'm all grown up and I'm just fine. You don't have to worry, okay?" She heard a deep sigh over the phone. She supposed she should have called him right away. Oh well, she was back now.

"Allie, want to meet me for lunch or dinner or something and you can fill me in on your visit home? What do you say? Do you have time?" Dave Benson, pastor of Grace Bible Church, always polite, always caring, and always there for her.

"Sure Dave, that would be great. How about dinner tomorrow night? The Black Angus again? They have those great steaks."

"The Black Angus it is. What time should I pick you up?"

"How about around five? Sound okay to you?"

"I'll be there. See you tomorrow." The phone went dead.

Chapter 6

She was back. Thank God, Allie was back and she sounded really good. Happy. Refreshed. Beautiful.

He had been worried to death about her. Was she okay? Had something happened either going up or coming back? Was she ever coming back or had she met someone in North Dakota and decided to stay there near her parents? He had felt as if he might actually die during her absence.

Allie's immorality, her ambivalent view of Christianity, her choice of "friends" to spend her time with, none of it mattered to him. Love was not a switch he could turn on and off at will. In spite of everything, he still loved her.

He dressed a little more carefully before leaving to pick her up. Nothing fancy, but just a little more tailored. He drew the line at a tie, though. He was still "cowboy" enough to ditch the tie. He didn't even wear one when he was preaching. No one ever seemed to mind.

He was fifteen minutes early, so rather than appear too anxious he parked two blocks away and listened to the radio to pass the time. At five o'clock on the dot he pulled up in front of her house, and, taking a deep breath, walked up to her front door. He didn't really know what to expect; what, if anything, had changed while she was gone?

She greeted him in a pair of black slacks paired with a plain white blouse. Simple pearl earrings graced her tiny ears. She was wearing minimal makeup and her hair was loose around her shoulders, shining, beckoning. She was as beautiful as ever, and her welcoming smile rendered her nearly ethereal.

"Right on time, as usual. Good to see you, Dave."

"Good to see you too, Allie. I missed you." He smiled down at her, his eyes fixed on her face. It was all too obvious that he really had missed her.

"Give me a hug, then?" She reached up for him and pulled him into a tight hug. It appeared she had missed him also.

He hugged her back, trying his best to keep things platonic and friendly. Normal. It was hard, and he wrestled within himself to release her before he gave himself away.

"You look great, Allie. Beautiful, as usual."

"Thanks, Preach. You're always so complimentary." She smiled up at him again.

"Are you hungry, Allie? Ready to head out?"

"Sure am. Lead the way."

Dave couldn't help himself. He reached for her hand as they walked to his pickup. The smile never left his face.

The food at the restaurant was good as always, and they were enjoying the evening, just like old times. Conversation was always easy between them with never a lapse. There was always something to talk about. Finally, Dave had to ask the question that was burning within him. He had to know. He cleared his throat and asked as casually as he could, "Have you seen Doug since you got back?" He couldn't look at her when he asked that question, but seemed instead to concentrate on his plate.

Allie was slow to answer as she seemed to be thinking over her response. "No, I haven't."

"You haven't? Did you call him?" He was holding his breath yet again as he waited for her answer.

"Actually, no, I didn't call him. I'm not sure that I'm going to."

"Why not? I thought you two were getting pretty close." The food turned sour in his mouth.

"I don't know. I'm not sure why I haven't. Guess I don't really miss him too much."

She smiled up at him, at the look she saw on his face.

"You know, Dave, Doug's a pretty good dancer and he's fun to be around, but if you'll take me dancing on Wednesdays, I'd much rather go with you. What do you say?"

"Why me?" His face looked puzzled.

"Because you're a better dancer, silly. And you're a pretty safe date, too." She laughed out loud.

"But I thought . . ."

"You thought what, exactly, Dave?"

"You two were spending an awful lot of time together, and, well, he's probably more fun than an old man like me." There, he said it. He hadn't said what he really wanted to, but he didn't know how to go about asking a girl if she was tired of sleeping with a man. Some things you just didn't do.

Allie seemed to suspect that Dave knew more than he was letting on. She looked up at him slyly, the smile gone from her face.

"I'm sure as a preacher you've heard it all by now. I'll confess, Doug was fun and he was good in bed. I enjoyed his company. But I think I'm over him now." She leaned back in her chair and then blurted out, "Maybe I'll work on getting you into my bed; what do you say?"

Dave turned absolutely white and Allie burst out laughing at the sight.

"Dave, I'm joking, okay? Don't be so serious, dummy. I would never pull something like that with you. Relax. We have too much fun to be ruining everything that way." She couldn't hold her laughter in and took a sip of her wine in an effort to compose herself.

Dave wasn't laughing. *Woman, if you only knew. It's definitely not funny. "She had blue eyes and blue jeans . . ."* He was at a loss for words, speechless. She had come way too close to the mark.

Allie reached over and handed Dave his wine glass. "Here, take a sip and settle down.

I was only kidding, for heaven's sake."

"It wasn't funny, Allie." He took a gulp of the wine. His color slowly returned and he kept his face averted from hers. "Not funny at all."

"No, I'm sorry. Am I forgiven?" She leaned over and placed her soft hand over his. "I won't say anything like that ever again, okay? I know you wouldn't be interested. You're a lot like Pen, you know? I couldn't get him do to anything with me either." She was smiling again, now. "I must be losing my touch!"

Dave remembered how Allie had tried so hard to pin her pregnancy on his friend, Aspen Windchase. She had done her best, hoping he would accept the baby as his and marry her, allowing her to keep up appearances and keep her baby. But it hadn't happened, and Pen's sister was now raising the child that could have stayed with her.

Back to the present. "No, Allie, I don't think you've lost your touch, as you call it. Not in the least. You are a very attractive woman, one that any man would be proud to be seen with." He meant every word. "What do you say, woman? Shall we go on to safer subjects?"

"Sure. So tell me, what did you do while I was gone? Anything special you want to talk about?"

Aside from missing you so much I could hardly function? "No, not really. Just the usual stuff. A couple of funerals and lots of home visits. A pastor's work is never done, you know."

Easy conversation returned, and once again they drank their wine and relaxed. It was a good night.

Dave took her home soon after, driving as slowly as he dared without arousing suspicion. When they arrived, Allie invited him in for coffee, now that Joe was gone and she had the house to herself.

"Coffee, Preach?"

He didn't hesitate. "Sure, I'd love a cup. I think I probably need it after that wine."

Once in the house, he followed her into the kitchen when she went to make the coffee. It vaguely occurred to him that he had probably had one glass of wine too many, and while he had felt safe driving, he was definitely a little more relaxed than normal.

Allie's back was in front of him, and before he realized what he was doing, he found his arms wrapped around her as he held her close. Then, ever so slowly, he turned her to face him, and, lowering his head, he claimed the lips that had been calling to him since he had first laid eyes on her. Groaning, he deepened the kiss when he felt her eager response. He was feeling things he hadn't felt in years, decades in fact. And she felt so good. He was lost in her.

Forever passed before he came to his senses and he released her.

"I'm sorry, Allie. I don't know what came over me. The wine, I guess." He was stumbling over the words, nearly stammering. Breathing hard, he made a desperate effort to catch his breath.

"Well, you didn't see me pushing you away, did you?" She was smiling at him, a rather dazed look on her face.

He tried to make an excuse for himself. "See, you shouldn't have made that joke about getting me into your bed back at the restaurant. Look what happened!"

"Well, I might have been joking then, but I'm not joking now. I liked it, Dave. I told you before, the last time you kissed me, that you were pretty good, but frankly, I had no idea."

He felt stupid. Clumsy. But he wasn't sorry at all. He wanted very much to kiss her again. But before he could put his desires into action, Allie was reaching for him.

"Kiss me again, Preach." Her mouth found his in the next instant.

The coffee was forgotten. Allie maintained the kiss, and began slowly guiding him down the hallway to her room. She obviously wanted more from him, and he came to his senses only when he felt the bed behind his knees. Suddenly, he pushed her roughly away from him. His whole body was shaking, and his confusion was obvious. Silently, Dave Benson turned away and walked down the hall and out of the door.

Allie watched him leave, making no effort to stop him.

He sat in the pickup for some time before he started the engine and headed for home.

What have I done? Only what I have wanted to do all along, it seems. I can never do that again. I can never see her again. There's no way I can NOT kiss her again. If I am around her, I will be unable to control myself. It's simple, really. I'm a man, she's a woman, and the result is only natural. Is that so wrong? For me, yes. Will I stop? No. I can't. I'm sorry, Lord, but I don't think that I can give her up. The fact is, I don't want to. I want more of her. God help me, I want all of her.

He found himself crying as he drove. He could still feel her lips on his. He could feel her arms around him, warming him to his very core. Even as he drove home, he wanted to go back and start again.

The next day, Dave was back at work, but his mind was elsewhere. *"The devil in blue jeans."* He prepared his sermon for Sunday, but asked his associate pastor to take over the service for him. For the next two weeks Dave led no services. It was obvious to others that something was wrong, but no one seemed to have any idea what to do, so they all left him alone. He did not see Allie, nor did he call her. He thought he might die.

It was July now, and one day he called his friend, Gus, asking if they could get together. Gus offered to meet him for lunch, but Dave declined, asking if they could meet at the end of the stable's driveway. They arranged to meet later that afternoon.

Dave was waiting when Gus pulled up and parked next to Dave's pickup. He got out and walked over to where Dave was sitting, staring vacantly through the windshield.

"Dave? Hello?" Gus tapped on the door to get his attention.

"What? Oh, hi Gus. Thanks for coming." Realizing finally that Gus had arrived and was waiting for him, he exited the vehicle and embraced his friend in a warm hug.

"Good to see you too, Dave." Gus laughed at his friend's apparent urgency. "What's going on? Why didn't you want to just come on up to the stable? We could have sat comfortably around the table with a good cup of coffee, and I know Raven would love to see you. You should see Catherine and how big she's getting!"

"I don't want to see anyone but you today, Gus. Sorry." He motioned with his hand, "Let's sit on the tailgate, shall we?"

"Must be serious, huh? When you want to talk without coffee I'm pretty sure something's up." Gus smiled, but it didn't reach his eyes as he followed his friend to the back of the pickup.

When they were seated, Dave finally took a deep breath and began.

"Where to start, Gus? I don't really know. I don't know much of anything right now, in fact."

"Well, you know what they say, just start at the beginning. Go ahead." Keeping his head down, Gus waited patiently for Dave to break his silence.

"Gus, I'm in trouble. Deep trouble, and I don't know how to get out of it. The fact is, I don't really think I can do anything. I need your advice." He sighed, deeply.

Gus waited wordlessly for his friend to continue.

"Gus, I don't really know how to say this, but I'm in love. I mean really in love and I don't know what to do about it."

Gus laughed out loud. "Well good for you, Dave. It's about time you found a good woman to share your life with. You've been alone for a very long time now. I don't know why you say you're in trouble—who's the lucky girl? Anyone I know?"

"It's Allie, Gus. God help me, I'm in love with Allie Morgan."

The smile instantly left Gus's face. "Allie? Catherine's mother? That Allie?"

"Yup. That Allie."

"How . . . ? Stupid question. Let me back up. When did this all start?"

"Pretty much the first time I ever laid eyes on her."

"When you were staying in Billings with Pen?"

"Right. She was trying to pin her pregnancy on Pen when I first met her. She came to the house. I remember the knock on the door and when I opened it, there she was. The second time I saw her I was totally lost."

"Oh boy. Dave, I don't know what to say. I'm sorry."

"Yeah. I don't either. I'm old enough to be her father, Gus. I'm an old man!"

"Oh, you're not that old, but yes, you are a little long in the tooth for that girl. Does she know how you feel?"

"I don't think so, but I don't know for sure. I made a fool of myself a couple of weeks ago at her house, but I blamed it on the wine."

"Wine? You were drinking?"

"Sure was. At the Black Angus."

"You were having wine in public? With Allie?"

"Yup. I figured I probably shouldn't, but I reasoned my way around it, went ahead and did it anyway."

Gus shook his head. "Dave, how far have you gone with her? I'm assuming not very far if you don't know whether or not she is aware of your feelings, am I right?"

"I've taken her dancing at the Mixer's Club. I kissed her, well, it was more like she kissed me. But it's happened a couple of times now. The last time I'm the one who started it."

Gus whistled through his teeth. "Well, I know why you wanted to talk, Dave. But you don't need advice from me. You already know the answer to everything. You're a pastor, Dave, and a good one, but that church will run you out on a rail if this all comes to light. You know that." He thought a moment and then added, "Unless, of course, you marry her. Any possibility of that?"

"I don't think she'll have me, Gus. She's not a born-again believer and being a pastor's wife is abhorrent to her. And no, I certainly haven't brought the subject up with her. It's way too soon, and besides, I know she's someone I can never marry and remain a pastor. It would be her or the ministry. What kind of a choice is that?" He couldn't bring himself to tell Gus about her promiscuity. He wasn't that brave.

"What do you want me to say, Dave? What do you think I can do to help you?"

"Actually, I know there's nothing you can do or say to help me. I just had to bare my soul to someone, and you're the best friend I have, so you were the one chosen to hear me out. I guess maybe deep inside I had a shred of hope that you would tell me it was going to be okay, that things could work out with her. I knew better, of course. She's a nice girl, a fun person to be around, and she's beautiful. But she's also no candidate for a minister's wife. I'm in real trouble here, and I'm afraid of how this is all going to turn out."

Gus put his arm around his friend's shoulder and pulled him close."I don't think I can help you with this, Dave. It's something you're going to have to work through yourself. But I'm here for you, anytime, anywhere. You need to talk, I'm here to listen. You know that I fully understand what you're going through, don't you? It was the same for me with Raven. I had to leave her for both our sakes, but in the end I had to at least be near her, even if I couldn't actually be with her. Anyway, you need me, you just call."

"Thanks, Gus. I don't know what else to say. I got myself into this mess and somehow I'll have to find the strength to pull myself out of it. But I just don't see how I'm going to do it. I feel like I can't breathe without her. I've managed to stay away from her for two whole weeks now, but I don't know how much longer I can hold out." He sighed deeply and turned his head away, covertly wiping a stray drop of moisture from his eye. Suddenly he dropped to his feet and waited for Gus to do the same. Without another word to his friend, he closed the tailgate, got back into the pickup, and drove away.

Gus watched his friend leave, his face lined with worry.

Chapter 7

Allie was getting restless. She had worked steadily ever since she was sixteen, and inactivity didn't sit well with her. She looked up all the care facilities in and around Bozeman, and, picking out the top three that interested her, determined to visit each of them in the next few days and pick where she wanted to apply for work. One morning she dressed carefully, put several copies of her resume in her purse and was heading out the door when the phone rang. She shut the door and ran the few steps to answer the phone. It was her mother.

"Allie?"

"Hi, Mom. What a pleasant surprise. What's up?"

"Well, your father and I have been talking, and we've decided we'd like to come visit you for a week or so, it that's all right with you. What do you think?"

"That would be great! Are you just coming to visit or do you have specific plans?"

"Well, you said you had plenty of room in your house, so we thought maybe we could use your place as a base of sorts, and from there we could visit Yellowstone Park, maybe Glacier Park, Big Sky, you know, all the fun places." Her excitement could be heard in her voice. "Your dad and I have never taken a real vacation, and we aren't getting any younger. I know we just saw you, but we can never get enough of our beautiful daughter."

"Oh Mom!"

"Now, if we will be an inconvenience to you, you just say so. We don't want to impose."

"No problem at all. In fact, I was just going to go look for a job, but if you're planning to come down, I think I'll wait until you leave and maybe I'll tag along with you while you're here, if that's okay with you?"

"That would be wonderful. We'd love it if you came along with us."

"So, when are you planning on coming?" Allie could feel herself getting excited at the prospect of spending some vacation time with her parents. "How soon can you be here?"

"If we come in three days will that be too soon?"

"Perfect. I'll see you both in three days and we can plan from there. This is going to be fun!"

"Thanks, Allie. See you soon!"

She left her purse on the couch and went to the kitchen to make herself a cup of coffee. Her parents were coming to visit; she was more than pleased. A job could wait!

Her parents arrived in the promised three days. They spent one day resting up from the drive over and planning their tour of the Big Sky state. The next two weeks were spent touring the parks and tourist spots within driving range of Bozeman. Some places were too far from Bozeman to make it back every night and they spent the occasional night or two in motels. Allie and her parents were more like friends now, the lines between parent and child blurring as they spent more time together. Montana is a big state, and they managed to see most of it. It was the vacation of a lifetime.

Allie had not noticed that her friend Dave had not contacted her in weeks.

All too soon it was time for her parents to head back home. Good-byes were said, tears shed, and hugs so tight they were meant to last a lifetime. Waving cheerfully, they drove off, tired and happy, looking forward to getting back to their own home once more.

They had only been gone from Bozeman for about three hours when the unthinkable happened. Driving up Highway 89 north of Wilsall, they were admiring a herd of antelope on the east side of the road when a bull moose suddenly appeared in front of them. They never saw the animal as they hit it head on. All fifteen hundred pounds of moose crashed through the windshield, totaling the car and killing the occupants instantly. The wreckage wasn't noticed for two hours, since traffic is sparse on that mostly deserted stretch of highway. It was two hours after that before the next of kin was notified.

Allie sat, stunned into silence, as the news was delivered to her over the phone. Her parents were gone. She needed to go to White Sulphur Springs to identify their bodies and collect their personal effects from the car. She had no idea how she could accomplish any of that. She sat there for what seemed like hours, unable to move, unable to think coherently.

She felt as if she was drowning, and she couldn't swim. She couldn't even tread water. Where to start?

She called her best friend, Dave. He was the only person she could think of, and she desperately needed someone. The phone rang several times before the answering machine came on. She hung the phone up. She didn't want to talk to a machine; she wanted to talk to her friend. Waiting only a few minutes, she called again, this time leaving a message for Dave to please come as soon as he could. Then she found the afghan on the back of the couch, and, curling herself up in it, she sat there in the dark and waited.

Dave didn't get the message until nearly eleven o'clock that evening. The caller didn't leave her name, only a short message to please come as soon as he could. He didn't need her name—he would know Allie's voice anywhere.

He wasn't sure what he should do. He had managed to stay away from the woman for nearly a month. He hadn't called or driven by her house; he was doing his best to erase her from his mind, his heart, and his life. He had been able to get back to preaching again, and was once more in intimate communion with God. It hadn't been easy, but he had been doing his level best. And now she had called. His heart had skipped a beat when he heard her voice. What would he do? Should he call her to see what she wanted or just go to her as she had requested. His options barely registered; he grabbed his coat and ran to his pickup. She had called and he would go.

He drove as fast as he dared to get to her. Pulling up in front of her house, he was at her front door in record time. He found he was sweating profusely and his heart was pounding as he rang the bell. He heard a faint call for him to come in, and, finding the door unlocked, he entered the darkened house.

"Allie?" He nearly stumbled in the darkness. There wasn't a single light on anywhere. "Allie, where are you? Are you here?"

"Yes, I'm here. In the living room." Her voice was flat, toneless. Dead.

He hadn't thought it mattered why she had called, it was enough that she had. Now, as he heard her emotionless voice, he knew something was terribly wrong. He was terrified as he made his way in the darkness to the living room where she waited for him.

He turned on the lights as he went further into the house. Finally he found her hiding under the afghan on the couch, her face pale, devoid of any color. He was with her in an instant, kneeling in front of her, his hand on her knee.

"Allie, what is it? What's wrong? Are you sick?" He had seen many people in this state before, and it always involved some sort of tragedy. *You can't be ill, Allie. You can't be.*

Suddenly she was reaching for him, both arms outstretched, searching for the comfort she instinctively knew only he could give her.

"Hold me, please. Hold me, Dave."

Rising from his knees he moved to sit next to her on the couch, gathering her into the safety of his arms. "It's okay, Allie, whatever it is, it's going to be okay. I'm here. I won't let anything happen to you."

The comfort and support he offered were her undoing, and she began crying at last. Deep, gulping sobs found their way out as she clung to him in her desperation.

"Allie? What . . . ?"

But she couldn't speak, she was crying too hard, her whole body shaking in spasms with her agony. Dave sat quietly and held her until she was able to speak again, his chin resting on her head.

Finally, the tears slowed, and her body calmed.

"Dave, my parents are dead." Her voice was barely a whisper. "They hit a moose." At this she suddenly began to laugh hysterically. "Can you believe it? A moose? Nobody hits a moose, for heaven's sake." Her laughter became almost a shriek.

"Allie, stop." He shook her gently, hoping to bring her back to reality.

Her eyes glazed as she looked up at him. "A stupid moose, Dave. And now they're gone. They were just here this morning. And now . . . they're gone. Just like that. In an instant. How can that be?"

Dave's eyes glistened as all the love he had tried so hard to cast aside washed over him yet again, and her pain became his. He saw her as she was, her skin pale, her eyes dull, her hair matted and straggly, and she was as beautiful as ever to him.

"I'm so sorry, Allie. So sorry. But I'm here now, and we'll get you through this. What do we need to do first? Where are they?"

"White Sulphur Springs. I have to go up there. . ."

"All right. We'll head up there first thing in the morning."

"We?"

"I'm not leaving you, Allie. I'll drive you up there and help you with whatever you need to do. I know you probably won't sleep much, but you really need to if you can. You're going to need all the rest you can get."

"You'll stay with me tonight?"

"I'll stay. I told you I won't leave you." *I don't think I can ever leave you again.*

She made herself comfortable against his chest, and her exhaustion overcame her at last. She slept.

Dave remained awake for some time, thinking. He had tried so very hard to leave her, and now he was back. It was as if they had never been apart. Those weeks away from her were erased and he was back where he had so longed to be. What was the point of trying to stay away? All his efforts had been useless. He loved her and wanted her just as much as he ever had. Nothing had changed except his resolve. He had no intention of trying to free himself from her again. He was back and he would stay.

In the morning he made a few calls to the church, explaining that he would be out of town for an undetermined period of time due to the deaths of a close friend's parents. He would be heading for North Dakota with her if she wanted him to come. Allie had no siblings so she would be responsible for disposing of their home and belongings, and he was sure she would need his help. He instructed her to pack her things while he went home to pack his.

She didn't want him to leave her for even that long, but this would save some time. He was back in an hour.

It was a two-hour drive to White Sulphur Springs and they made the trip in silence. Dave took her to the Twichel Funeral Home where arrangements were made for burial in Mandan, North Dakota. Two hours later they were on their way east. It was about five hundred and forty miles to Mandan; it would take them nearly eight hours to make the drive to her parents' house. The trip was a silent one; they arrived around eight that evening.

The next few weeks were frantically busy as they made funeral arrangements, the funeral itself, sorting through and emptying the house, and then listing it for sale. Dave helped her as much as he could; conversation was sparse. There wasn't much he could say, anyway. She certainly didn't need to hear any trite "preachy" comments, so he did what he could to help and stayed quiet for the most part. How he wanted to be holding and comforting her! But she seemed to have erected an invisible barrier between them. Like an ice queen, she was unapproachable. It should have made it easier for him to distance himself emotionally, but it didn't. His head wanted to take advantage of this distance, but his heart wouldn't let him.

Finally it was time to head back to Bozeman. Allie kept only a few personal items having a lot of sentimental value; everything else had been sold and the estate settled. She had inherited a sizeable amount of cash; she wouldn't need to work anytime soon unless she wanted to. They loaded up his pickup and drove toward Montana early one morning.

As Mandan faded into the distance, Allie finally allowed herself to "feel." She was beginning to mourn, something she had not allowed herself to do up until now. She rested her head against the passenger window, closed her eyes in exhaustion, and allowed the tears to come. Slowly, at first, and then she couldn't wipe them away fast enough.

"Sorry, Dave. I can't help it."

"That's all right, Allie, you go right ahead. I know you cried a lot when you first got the news, but you never allowed yourself to actually grieve. It has to happen sometime and now is as good as any." He glanced over at her. "Want me to pull over for a while?"

"No. I'll be fine. Just keep driving."

Finally she began to talk, going back over her life, remembering her parents and their relationship. They had been a truly loving family.

"I really wish I had some siblings, you know? It would be a lot easier if I had some family left, but now it's just me. I'm all alone and I don't like it very much."

"I'm here, though. Doesn't that help?"

"Oh, sure, Dave. It helps, but you're not family. You're a good friend, but you're a pastor and that's different."

"I'm still a man, Allie, and I really care about you, you know that."

"Yeah, I know. But right now I wish you were a brother instead."

He let the comment slide for now, but it stung.

Allie talked all the way home. It was a one-sided conversation; she expected no responses from Dave. She just needed to talk.

Finally, they arrived back at her home in Bozeman. They unpacked the pickup and Dave faced the reality that it was time for him to leave. Again. He picked up his hat and headed for the front door.

"Guess I'll see you around, Allie. Call me if you need anything, okay?" He dreaded leaving her yet again.

"Yeah, okay. Thanks for everything."

He walked out and did not look back. He had promised himself that he would not leave her again, but she hadn't asked him to stay. His heart clenched in his chest. She hadn't asked him for anything. She didn't need him anymore. Somehow he would have to find a way to live without her. He had no idea how to do that. No idea at all.

Chapter 8

Allie spent the next week alone in the house. Finally it occurred to her that she needed groceries; she couldn't live forever on canned soup. She called Dave. She didn't want to take a cab to go to the grocery store, and Dave was a lot more fun to be around than some cranky old cab driver.

Before her friend showed up, she had decided it was time to buy a car. Rather than groceries, she needed her own source of transportation more. When the knock came, she was waiting.

"Ready? We're going to the grocery store, right?"

"You know, I think I've changed my mind. I want to buy a car. Can you take me to one of the dealers?"

"A car? Isn't it a little soon since, well, you know? Don't you want to think about this a little? Do you even know what kind of a car you want?"

"I've got the money now, and I've got the time. Yes, I want a car. Will you take me and help me pick one out? Guys always know more about these things." She smiled coyly at her friend, not that she needed to. She knew Dave well enough to know he would do pretty much whatever she asked him to, and today she wanted him to help her buy a new car.

"Okay, if you're sure that's what you want. But don't you think you need food more? You look like you've lost a couple of pounds since we got back from North Dakota."

She supposed she had lost some weight. Her jeans did seem to have a little more room in them. Oh well, losing a few pounds never hurt anyone.

"I'm fine. Let's go find a car for me." She tossed her hair to one side and led the way to his pickup.

Three hours later she was the proud owner of a light blue Camry. She would have preferred a flashy convertible, but convertibles were rather impractical in Montana as there weren't many favorable days to put the top down. Dave left her at the dealership after the purchase was completed. She didn't see him for the next several days and it never occurred to her to call him.

She went shopping for groceries, then clothes, and finally furniture. Her parents had left her a great deal of money and she began spending at a prodigious rate, which was totally out of character for her. Allie had always been careful with money, but not anymore. And she was getting restless. It began to bother her, this "feeling" that was keeping her somewhat on edge. She started hanging out in the casinos, which were on every corner, it seemed. She won sometimes and she lost even more, but she didn't care. It was a way to kill time. It didn't take her long to start hanging out at the Mixer's Club again.

Doug was still showing up there at times, and she picked up where she had left off with him, drinking and going to motels. For some reason she didn't understand, she did not invite him to her house for their trysts. Doug was still cute and fun, but not someone she wanted on a permanent basis.

She was on an emotional roller coaster of sorts. She got bored easily and remained restless. She began filling her time with any and every pleasure she could think of, but nothing changed for her. She started drinking more and even took up smoking. Nothing helped. She was obviously on a downward spiral but for some reason she didn't see it as such; she didn't really want her life to be different. She was enjoying her new vices. With no schedules to meet and no pretenses to keep up, she was living her life exactly as she chose with no limits.

But her restlessness grew. She became a regular at Mixer's, and while she was flirting with many of the men there, unless she was with Doug, she went home alone. To her credit she never drove, and always took a cab both ways rather than attempting to drive under the influence. But filling her life with "everything" only seemed to leave her feeling even more empty. She stayed up later at night and slept in until nearly noon every day. She had nowhere to go and no one special to see. While she thought about going back to work occasionally, the thought of working again was not appealing. There was a "hole" somewhere inside of her that she couldn't seem to fill, so she drank more, smoked more, and flirted more. In public she smiled and laughed most of the time, while the depression settled over her at home. She had no idea she was in trouble. Dave never entered her mind; she didn't need a preacher in her life; she needed . . . what? She had no idea.

The bar was smoke filled, as usual. She had no dearth of dance partners or men willing to buy her drinks. Cigarettes were hers for the asking. As she drank she became more and more relaxed. Tonight, for some reason, her control seemed to be slipping away.

Something was really off and she couldn't quite put her finger on whatever "it" was. The men were getting friendlier and she began letting her guard down. While she was enjoying the attention her outgoing personality and good looks were generating, none of the men held any interest for her. Doug wasn't here tonight, and she found herself wanting . . . someone.

One of the older men finally noticed that Allie seemed to be heading for trouble. She could barely stand anymore and dancing consisted of her partner of the moment holding her up as she managed to sway to the music. A fatherly type of man, John Anderson casually walked over to her table, and, sitting down as if he belonged there, politely asked the other two men ogling her to leave, which they did.

"Are you all right? You don't look so good, young lady." John's liquid brown eyes showed his concern, as did the furrows between his graying brows.

Her words were slurred, her eyes glazed. "I think I am. I guess. No, wait, I don't think I'm doing so good after all." She tried to smile at her new companion but was unable to make eye contact and she slowly lowered her head to rest it on the table.

"Would you like me to take you home, honey?"

"No, thank you. Kind of you to offer, but I don't know you, you know?" It was obvious she was having trouble getting the words out.

"Well, if you won't let me take you home, is there someone you'd like me to call? You're here alone, aren't you? Or can I call you a cab?"

She began to wave the man off, but then something clicked in her befuddled brain. "Can you call my friend Dave for me?"

"Dave? Dave who?"

"Just Dave. My friend. I'm pretty sure he'll come get me. He always comes when I call him, you know?"

"Sure, I'll call him. Do you know his number?"

It took her several tries, but she finally managed to get his number right. "What's your name, sweetheart? Who shall I say wants him to come?"

"Oh, he'll know. It doesn't matter anyway. He'll come. Just tell him I need a ride home." Folding her arms on the table, she was nearly asleep in seconds.

John left her to make the call.

Dave was at the bar in less than twenty minutes. The caller had said only that a very pretty young lady at Mixer's was in need of a ride home and that perhaps Dave should hurry. She had told him she was sure Dave would come, but hadn't given her name. She said Dave would know who she was.

She awoke to someone's arm around her shoulder and a soft voice in her ear. "Allie, it's me, Dave. Time to wake up, my girl."

"Dave, is that you? She raised her head but was unable to focus. Her head was swimming, but she recognized her friend's voice.

"Yup, it's me. In the flesh. I heard you needed a ride, so here's your escort home." His arm around her shoulder was warm and secure. Comforting. She was safe with

Dave. Her head relaxed on his arm and she began drifting off again.

"Thanks for coming. You're still my friend, aren't you, Dave." It was a statement, not a question.

"Sure, Allie. I'll always be your friend." He stroked her hair, slowly molding his big hand to cup her head. Finally he bent to brush a soft kiss on her crown.

Allie never noticed, but snuggled closer into her friend's arm. "You feel so good, Dave. Can't we just stay like this? Huh?"

He gently removed his arm, forcing her to wake up. Putting one arm around her waist he pulled her up and to his side, wrapping her arm around his shoulder, and then escorted her to the door and out to his pickup. Gently placing her in the passenger seat, he fastened her seatbelt. She remained more asleep than awake.

Dave drove to her house slowly, and once there, helped her into the living room where he laid her on the couch. Covering her with the afghan, he gazed at her for a moment and then turned to go.

"Don't, Dave. Don't go. Stay with me, please?" Her voice came across less slurred; she was waking up as the alcohol began to wear off.

"I really shouldn't stay, Allie. I need to go." He kept his back to her.

"No, stay. I need you." She struggled to a sitting position and patted the seat beside her. "Sit here with me for a while. I haven't seen you in, what, forever?"

He turned, slowly, reluctantly, and then sighed deeply. "Want some coffee to try to sober up a little?"

"Yes, please, that sounds wonderful." Right now she would do anything to keep him with her. She hadn't realized how much she had missed this man.

"Okay. Coffee it is. I'll be right back."

It was only a few minutes before he returned with two cups of freshly brewed coffee. He went to one of the chairs to sit, but she patted the seat on the couch beside her again, and he changed course to sit there. She moved even closer to him, leaning her head on his shoulder.

"Thanks." It was said softly, barely audible.

"You're welcome."

"I knew you would come. You've always come when I ask for you." She started to grasp his arm with her free hand.

"Careful! You're going to spill my coffee, woman!" He balanced his cup carefully as she wrenched his arm, but he was smiling at her.

"Okay, okay, I'll be careful. Drink in peace, friend." She smiled back at him.

They sat silently for a while, each lost in their own thoughts, sipping their coffee, but it wasn't long before Allie's hand started to drift a little, the remains of her coffee coming dangerously close to the rim of the cup. Dave reached over quickly, taking the cup from her loosening grasp."

"Here, let me have that. You're about to spill it everywhere, Allie."

Allie gave a little moan as she relinquished the cup, and then rested her head on Dave's shoulder, instantly asleep once more.

Dave managed to set both cups on the end table just before her head made it to his shoulder and he was no longer able to move. Watching her carefully, he raised his arm and gently lowered her until she was resting comfortably on his lap. She was sound asleep.

Finally, he was free to do things with her that he had never trusted himself to do before. Oh, it was nothing nefarious, but since he was pretty sure she wouldn't remember any of this in the morning, he allowed himself to take a few small liberties.

He simply stared at her for several long minutes, lost in the nearness of her. He had missed her so! He had promised he would never leave this woman when he took her to North Dakota after her parents had passed away in that awful accident, but she hadn't wanted him around after they returned to Bozeman. She hadn't called, hadn't asked him for anything. It had nearly killed him to keep himself from calling her, but he had done it. It was for the best, he knew, but he didn't want what was best, he wanted Allie.

His hand drifted to her face and then softly, gently, he began to caress her cheek. He pulled the loose strands of strawberry blonde hair away from her face, her beautiful, shimmery hair. His forefinger traced the line of her eyebrow, and then, even more gently, he traced the outline of her lips. He remembered kissing her those few times— they weren't nearly enough.

When he had gotten that call from a man by the name of John Anderson, informing him that a young woman at the Mixer's bar needed a ride home, he knew instantly it was Allie. He had been worried sick all the way to the bar, hoping she wasn't in any real trouble. John hadn't said too much, only that Dave should come right away. His imagination had run wild, and the relief he had felt when he saw that she was only drunk had left him nearly weak. A drunken Allie he could handle. It made him sad to see her like that, but he was so grateful she had asked for him that he didn't really care if she was passed out or not. John had stayed with her until Dave arrived, making sure that no men tried to take advantage of her. Dave had thanked him profusely, all the while noting that John wasn't someone he knew. He was thankful for that.

His gaze remained fixed on her face. Finally, he bent his head and kissed her forehead. It wasn't enough for him. He tasted her lips next, ever so gently at first, and then as his passion overcame him, he deepened the kiss. Allie, hovering on the edge of wakefulness, responded with genuine feeling. Her hands came up to frame Dave's face as she pulled him even closer.

Suddenly, as quickly as she had responded to his kiss, she was asleep once more. The moment passed. Dave heard himself as he exhaled; he felt more alive than he had in years.

She might be drunk, but she had responded to him in a way he had only dreamed about.

The progress he had made in removing her from his life vanished in those few moments of intimacy. It was as if he had never left her. *"Somebody's knockin'."* Again.

Chapter 9

It was morning. Dave was still seated on the couch with Allie's head resting on his lap when he came slowly awake to his unfamiliar surroundings. During the night he had pulled the afghan up to cover both of them, and he had obviously drifted off at some point himself. The sun's rays were streaming through the living room picture window, trying valiantly to penetrate the smudges that had accumulated over the weeks she had failed to wash it.

He allowed his gaze to leave Allie and wander around the room. The dirty window caught his eye first; it was hard to miss. He noted the fine layer of dust coating every flat surface. A cobweb decorated the lamp on the end table. The occasional small scrap of paper could be found blending into the carpet here and there. Allie obviously had not cleaned the house in weeks. It was not like her at all. She had always been a neat and tidy person. What was going on? Was she having that much trouble dealing with the death of her parents? It looked to him as if some "pastor talk" might be in order when she was ready for it. He could wait.

Sometime later Allie finally woke up. She yawned and stretched, raising her arms high above her head, nearly hitting Dave in his face. She laughed.

"You're still here?"

"What, did you think I'd just bring you home and leave you?" He was smiling down at her. He had no idea his love was shining gloriously in his eyes.

"Well, I haven't called you in weeks so I thought, well, yeah, I thought you would probably drop me off and go on home." She had apparently forgotten that she had asked him to stay last night.

"Guess you thought wrong." His face clouded suddenly. "Wait, are you upset that I stayed? I can leave right now if you want me to."

"No, silly. I like having you around. You have a very comfortable lap, did you know that?"

"Glad to be of service, ma'am. You can use it anytime. I could have used a lap of my own though. Your couch is comfortable, but a bed is a lot more so." His face reddened at the possible implication after the liberties he had taken with her last night. How much did she remember? He had no idea and no way to find out without asking her.

She sat up slowly, holding her head as she did so. "Oh, brother, does my head ever hurt. Guess I was pretty drunk last night, wasn't I? I had fun, though."

"Yup, you were pretty drunk. You were nearly passed out when I got there. Allie, why did you drink so much? Want to talk about it?"

She ignored his questions. "Wish you had come earlier. I remember you're a pretty good dancer, and we could have had some fun together."

He looked at her and rolled his eyes. "Allie, I . . ."

"You what, Preach? You didn't like dancing with me?"

"It's not that, exactly."

"Well, you sure acted like you were enjoying it when you took me a few months ago." She leaned back into the couch and closed her eyes. "It's a lot more fun at that bar with you, Dave. Take me dancing again next week?"

"No, I don't think that's a good idea. It wasn't before and it isn't now."

Allie hadn't missed that look in Dave's eyes when he smiled at her earlier. She played him, now.

"Would you rather I danced with those other men at that bar, then?"

"Allie, you know I don't approve of that. You really shouldn't be hanging out in bars anyway."

"Well, the only way to take care of that situation is to take me yourself. Now, if you don't care and you really don't want to, well, that's that. But I'd rather you took me. How about next week?"

"Can we talk about it later?"

"I guess. But next week will be here pretty fast!" She began to fidget where she sat, and then suddenly sat up.

"I think I need a smoke. Have you seen my cigarettes anywhere around here?"

"Since when do you smoke, Allie?"

"Since, oh, I don't know. Anyway, I want one now. Where's my purse?"

"It's on the kitchen table where I left it last night."

She left the room but returned soon with a pack and a lighter in her hands. Sitting next to him on the couch, she looked at him coyly as she handed him the lighter.

"Light one for me?"

"Allie, you really shouldn't."

"Will you light it for me or not? Don't preach to me, just light it for me."

He did as she asked. It was always hard for him to go into a bar. A former heavy smoker himself, the heady smell of a cigarette was always a torture for him. He had never stopped wanting to smoke, and only his commitment to God and his new life in Christ had kept him from it all these years. Now he was deliberately inhaling that smoke first hand, right in front of his face. It was all he could do not to take the cigarette from her and suck in one good, strong, deep hit of that smoke. His insides were churning. He knew he should leave right now, but his desire to stay with her won. He folded his hands in his lap and settled himself for the time being. His craving for a cigarette was suddenly on par with his craving for the woman herself.

Steeling himself against the temptation, he leaned away from her, trying to remove himself from that wonderful smell that permeated the room each time she exhaled.

She laughed at him. She knew it wasn't kind, but she did it anyway. "What's the matter, Dave? Does my smoking make you want a cigarette yourself? You're welcome to one of mine. Here." She pulled a single cigarette from the pack and held it out to him. "Go on, take it. It won't bite you." She laughed again.

"Allie, stop it. If you keep this up I'm leaving."

"Spoilsport! Go on, then, go on home. You've done your duty by bringing me home, and I thank you for it."

"You're mad now?"

"No, Preach, I'm not mad. But I know you're a busy person, so it's fine, you can head out. I have a lot to do today so I really guess I should get to it."

Dave looked at her, a long, hard stare. What was going on here?

"Come on. I'll walk you to the door." She put her cigarette in a waiting ashtray and rose to her feet, encasing one of Dave's arms in her own, slowly guiding him to the door.

Dave allowed himself to be led, confusion written all over his face. What was going on with her, anyway?

And then Allie did the unthinkable. Right in front of the door, she spun around to face him, grabbed his face with both hands, and, pulling him to her she proceeded to kiss him long and hard, tasting him, moving against him, putting everything she had into that kiss.

He kissed her back, then pulled roughly away from her and rapidly left the house. He heard her soft chuckle as he nearly ran to his pickup.

Allie wrapped her arms around herself as the door slammed behind her friend, and then, still laughing, she returned to the couch. She sat and finished that cigarette she had started, laughing out loud again, and then rose to go take a much-needed shower. Men were so very predictable!

She stood under the hot, steaming stream until the water began to turn tepid. Exiting the shower, she remotely noticed that the room was steamed, the mirror fogged. Her mind seemed numb. It was as if she was watching herself from across the room, totally detached. Shaking her head, she began to dry off with the thirsty towel, but seemed to be having trouble drying her face. It stayed wet. Finally ,she sank to the floor, holding the towel in front of her, sitting cross-legged on the carpet.

She was crying noiselessly. It finally registered and she came back to herself. Yes, she was definitely crying. *What am I crying about? I'm fine. I'm happy. I have plenty of money and I'm living exactly as I wish.* She blew her nose in the towel, not thinking and then got to her feet. She threw the towel into the dirty clothes hamper and went to get dressed, but found herself was crying once more. *Enough of this!*

She suddenly realized she was pacing the length and breadth of her bedroom, back and forth, back and forth, still crying. Finally she forced herself to stop, and tried to think rationally, but it was no use. Her fist pounded the nightstand by the bed. *No!* And she heard herself beginning to voice random thoughts. The words came softly at first, but the volume and tempo of her vocalizations steadily increased. It wasn't long before she was shouting loudly into the empty house, sobbing at the same time.

Allie was angry. She was more than angry. Words were inadequate to express the overwhelming enormity of her anger. She clenched and unclenched her fists as she began to pace the whole house. Looming over the essence of nearly everything she screamed was the one word, *"Why?"*

It had all been for nothing, in the end, and she put the blame for everything squarely on God. He was the final authority, wasn't He? She had loved her patient, Joe, and he was dead. Her parents, how she had loved and adored them! And a moose? That just didn't make any sense. They were now dead. And the root of the whole mess was the fact that she had given her baby away. Catherine was *her* baby, not Raven's. If only she had known everything would turn out like this she would never have given up her baby. Never.

And just where was she now? Hanging out in bars, smoking, drinking more and more, and for what? What was the point? Life had absolutely no meaning for her anymore.

Hours later exhaustion finally overcame her. Going into the kitchen she found the bottle of Crown Royal and drank directly from the bottle. She wanted oblivion from her present state. Still naked, she took the bottle to the living room and sat heavily on the couch. After one more strong swallow from the bottle, she capped it, sat it on the floor at her feet, and, covering herself with the ever-present afghan, sank into that oblivion she longed for so desperately.

When she awoke, it was afternoon and the sun was starting its descent. She was rational now, and she recognized her deep-seated anger for what it was. But she was able to think clearly and she began going over her list of grievances once more.

Her parents were dead. Both of them were gone and death being the finality that it was, there was nothing that could be done about that. Joe was also gone, and again, nothing could be done to change that.

She was lonely. It would help to go back to work, but she really didn't want to do that just yet, and with the money her parents had left her, she didn't need to. She could put that work "thing" on hold, at least for the time being. It was an option for the future.

But her baby? Her baby was alive and flourishing with another woman. As long as Catherine was out there, maybe Allie had some sort of a chance. Maybe there was some way she could get her daughter back. Short of getting her permanently, at least there should be a way for her to see Catherine regularly. Maybe. But how to do it?

Sometime later the solution came to her. Dave. She could use her pastor friend Dave. When she had been resting on his lap on the couch she had seen it in his eyes; he was in love with her. She had literally seen his heart in his eyes, and Allie was not a stupid girl. She liked Dave, she really did, but she was not in love with him. It occurred to her that she might be able to be around Catherine if she used Dave to get there. But how? She would have to make a plan, a good one. Perhaps she could have it all, if she was just clever enough.

She recognized the fact that she would have to use her friend, and perhaps not in a nice way. It might be unfair to him, but if it meant getting her way, she would do whatever it took to achieve her goals.

She dwelt on her situation the rest of the day and well into the night, trying to formulate a plan. She smiled when it finally came to her. She would use Dave's obvious love for her to get to Catherine. Raven and Gus, Catherine's adoptive parents, were regular churchgoers at Dave's church. It would mean she would have to start attending Grace Bible Church, but she guessed there were worse things in life than going to church steadily. But no one could know exactly why she was starting to attend. She would couch it in terms of her relationship with Dave. Yes, her plan just might work. She would start tomorrow.

Chapter 10

Dave felt like he had been blindsided. He had been working so hard to stifle his feelings for Allie, and then two days ago she had called him back into her life after weeks of absence. While he was still in love with her, he had finally gotten at least a little control over his emotions where she was concerned. She had asked him to take her home from the bar, and, as expected, he had come running. In all fairness, he told himself, he would have done the same for anyone. But Allie was special and his response was visceral. Then she had made it worse for him by asking him to stay with her that night. But the final blow had come when she had kissed him goodbye at the door as he was leaving. It hadn't been just a kiss between friends, it had been a womanly kiss, full of promise and seduction. His relapse was complete.

He found himself once again thinking about her at all hours of the day and night, seeing her face in his mind, her smile, her hair. Her kiss, over and over. He wanted more. He wasn't allowed to have what he wanted. *If only she would become a Christian. If only . . .*

He spent what seemed like hours trying to think up some excuse to call her. Finally, he settled on the only logical one: dinner. They used to spend time at restaurants together as friends, so why couldn't they do so again? It was harmless enough as long as he kept his hands to himself. She probably needed someone to talk to anyway, and who better than a pastor friend? Who better than him?

He called her the next afternoon.

"Allie? It's me, Dave. Just wondering how you're doing after your night on the town. Are you all right now?"

Her laugh was light, happy.

"I'm fine, Dave. Actually, I was just thinking about you. We haven't been out for a meal in ages. How about dinner one of these evenings? Do you think you have time for me?"

Do I have time for you? If only I didn't! "That sounds great. How about tomorrow, say around five again? I'll pick you up so you don't have to drive. How does that sound?"

"See you tomorrow, then. Take care."

"You too. Sleep well." He hung up the phone, and then sat staring at it for what seemed like ages. She wanted to see him again; that kiss had been almost a promise, it seemed. She had terrified him. He had loved it.

He picked her up promptly at five the next evening. Allie was wearing new dark denim blue jeans and a semi sheer lacy blouse with pearl buttons. She looked fabulous, as always. They drove to the Black Angus again, their favorite place to dine in Bozeman. The interior was muted and cozy with booths encased in dark, smoky glass, making them basically private. The atmosphere suited them both for different reasons.

"Wine with dinner, Dave?"

He started to protest the idea but she cut him off.

"We've had wine before and it was okay with you. I think you enjoyed it, didn't you?"

"Well, yes, I did. But you seem to forget that I'm a minister and it really doesn't look good, remember?"

"I bet the Bible doesn't say one thing about drinking a little wine, does it? Come on, let's enjoy some together."

He gave in, his resistance lower than ever before. Glancing around their booth, he felt comfortable and invisible. "Okay. But just one glass, right?"

She laughed at him again. She was full of laughter tonight, it seemed. "Whatever you say, Preach. One or ten, whatever you say." She tossed her head making her hair swing provocatively.

The motion did not go unnoticed by her dinner companion. His eyes glistened in the darkened booth, shining with his emotion. She was so beautiful. He wanted her more than ever.

They talked, they laughed, and they drank wine. Allie was friendly but not overly so. She was back to her old winsome self; easy, confident, and pleasant to be around. Too soon it was time to take her home.

Dave hated to see the evening end, but he had a busy day tomorrow and besides, he didn't want to push anything. Her kiss had been all too inviting, but he was going to try his best to keep himself under control. He couldn't help but wonder how the evening was going to end, however. Would she kiss him again? He wouldn't initiate anything, but he sure wouldn't turn down another kiss like the one she had given him the other night. Not for all the wheat in Montana.

They pulled up in front of her house and he got out to walk her to the front door. "Oh, you don't have to walk me in, Dave. It's okay. It's not like it's a date or anything. We're just friends, after all."

"No, I wouldn't feel right if I didn't walk you to the door at least." He laughed. "It's just not done that way." Feeling brave, he took her arm in his and escorted her up the walk.

"Well, thanks for another very lovely dinner. I always enjoy spending time with you."

"I like spending time with you too, Allie. You know that, I think." He stood, waiting, trying not to look expectant.

"See you around, Preach. Thanks again." She raised her head and gave him a quick, light kiss on his cheek. "Dinner again, maybe next week?"

"Sure. Want me to call you?"

"That would be great. Talk to you soon, then. Good night." She turned and was gone.

Dave stood there for several seconds, stunned. *What did you think, stupid? Thought she was going to kiss you again or something? Dream on. Things were different, before. You might love her but you're still only a good friend to her. Get real.*

His head lowered, he turned and walked slowly back to his pickup. Allie watched from her window. She smiled as he walked away.

He called her the following Tuesday, having managed to wait exactly one week before calling her again, relying on her veiled promise to go out to dinner with him again. In fact, she had never refused his invitations to lunches or dinners, but he didn't want to push it either. There could always be a first time for her to refuse, and the last thing he wanted was for her to turn him down.

This time they went to the Stockman in Livingston. Dave thought it less likely that he might run into one of his parishioners, and while it was a bar, it did have a separate eating area and was known around town for great food. Like most bars, the lights were dimmed, making for an intimate dining atmosphere. The conversation flowed easily, as it always did between them, and the time flew.

She lit her first cigarette as soon as she finished her meal. "Allie, do you have to?"

"Do I have to what, exactly?"

"Smoke."

"Oh, don't be such a prude. I happen to like the taste of them and I also happen to be over twenty-one."

"What if I ask you nicely?"

"Later. I'll just have a couple more and then that's it for tonight. Okay?"

"Okay." What could he say? He couldn't tell her how that smell was so addicting for him. How he used to be a chain smoker but had quit years ago. How he still craved one nearly every day.

Tonight beer was the drink of choice, and after three glasses, each one accompanied by a cigarette, Allie brought up the subject of dancing again. She crossed her arms on the table in front of her, and leaned forward toward her dinner companion.

"Dave, I have a favor to ask." Her eyes were shining, liquid, inviting.

"Sure, Allie, you know I'll try to help you in any way I can. What do you need?"

She leaned a little closer, her blouse gaping just enough to allow Dave a tantalizing glimpse of her cleavage. He swallowed, hard.

"Take me dancing tomorrow? Please?" She was smiling that irresistible smile of hers again.

"Allie, I'm a pastor, remember? I don't dance, girl." With an effort he turned his eyes away from the obvious display before him.

"You took me before and we had fun, didn't we? I know I did, and I'm pretty sure you weren't too miserable yourself."

"Well, you're right, I wasn't exactly miserable. But Allie, it just isn't right. How about we just do dinner again instead?"

Allie straightened up in her chair, uncrossing her arms and placing her hands in her lap.

"If you can take me once, you can take me again, I think. It didn't kill you before and it won't kill you tomorrow either. Come on, Preach, you're a great dancer and it was fun."

"Allie, I . . ."

"You what, exactly? Scared or something?" She began to taunt him.

"No, I'm not scared. I think you know me better than that. But it's just not right. I shouldn't be in bars, dancing."

"Well, I miss it, so I plan to go to Mixer's, tomorrow. If you won't take me, then fine. I'm sure I can find someone to dance with me, but I'd still rather it was you." She laughed at him. "At least you can probably keep me from making a fool of myself in public. I probably won't be drinking too much if you're with me. Please?"

That was the clincher for Dave. The thought of Allie dancing with other men, drinking with them and then—what if Doug was there and they—memories of watching her lead Doug into a motel room came rushing back, overwhelming him. He closed eyes in defeat.

"Okay. I'll take you. But dancing only and I can't stay late. I'll get my associate to take over the Wednesday evening service for me. But Allie, I can't be doing this every week, you know? Can't we find something else to do? How about a movie some evening instead?"

"I'll think about it, Dave, but tomorrow you'll take me, right?"
"Yes, I'll take you. What time should I pick you up, then?"

"How about seven? I'll try not to keep you out too late, how does that sound?" Sudden inspiration hit Dave and he decided to give it a try.

"Allie, how about we make a deal?"

"What kind of a deal, exactly?" Her face betrayed her hesitation.

"I'll take you dancing tomorrow if you'll come to church Sunday. I do something with you that you like and you do something with me that I like. Fair?"

She closed her eyes as she contemplated his proposition. "Okay, I'll come to church, but only once, and not this week. But I will come one of these weeks. Good enough for you?"

His heart sang in his chest. She had agreed to attend a Sunday service. Perhaps she was going to be open to the Gospel after all. Maybe there was hope that she would become a true believer, and that meant that there might be a chance for him.

"Fair enough. But you promised to come and I won't let you off the hook on that one. If not this Sunday, how about next week?"

"Don't push me on this, Dave. I said I'd come, and I will, but it will be when I'm ready. I haven't been in church for years and I have to psych myself up for it. It might take me a while to get there." She smiled at him again.

"But you will come?" His eagerness rang in his voice.

"Yes, I said I would, and I will. I'll let you know when. In the meantime, be sure to wear your dancing shoes tomorrow night. I'll be wearing mine!" She beamed at him.

Dave drove back to Bozeman as slowly as he dared. His three beers were well out of his system and he was confident he was sober enough to drive. Allie, however, had managed to down two more beers before they left and seemed a little light-headed. Halfway to Bozeman she managed to slide across the bench seat and leaned against her escort, her head coming to rest on his shoulder. Unconsciously his arm found its way around her and he pulled her close. He reduced his speed a little more.

She was sleeping, it seemed. Every now and then he lowered his eyes to gaze at his passenger. Twice his lips found their way of their own accord to the top of her head; a feather-light kiss and then a deep breath, inhaling the fragrant scent of her. He found he was grateful for the beers that had induced her sleep. Somehow he needed to keep his love a secret from her if he could. He had no idea his eyes had already betrayed him.

He pulled up in front of her house and turned the engine off. Unwilling to lose her to the night, he sat with his arm around her for some time. Finally, she stirred and then sat up abruptly.

"Oh my! I'm sorry, Dave, I didn't mean to . . ."

"It's fine, Allie. I don't mind. You felt kind of good, actually." He smiled at her. "Don't let it go to your head, though. I'm still a preacher, remember?"

"Silly!" She smoothed her tumbled hair from her face and yawned deeply. "Thanks for a great evening. Dinner with you is always fun for me."

They exchanged glances, each trying to read something in the other's expression.

Suddenly Allie raised her face and gave him a sweet kiss on the cheek. "Thanks again. I can walk myself in tonight."

Before he could restrain her or make any comment, Allie slid to the other side of the seat, reached for the door and was out in seconds. Waving at him through the window, she turned quickly and ran up the steps to her front door. She did not look back.

Dave watched her go, puzzled. A kiss on his cheek? He blushed as he remembered the kiss she had given him the other day. He wanted her to kiss him again like that. Deep. Memorable. Addicting.

He fought with himself most of that night, lying awake, chastising himself, trying to find a way out of taking her dancing. He tried, but he knew his heart wasn't in the denial. The truth was, he wanted desperately to take her dancing. He wanted to be in that smoke-filled bar, holding her tightly in his arms. He wanted to feel her, smell her, and hold her. He liked the taste of beer and he wanted the freedom once more to drink it as he liked. Not to excess, he told himself, but some, just for the taste of it. He wanted much more than that, but these thoughts were as far as he allowed himself to go. He wrestled with the fact that he was skipping his church duties for a woman and a truly sinful atmosphere. He wanted it all, however, the woman and the bar. There was no denying that. He found himself pushing God further and further from his thoughts as those of the woman he loved took over.

He picked her up the next evening as he had promised. His eyes shone as she met him at the door; Allie was indeed beautiful.

She put her arm through his, smiling at him the whole time.

"Thanks, Preach. We're going to have fun tonight, aren't we?" She gave his arm a quick squeeze.

"Sure, Allie. We'll have a good time, I think." He grimaced as a quick thought of church and the missed prayer service raced through his mind, but it was quickly gone, replaced by Allie's wonderful smile of promise.

Since Allie had started smoking, he found himself wanting a cigarette more and more.

As they entered the bar, the smell nearly overwhelmed him. They found a table, she lit up a cigarette, and before he realized it, he was asking her for a smoke.

"Allie, do you think . . . well . . . ."

"What, Dave, do I think what exactly?" Turning her head, she casually exhaled to the side, the smoke visible to his yearning eyes.

"Can I have a cigarette, please? Just one."

"Dave, you don't smoke. What do you want a cigarette for? They're not good for you, you know!" She puffed hers again.

"I know, I know. I quit years ago, but I just really want one now. Just one. I'll just have one. That's enough, I think."

Allie laughed as she pulled the half-empty pack from her purse and handed it to her escort.

"Here, have one on me. But you said only one, and I'm going to hold you to it, Preach."

He pulled one from the package and she lit it for him with her own. He inhaled deeply at the familiar odor. His eyes closed in pure pleasure. He had forgotten how good a cigarette was. Unhealthy, perhaps, but wonderful.

They each ordered a beer, and sat comfortably, smoking and drinking. Church was completely forgotten and Dave's past life came surging back for him. Bars, women, smoke, drinks. It felt good, like an old sheepskin jacket he once owned. He let the warm feelings envelope him, and he smiled softly. No wonder people sinned so easily. Sin felt good, so deceptively good.

Allie was drinking beer, two to his one. She was getting tipsy, just the way she seemed to want to be.

"Dance with me now, Preach? You've finished your cigarette."

"Sure, Allie. Let's hit the floor." He rose to his feet, holding his hand out to her in an invitation.

Most of the dances were slow ones, country western tunes, melancholy and inviting in a way. Dave lost himself in the music and Allie. He found himself pulling her closer and closer to himself, loving how she felt, how she smelled. It was all so good. So very, very good.

They stayed until closing time, drinking and dancing. Dave was true to his word and did not ask for another cigarette, but he did continue drinking the occasional beer. He felt slightly light-headed when it was time to drive home, but he was confident he could drive safely. Her home was not far away, and he could take the side streets. They arrived around three in the morning.

Allie allowed him to walk her to her front door this time, leaning heavily against him as they walked. She was a little happy, but not really drunk, not like the other day when that Mr. Anderson had called him to come and take her home.

"Dave, I think you'd better come in and stay for a while. You're not completely sober." She was smiling broadly at him again.

"Oh, I think I can make it home okay. I made it this far." The last thing he wanted to do was to go home, but he knew he shouldn't be staying. He wasn't sure he would be able to control himself alone with Allie after a few beers.

"You sure?"

"I'm sure. I'll call you, okay?"

"Okay. You call me when you miss me."

He heard himself mumbling unintelligibly. "I miss you already, woman."

In what seemed like slow motion, Allie reached for him, and pulling his head down, she kissed him again as she had done the other day. A scorching, seductive kiss as she put everything she had into it."

Pulling away only slightly, she breathed the words into his open mouth ever so softly. "Thanks for a great night, Preach." Then she turned and was gone.

At home, in his bed, Dave Benson never noticed the tears that seeped slowly, silently down his cheeks. Despair seeped into him as he relived the night with Allie. What had he done? What was he going to do? How could he possibly give her up? He couldn't. He wouldn't.

Chapter 11

The next morning, he called his friend Gus again.

"Gus, it's Dave. Got time for me again sometime today?"

"Sure, Dave. What's up?"

"More of the same, Gus. I just really need to talk to someone, and you're my best friend so you get the pleasure, it you don't mind too much." He was desperate. They made arrangements to meet later that afternoon, this time at a small café in Belgrade. Dave wanted at least a little privacy.

The look on Gus's face betrayed his concern as he walked to the table where Dave was waiting for him.

"Coffee, Gus?"

"Sure. Black, as usual." Gus took the empty chair across from his friend, sliding easily onto the seat.

"You look terrible, if I do say so, Dave. What on earth is going on with you?"

"Gus, it's Allie. No, wait, it's me, not her. I can't blame her for anything. This is all my doing and my problem."

"Okay, so take it one step at a time for me here. What do you think you have to blame yourself for that's so upsetting to you?" He stared at his friend hard, eye to eye, unblinking, and then took a deep breath.

"Dave, you haven't . . ."

"Haven't what, Gus? Haven't fallen even more in love with a woman young enough to be my daughter? Haven't relapsed into some old habits I thought were long out of my system? Haven't found thoughts of her pushing my communion with Christ out of my head? Haven't kissed her? Haven't told her how I feel? I haven't what, exactly?"

Gus sighed deeply, his concern and sorrow for his good friend and pastor written all over his face. "Does she know? Does she know how much you love her? Have you told her?"

"No, I don't think she knows. Oh, I'm sure she knows I like her a lot. How could she miss that one? I take her out to dinner, I rescue her when she needs rescuing." He paused. "I took her dancing at the Mixer's bar last night. Again."

Gus stared at his friend. "You took her where? You did what?"

"She wanted me to take her dancing, so I did. And that's not all I did, Gus."

"What else do you want to tell me here?"

"I had a few beers and a cigarette. Me. I did that."

"I thought you quit smoking years ago, Dave. And I know you quit drinking. You're a pastor now, a born-again Christian. A leader. You had a cigarette?"

"Yup. Gus, it was so good, smoking again. It's like that heroin I used to do—I can't get enough of it. I find myself wanting a cigarette nearly every waking moment now. I know I shouldn't have had that one, but . . ."

"Go on, but what?"

"Well, Allie has started smoking and being around her, well, it just got to me. I asked her for one and she gave it to me."

"Was she laughing, Dave?"

"No, she actually told me it wasn't good for me and tried to talk me out of it. But I wanted it, Gus. I really, really wanted it. So she gave one to me. I promised her it would only be one, and I kept my promise, but it was hard, let me tell you. I want one right now, and I suppose if there was one available I'd go ahead and smoke it."

"Well, Dave, a cigarette isn't the end of the world for you. Not good sense, but let's get practical here. So you relapsed in that department. Not healthy, but not a qualification one way or the other for a pastor. They won't kick you out for smoking once in a while. Rest easy on that one, my friend."

"And the beer? What about the beer? What about hanging out in a bar? What about the dancing? Gus, what on earth am I going to do?" He hung his head in his hands, defeated.

Softly, barely audible, Gus asked, "Have you slept with her?"

Dave was suddenly enveloped in a silence so pronounced he found it difficult to even blink. There. It was out. The topic he had been trying so desperately to keep from even entering his mind. But there it was. Gus seemed to know what was really on his mind.

"No, I haven't."

Gus' sigh of relief was audible.

Dave raised his head and looked his friend steadily in the eyes. "But Gus, I want to. I want to so bad you can't imagine."

"Well, that's where you're wrong, Dave. I most certainly can relate to how you feel, I'm married to Raven, remember? I still think of how it was for me when she didn't even know I existed as a man. There isn't a man in this world that wouldn't want to, well, you know what I mean. So yes, I do know how you feel, and frankly I wouldn't wish that feeling on anyone. I'm sorry, Dave, I really am."

"Yeah. I'm sorry too. It's coming, Gus. I can feel it in my bones. I'm caught in a web of my own making and I'm too weak to break away. The sad truth is I don't really want to get away. I love her, Gus. I love her and I want to marry her. Somehow, some way, there just has to be a way. But even if I find that way, I don't know if she'd have me. I don't really know how she feels about me."

"Well, we know she obviously likes your company or she wouldn't be going out with you."

"Liking me and loving me enough to marry me are two different things. You know that as well as I do. Besides, I can "legally" do a lot of things as a pastor, but you and I both know that I can't marry someone who is not a Christian and remain a pastor. It just won't work. I don't think she'd even consider marrying a minister anyway. No way."

"So, what now, Dave. How can I help?"

"You've helped me just by listening to my pitiful story, Gus. Other than that, I need your prayers, my friend. I need them badly. Please pray for me to have the strength to get through this. To get through it and past it." He was quiet for a moment.

"Gus, do you remember that song from years ago called *Somebody's Knockin'?*"

Gus was pensive for a moment before replying, "Yeah, I remember it. What about it?"

Dave softly sang the words to the first verse:

"Somebody's knockin',
should I let him in?
Lord, it's the devil,
would you look at him?
I've heard about him
but I never dreamed,
He'd have blue eyes and blue jeans..."

"I never dreamed the devil would be a woman, and she'd have blue eyes and blue jeans."

"Are you trying to compare Allie to the devil?"

"No, but the devil is all about temptation, and Allie is the biggest temptation I think I've ever run across."

"Not fair, is it, Dave? What about heroin, cigarettes, and booze? Aren't they the biggest ones?"

"Before I became a Christian those vices just sort of went with my lifestyle. But I got saved, Gus. I got saved big time. And now . . . she has blue eyes and blue jeans. And I'm lost."

Gus sat quietly, eyes downcast. He took a sip of his coffee, then looked up at his good friend. "I'm probably asking a really stupid question here, but is there any chance at all that you can just walk away from her? What about quitting the church here in Bozeman and applying for a position elsewhere? Maybe out of the state?"

"Nope. Can't do it. It's too late for that. I tried and I was actually doing fairly well for a few weeks. I didn't call her and she didn't call me. Then her parents were killed in a freak car accident with a moose, and she called me for help. I went with her to Mandan to help her with the funeral arrangements and taking care of the estate, and I've been locked right back in ever since."

"Why did you have to go, Dave? Doesn't she have any brothers or sisters that could have helped her out?"

"She's an only child, so no, she had no one to help her besides me. And Gus, I have to admit, I was so happy she called me! I was so miserable without her, you just don't understand. No, wait, there's Raven. You're right, you do understand. I forgot."

"I guess I'll just have to pray really hard then. I'm assuming you won't want Raven and Pen to know anything about this, right? They could be praying too, you know."

"No, I don't want anyone else to know. I'm too ashamed, Gus. I never in my wildest dreams thought anything like this could ever happen to me. Not to me." He shook his head slowly, then turned and stared silently into space. Finally he rose to his feet, his gaze returning to his good friend.

"Thanks for coming, Gus. Even though I know you really can't help me, it felt good to bare my soul a little. I know you'll keep everything I've told you to yourself. I know too that you'll pray for me." He turned and left his friend sitting at the table with his cold coffee.

Pouring his heart out to his friend was cathartic and sobering. It was late afternoon when he opened his front door, and, locking it behind him, walked slowly through the house to his bedroom. He removed his jacket and kicked his boots off, then wordlessly sank to his knees on the carpet. He lowered his head and began praying silently to his God. Pouring out his heart, it took only a few sentences before his words ran out. He had nothing left to say. God knew it all already anyway; words were superfluous. Becoming weak with emotion, he lowered himself to a prone position, his arms outstretched, his body forming the shape of a cross on the floor. His forehead pressed into the carpet, he found himself groaning softly, unintelligible sounds with no meaning escaping into the bedroom. At one point he pounded his fists onto the floor in his agony. Finally he turned his head to the side and succumbed to the deep sleep of total exhaustion. He knew God had heard him and he rested in that fact.

Morning found him still on the floor, stiff and cold. Slowly, he got to his feet. He had prayed as he had never prayed before in his life, expecting to be released from the temptations that were bearing down on him. But he found that was not the case. Allie was still burning on his mind. What was wrong? *God? Why? Where are You?*

There was no reply in his spirit; there didn't need to be. He knew the answer already. He had prayed for an "easy out," but the simple truth was that he didn't want out. Not really. Not in the deepest part of his being. He still wanted Allie. He wanted to retain control of his life in his own way. There would be no simple relief for him. He was sorry—very, very sorry, but he was not truly repentant. His prayer time became shorter and shorter from that day on, and thoughts of Allie took up more and more of his time. He was walking away from God, and while deep inside he realized that fact, he did nothing to reverse it.

Chapter 12

Allie now had the semblance of a plan in her head. She had lost everything of importance in her life, and while some things could never be replaced or restored, one thing remained that could, if she was shrewd enough, possibly be set right. She could get her daughter back. It would take a lot of planning and time, but in her heart she was certain it could be accomplished. She realized that fair play was out of the question. She knew she could do nothing openly, but would have to tread very cautiously indeed. She would get to her daughter through her pastor friend, Dave Benson.

She had known for some time that Dave was in love with her. It was sad, really, because she also realized that he was actually nothing more than a good friend to her, and while Allie was basically a "good girl," she had no qualms whatsoever about using her friend to get what she wanted. The way to Catherine lay through Dave, who was good friends with the adoptive parents of her child. If she was smart and took it slow, she planned to get to Catherine through him.

Where to start? She would have to go to church, probably more than once. No one could keep her away from a church, and Dave would be so happy that she was attending she knew she would be welcomed warmly. Yes, that was how to start.

On Saturday, she began. She called Dave around ten in the morning, taking him completely by surprise.

"Dave, it's me." Her voice betrayed the smile she had plastered on her face.

"Oh, hi Allie. You surprised me; I wasn't expecting to hear from you today." His pleasure at hearing her voice came through the phone. "Always nice to hear from you, my friend. What's up?"

"Well, remember that I promised to come to church if you would take me dancing?"

"Sure, I remember. How could I forget that?"

"Well, how about tomorrow?"

"Tomorrow? I thought you said you wouldn't be coming for some time?"

"Well, if you don't want me to come . . ." Her voice trailed off as she smiled to herself.

"No, no, it's not that. Of course I want you to come. Tomorrow, you say?"

"Yes, tomorrow. But what time should I show up?"

"The service starts at ten, so if you show up by nine-thirty or nine-forty-five that should be fine."

"Are you preaching tomorrow or is that associate pastor doing the honors?"

"Does it matter?"

"Not at all, but if you aren't preaching can you sit with me? Or would that not be a good thing for you to do?"

He laughed, a warm, pleasing sound. "Sorry, I can't sit with you since I am indeed giving the message. But I'm sure you can find a good seat in the back if you're nervous about coming. And the people are all very friendly, so don't worry."

"Oh, I'm not worried, not at all." *Quite the opposite. I'm excited.*

"Allie, thanks for calling, and thanks for agreeing to come. I'll be looking for you."

"I have a small request, though."

"What small request would that be, woman?"

"Take me out to lunch afterward?"

"You got it. Lunch it is. You can pick the place. Your wish is my command."

"Thanks, Dave. See you tomorrow."

"See you. Thanks for calling."

Allie hung up the phone, her face a mask, devoid of emotion. Step one was accomplished and no one was the wiser. With any luck at all, Raven and Gus would be there tomorrow, and they would have Catherine with them. She would at least be able to see her baby if only from a distance. She would probably have to become a regular at church, but she could handle that. And she would have to play Dave as she had never played a man before in her life; he was the key, the go-between.

The next morning she showered and dressed carefully. Everything had to be perfect to pull this off. She had to look stunning and sexy for Dave, but not overtly to the point that anyone would notice but him. Knowing the man was in love with her ensured that he would see what other casual observers would most likely miss. She was dressing for him, but also with the goal of remaining anonymous. She thought about her hair for some time. She wanted to look good, not too obvious in any way, but different from her usual look. The last thing she wanted was for Raven and Gus to recognize her; she wanted to blend in with the crowd and not stand out in any way, wanting to see without being seen. Pulling her hair back into a tight bun, with tan slacks and a matching blazer, she actually looked nothing like her usual self. A hat retrieved from the back of her closet completed the look. Gazing at her reflection in the hall mirror, she barely recognized herself. With her hair up and extra makeup, her appearance was totally different from her everyday look. She looked very sophisticated, nothing like a native Montanan.

She arrived early and parked in the back of the parking lot, leaving herself a good view of most of the vehicles. If Raven and Gus showed up she wanted to enter the building after them, planning on their gazes being toward the front of the church when she came in to sit. She would take a back pew and hopefully remain out of their sight while allowing her to watch them covertly from behind, and hopefully get a glimpse of Catherine.

She waited until nearly ten o'clock, but saw no sign of the couple. They hadn't come this morning! Her plan was all a waste of her time. She debated whether to go in or not, since her main objective had been ruined, and in the end started the car and drove home. Church could wait for another week. If she couldn't see Catherine she really didn't want any part of church.

Dave finally called her later that afternoon.

"Allie? I looked for you this morning but didn't see you anywhere. Did you change your mind? You didn't come?"

"Yeah, sorry, I chickened out. I actually made it to the parking lot, but, well, it's been an awful long time since I was in church and I guess I just got cold feet. Are you mad?"

"No, not mad, just disappointed. I was really hoping you would come. You could critique my preaching, maybe give me some helpful hints, you know?"

"I'm sorry, Dave. I really am. Can we do lunch anyway or do you have other plans?"

"Lunch would be great. Can I pick you up?"

"Anytime, cowboy. I'll be ready, and we can talk some more over food. Okay?"

"I'll be there shortly. See you soon."

She hurried down the hall to her bedroom where she hastily let her hair down and then went to the bathroom where she carefully removed the extra makeup she had applied earlier. She wanted to save her "disguise" for another Sunday when it was needed. For Dave, the look would be her usual.

When the doorbell rang, Allie greeted her friend with a warm smile and her normal casual look. Her hair was soft and shiny, swinging easily around her shoulders. The dark indigo jeans were back, and paired with a soft pink blouse, Allie looked young, innocent, and lovely.

They went to the Bacchus downtown and settled themselves comfortably in one of the many booths.

"So, you made it as far as the parking lot this morning, but then changed your mind and left?"

"That's pretty much what happened. Sorry, like I said."

"Did something happen? Did someone say something to you? I never took you for a timid person, so I have trouble believing you were too scared to come in."

"Well, I wasn't really scared, and no, no one said anything to me. I never even got out of the car. I just, well . . ."

"At any rate, I'm sorry you didn't come in. I was really hoping to see you there, you know?"

"Tell you what—I promise I'll be there next Sunday, okay? Scout's honor, I will."

The waitress brought their meals and they concentrated on eating for the next few moments. Then Allie had an idea, and putting her fork down, she propped her elbows on the table, lacing her fingers together, and rested her chin on them.

"I have an idea."

Dave rolled his eyes in mock dismay.

"What now? It's Sunday and I can guarantee you I am definitely not taking you dancing today!"

"No, silly, no dancing today. That's reserved for Wednesday evenings. How about a movie this afternoon?"

"A movie?" His face registered confusion, his brows furrowed.

"Sure. A movie. Why not? Or don't preachers go to movies either?" She turned on the charm, smiling that warm smile she was so good at."

Dave tipped his head back and laughed out loud. "Do you have any idea how many years it's been since I went to a movie? And yes, I think it's okay for a preacher to go to the movies as long as it isn't R rated or anything." He laughed again at the idea.

"Well, let's see what's playing and what time the next show starts. And I'm warning you—I want a large popcorn and a soda to go with it."

"You got it, my girl."

They finished their meal then walked outside to see what was playing. They were in luck, as one of the theaters was running a G rated film. They were in time for the late afternoon showing, and, as promised, Dave purchased a large bucket of buttered popcorn and a large soda for Allie. He was going to get himself one of each also but Allie convinced him they could share the popcorn and just use two straws for the soda. He agreed.

Allie was looking forward to spending time in a darkened theater with her friend. She could use the time and location to her advantage. Watching closely, as Dave reached for some popcorn she was careful to reach in unison, forcing their fingers to touch. She smiled to herself in the darkness each time, assured of the effect the touching was having on Dave. One step at a time.

About halfway through the movie she casually leaned over and rested her head on his shoulder. She felt him stiffen for a brief moment before relaxing. He turned his head to look at her as she gazed back up at him with a smile, barely visible in the dimmed light. He smiled back. It was all the encouragement she needed; she didn't move for the rest of the movie.

When it was over, they walked out together, and once outside, Allie innocently reached over and took his hand in hers. He started to pull his hand away, but she tightened her grip and he relaxed once more. They remained holding hands all the way to his pickup.

When they arrived at her house Allie reached for his hand again as he escorted her to the front door. He glanced at her once with a puzzled look, but accepted her overt gesture without complaint.

"Thanks for a really nice afternoon, Dave. I had a lot of fun. You really are good company, you know." She seemed hesitant to release his hand.

"I had a nice time too. The movie was a good idea. I had forgotten how much fun they could be." He smiled at her.

"Dancing on Wednesday, Preach?"

"If you come to church Sunday then I promise I'll take you next Wednesday. Fair enough?"

She pouted. "I guess. Okay, I promise I'll be there Sunday, and I won't chicken out. So then we go dancing on Wednesday, right?"

"You keep your end of the bargain and I'll keep mine."

Before he could react, she planted a quick kiss on his cheek, then turned and entered the house, leaving him standing on the front porch in apparent confusion yet again. Finally, he sighed deeply, turned, and walked away.

On Sunday Allie kept her part of the bargain. She dressed in the same clothes she had worn the previous week since no one had seen her at the church. Once again she no longer looked like herself. Anyone who knew her casually probably wouldn't recognize her at first glance.

As before, she waited in the back of the parking lot, hoping to see Raven and Gus enter the church building, and this week she was rewarded for her patience. They arrived in good time, and holding her breath, she watched anxiously, hoping for a glimpse of her daughter. While she was unable to see Catherine's face, she was able to get a glimpse of two chubby legs with tiny feet encased in little pink booties. It was enough . . . it was nowhere near enough.

She waited several minutes before following them in, wanting the couple to be seated before she entered, hoping their attention would be elsewhere. It turned out just as she had hoped. Being regular church attendees, Raven and Gus had their favorite seats about halfway to the front of the sanctuary. Their gazes remained on the choir and Pastor Dave Benson, who was seated to one side. Catherine was out of sight, apparently seated on one of her parents' lap. Allie shook hands with the greeter, and taking a deep breath, claimed a seat on the end of the last pew. A few people glanced at her as she entered and sat down, but she didn't recognize anyone and they quickly lost interest.

She could see her friend Dave surveying the crowd, his eyes darting everywhere until he saw her. Their eyes met and she smiled at him, and then lowered her head coyly.

It was not her first time in a church, and the protocol came back to her quickly. She appeared relaxed and attentive, but she was in turmoil inside. All she could think about was seeing Catherine, and every so often she was rewarded with a quick glimpse as the baby changed position. And then, during a prayer as everyone stood, she saw her baby's face full on as Raven held her to her shoulder. She was beyond beautiful. Allie was smitten with an overpowering feeling of love.

Catherine seemed to find Allie's face among the crowd and stared at her birth mother full on. She had inherited her mother's light blue eyes, and Allie felt almost as if she was seeing herself in the mirror in some way. One tear stained her makeup, so carefully applied that morning.

The prayer concluded and everyone sat down. Catherine was removed from her sight again, but she had seen her, she had seen her baby. She had accomplished what she had come to do.

Dave soon approached the podium and began his sermon. Allie tried half-heartedly to listen at first, but her friend was going on about salvation and something about a personal relationship with Jesus. She didn't need that and didn't really care. She lost all interest in what he was saying and her mind once more filled with thoughts of Catherine, and how she was going to manage to see her again.

Soon Dave was finished and the final hymn was being sung, with everyone standing again. Allie lowered her face, turned and walked quickly out of the sanctuary and out to her car. She didn't want to talk to anyone, and she definitely didn't want Raven or Gus to see her. But she had kept her promise. She smiled to herself as she thought of her upcoming date with Dave. He was going to take her dancing again. Her plan was definitely going to work.

Chapter 13

Dave was nearly speechless when he saw Allie walk into the church and take her seat.

He almost failed to recognize her with her hair up under her hat and the excessive although tasteful makeup she was wearing. She had actually come just as she had promised. He was elated. He watched as she carefully chose a seat in the very back pew. He had been a pastor long enough to understand her choice—newcomers usually picked that seat, which enabled a quick and easy exit at the end of the service. He smiled as he watched her.

He had carefully prepared his sermon weeks ago in the hope that one day Allie might hear what he had to say. He had actually preached this basic sermon many times over the years, presenting the Gospel in the simplest terms he knew how to use, hoping that those who heard it would not miss the good news of salvation God provided for any who were willing to acknowledge Christ as Lord and Savior. Thrilled that she had come at last, he also noted almost to the second when her attention strayed and she was no longer listening to him. He carried on, however, not missing a beat. He also never saw the object of her newly focused attention.

He watched her leave as soon as the service concluded, her head down, walking swiftly as if on a mission. She was gone long before he walked to the back of the church where he stood to greet the parishioners as they exited.

Later, he sat motionless in his big easy chair in the living room, thinking, remembering. Had it only been a week ago that he and Allie had gone to the Bacchus for lunch and then to a movie? Only a week since they sat together in the darkened theater, their fingers meeting occasionally as they reached for popcorn at the same time? Only a week since Allie had rested her head on his shoulder, relaxed and seemingly pleased to be in that position?

Only a week since she had reached for his hand, holding it in public all the way back to his pickup? He remembered his slight hesitance about the public display of mild affection, but then dismissed it as he recalled how he had held her at Mixer's when they danced. There was certainly nothing wrong with holding a woman's hand in public. He was glad she had clasped his hand, taking the lead.

But what was Allie doing? Were her feelings changing toward him in some way he had failed to notice? She had obviously moved past just being friends. Friends usually didn't get that close, physically. Was she actually starting to see him as more than just a good friend? *Could it be that she finally sees me as a man, not just a friend or a preacher, but a man who sees her as much more than just a friend?*

He started thinking about his promise to take her back to the bar. He recognized that he should have reservations about his upcoming "date," but found himself looking forward to it, feeling both nervous, very much alive, and young again. Allie made him feel young and rejuvenated. He very much liked the feeling.

He wished she had mentioned going out for lunch again after church today, but she hadn't. He wanted to call her in the worst way, but steeled himself, deciding to wait until Tuesday evening. His rational, proper preacher self said he should wait in the hope that she might forget about dancing and the bar. His new eager self was certain she would not change her plans, and he actually wanted to take her dancing. He found himself putting his occupation completely out of his mind. He couldn't wait to pick her up and take her back to that bar for the evening. He couldn't wait to see if she would hold his hand and perhaps rest her head on his shoulder again. He leaned his head back against the chair and sighed deeply. How on earth was he going to make it until Wednesday?

Allie didn't make him wait until Tuesday to call her, but called him the next morning. "Dave?"

"Hi, Allie." He found his legs were shaking at the sound of her voice and he quickly sat on a nearby chair.

"You saw me Sunday, right? I came, just like I said I would."

"Sure, I saw you, but you left so fast I didn't get a chance to say hi to you." He knew why she had left so quickly, but he left the explanation to her.

"Oh, you know. It's been so long since I've been in a church, I, well, I . . ."

He laughed. "It's okay, Allie, I understand. You aren't the first one to grab the back pew, believe me. But I would have liked to at least have said hello to you before you left."

"We're talking now, though. That's good enough, don't you think?"

"Sure, it's good enough. While we're talking, what did you think of my sermon? Did you get anything out of it? Did you learn anything? Or was I too boring?"

"No, you weren't boring, but I had trouble concentrating. To tell you the truth I don't remember anything about it now. Sorry."

He sighed quietly. "Is there a specific reason you called?"

"Wednesday night, remember? I kept my promise now you have to keep yours, right?"

"I thought maybe you had forgotten about that dancing thing. Want to just go to dinner instead?" He waited breathlessly for her answer, wanting to do the right thing and hoping she didn't.

"Not a chance, Preach. Dancing, Wednesday evening. You can pick me up around seven if that works for you."

"Seven it is, then. See you Wednesday."

"Dave?"

"Yes?"

"Wear your dancing shoes, cowboy!" She hung up the phone.

That afternoon he went shopping for some new jeans and shirts. On Tuesday morning he got a haircut.

Wednesday came so slowly he found himself wanting a few beers just to calm himself down. He had no beer at his home, however, and he was smart enough to know he shouldn't be seen at a liquor store buying some. He shouldn't be observed anywhere buying beer. At least at Mixer's the odds were almost nil that he would be seen by anyone he knew.

He showered and shaved late that afternoon, and, donning one of his new outfits, checked his appearance in the hall mirror. Smiling, he nodded in satisfaction. He might be a lot older than Allie, but he wouldn't embarrass her with his looks. He still had "it" and he knew it.

Hoping not to appear too anxious, he purposely arrived fifteen minutes late. Allie greeted him at the front door with a slight pout on her pretty mouth, and looking more stunning than he had ever seen her. Tonight she wore a low-cut sleeveless, semi-transparent pale yellow blouse with pearl buttons, and the tightest indigo jeans he had ever seen on a woman. Her figure was perfect and he found himself staring at the hint of cleavage the shirt revealed.

"Dave?"

He couldn't look away. "Hmm?"

She reached over, and putting her index finger under his chin, gently tipped his head up, laughing as she did so.

"Oh, sorry."

"I was starting to wonder if you got cold feet or something. You're never late." She scowled at him, but her eyes were smiling.

"Well, being a woman you should know it takes a little time to look this good." He turned slowly around in a complete circle. "What do you think? Will I pass?"

She laughed, that light, provocative laugh that was uniquely her own.

"You'll definitely pass, cowboy. I like you like this way a lot better than the way you looked on Sunday. You look like a lot more fun tonight."

"Thanks, I think."

"We are, aren't we?"

"We are what, exactly?"

"Going to have fun!" She smiled up at him as she took his arm in hers and gave it a light squeeze.

Electricity raced through him at her touch. He smiled back at her. "Yup, we are. Shall we go? Your carriage awaits, miss."

Montana is far enough North that daylight hangs around until after ten o'clock in the evening during the summer months. Dave became a little uneasy at the exposure the light gave him and his "date." But once inside the bar, darkness entombed them, and his anxiety abated. Worldwide, the cover of darkness hid a multitude of actions, some sinful, some not. Dave felt hidden in the muted light the bar provided. He relaxed. He felt transported back many years when he had essentially lived in bars. It almost made him feel like he was home again, in a way.

This time he took the lead, and, clasping Allie's hand, escorted her to a table near the back of the bar, well hidden in the shadows.

"This okay with you, Allie, or do you want to sit closer to the band?" "This is perfect. We can talk and have a few drinks all by ourselves."

They sat close together so they could hear each other over the noise. Dave suddenly grew quiet, his anxiety returning with full force, not because of his surroundings or companion, but due to something else. He looked around the bar, staring intently at each man he saw, but he did not see the one he was actually looking for.

"What about Doug, Allie? Will he be coming tonight? Are you by any chance waiting for him to show up?"

"No, silly, I'm here with you tonight. Only you. My personal preacher."

He winced inwardly at her description of him, but just as quickly brushed it off. He was here, with the woman he loved, and she was returning every gesture he made in her direction. He planned to make the most of this evening while he had the chance to spend this time with her.

At her suggestion he went to the bar and returned with two ice cold beers. Allie raised her glass with a twinkle in her eye.

"Toast, Preach?"

"Sure, but what are we toasting?"

"How about us?"

"To us?" He looked genuinely puzzled.

"Why not? I think we look pretty good together."

"Well, okay. Toast." He raised his glass and they met with a light, tinkling sound. Allie was smiling broadly at him and he found himself grinning back at her.

"Dave, I really think it's time we acknowledged that we are maybe a little more than just friends, don't you think?"

Shock showed on his face. *More than friends? Had he heard her correctly?*

"More than friends? What are you saying, exactly, Allie?"

"Well, I find that you have grown on me over the past year. Can't help it, but I see you as a lot more than just a friend. I thought maybe you felt that way too, but maybe I'm wrong. Am I wrong, Preach?"

"Allie, you do know that I'm old enough to be your father, right?"

She threw her head back and laughed, a very hearty laugh.

"Of course I know that, silly. So what? Lots of women date older men." She leaned forward toward him, exposing a glimpse of cleavage again for his benefit. "Besides, you're an awfully handsome older man. I think I may have to keep you. What do you say?"

He had a hard time keeping his eyes averted from her chest. Swallowing hard, he finally raised his eyes to hers.

"If you say so, Allie."

"I most certainly do say so, Dave." She straightened up again. "Look, if you're not interested in me that way, I'll back off and I won't bother you ever again. I promise. But if you think of me as anything more than a friend, then I think we should go for it. Let's give it a shot and see where it leads."

"Allie . . ."

"Dave, neither of us is getting any younger, here. Don't you think we've wasted enough time as friends?" Suddenly she lowered her voice. "Or does my having had a baby turn you completely off? I guess I am officially an unwed mother, even though I'm not raising my baby, but maybe I'm not good enough for you, you being a preacher and all." Tears glistened in her eyes as she spoke.

He reached for her hands, and clasping them firmly in his own, he looked deeply into her eyes.

"Allie, don't ever say that, okay? You're more than good enough for me. You're more than good enough for any man and don't you forget it. Is that clear enough for you? None of us are perfect, you know. I have skeletons in my closet too. Jesus loves us all anyway." *I love you anyway.*

"I don't much care whether or not Jesus loves me, I want to know how you feel about me. Do you want to date me or not?"

"Well, if you're sure, then yes, I'd love to go out with you!" He wondered if she was being obtuse on purpose; surely she had some idea that he didn't exactly mind being with her.

"Then let's call tonight our first official date, what do you say?"

"A date, a real date, it is, then." His heart had begun beating so fast he thought his chest must be pounding visibly. He didn't have to dream about her anymore. She wanted to be seen with him; she wanted him.

"Now that the dating thing is out of the way, do you mind if I have another beer?"

"Not at all. I'll go get you one."

When he came back she took a sip of the cold brew and then lit a cigarette. "Want one?" She held the pack out for him.

"I shouldn't, you know I shouldn't, but I confess I really do want a smoke." He reached over and took one out of the pack.

"Here, let me." Allie reached over and deftly lit it for him. "I don't think smoking will keep you out of heaven, so you're safe."

He inhaled the smoke deeply, savoring it as it filled his lungs. How he had missed cigarettes! He may have quit years ago but the yearning for them had never left him. As a pastor he had removed himself from any environments where he was around the temptation, but in the bar it was overwhelming. If Allie hadn't started smoking, he could have resisted, but tonight, it just didn't seem to matter. He enjoyed the cigarette until it was completely gone.

They finished their cigarettes and their second beer as the music started, another one of those slow seductive bar songs. Allie looked at him and he rose to his feet, holding his hand out to her. She took it firmly and followed him out onto the dance floor.

Allie had been right when she said he was a good dancer. As with nearly everything he did, he was proficient, and dancing was second nature for him. He was a natural leader, smooth and commanding. The beer, the smoke-filled darkened room, and the music seduced him as much as Allie herself did. He put an arm around her waist and pulled her close.

Halfway into the song he pulled her closer yet; he met with no resistance. Allie put both arms around his neck and leaned into him. They swayed together with the music, lost in their own world.

Too soon it was over and Dave had to release her. They went back to their table and had another beer and another cigarette. Then they were dancing again. They stayed until the bar closed.

Dave had at least enough sense to sober up enough to be able to drive Allie home. He had stopped drinking two hours before it was time to leave, but he drove slowly, wanting the night and the mood to last as long as possible. Allie sat next to him on the bench seat, her head resting on his shoulder. *It may not be the same, and it may or may not be right, but I think maybe this is as close to heaven on earth as it gets.*

They pulled up in front of her house and he walked around to open the pickup door for her. Taking her hand, he held it as he escorted her to the front door.

"Coffee, Preach?" Her words were a little slurred and her cheeks were flushed.

Dave found himself staring at her in the darkness. It was so tempting to follow her inside, but he wasn't sure he could trust himself. He was feeling too good.

"No, I think you need to get to bed and I need to get home before the sun comes up. But I thank you for the offer. It would taste good, but no. Not tonight." He turned to leave but she reached for his arm and turned him back to face her.

"It's our first real date, Dave. Can't I have a kiss goodnight?"

She didn't have to ask him twice. Slowly, making it last as long as he could, he pulled her into his arms and lowered his head. The kiss was gentle, soft, but full of meaning and passion.

"Good night, Allison." He turned and was gone.

Chapter 14

Allie was surprised at how much she had enjoyed their first official date. Oh, she had been friends with Dave for well over a year now, and even though she had teased him with the occasional kiss, she had actually kept their relationship at the friendship level. While Allie knew she was never going to be in love with Dave, she was willing to keep him as a steady date. She had no doubt about his feelings for her. The man was totally besotted. She had seen it in his eyes more than once, and Dave wasn't a player. Her biggest worry now was how she was going to convince him to leave after she had Catherine back. She wouldn't need him anymore once that was accomplished. But in the meantime, she would have a good time with him, and treat him the way any man wanted to be treated.

The evening at Mixer's really had been fun. He was a fantastic dancer and handsome as they came. While she knew men eyed her a lot, she saw the women following Dave with their eyes. If she had not been with him he would only have left the bar alone because it was his choice. She wished he had come in for coffee. Her plans actually involved a lot more than a chaste good night kiss. But she supposed her plans would have to wait. First, the web must tighten significantly. She would have to become a regular at church.

On Friday she began her campaign of phone calls every other day. Dave was always fun to talk to anyway, thus calling him so frequently was no hardship. The conversations were usually fairly short, just enough to keep in contact. She did not mention that she would be back in church Sunday, but that was certainly her plan.

Saturday morning, Dave called his new steady girlfriend and asked her out for dinner; she immediately accepted. That evening he took her out for pizza, far more casual than the Black Angus. They flirted playfully with each other throughout the meal, but when he took her home he kissed her as he had after they went to Mixer's. She would have liked a deeper, more seductive kiss, but she would play this his way, at his speed.

Sunday morning she sat in the back pew as she had done the week before, leaving immediately when the service was finished.

She was able to get only a quick glimpse of Catherine, but that was enough. Thankfully, Raven and Gus again did not see her.

She became a regular attendee at Grace Bible Church. While it wasn't a huge church, it was big enough that she managed to avoid being seen by the Whittackers even though she usually managed to see her baby, if only briefly. Dave was usually preaching, but even though she appeared to focus on what he was saying, she seldom paid any real attention. She didn't really care about any of that. She was only there to see Catherine.

They went out to lunch and dinner at least once a week, but she didn't ask Dave to take her dancing for three weeks. She wanted him to be comfortable with them as a couple, and she understood that he wasn't pleased about going to the bar. On the other hand, she wasn't willing to give that up, either. Dating Allie meant spending time at Mixer's.

They held hands a lot, laughed a lot, and smoked quite a bit. Dave even gave her money for cigarettes, feeling guilty about bumming from her all the time. However, while getting past Dave's defenses was good for her plan, she also realized that smoking was not a good thing. While she was alone, she didn't care much one way or the other, but if she was actually planning on being with Catherine, smoking would have to go. She certainly couldn't do anything to harm her daughter in any way.

They were enjoying a pizza in the park one Sunday afternoon when she asked him to take her dancing again.

"Dave, I haven't asked you to take me to Mixer's for several weeks now, and I really want to go again. What do you say, are we on for Wednesday?" She saw his obvious hesitation before he answered.

"Allie, I really don't think we should go. I'm a pastor, remember? It just isn't right, you know"

"No, I don't know. You keep saying that over and over again, but you've taken me before and seemed to have a good time, so what's the problem? Are you going to turn into a prude on me now?" She pouted.

"Allie, I worry about being seen in this town. I may not be doing anything technically wrong, per se, but it just doesn't look good.

We've been having a good time together, doing normal dating stuff, haven't we? Do we really need to go dancing again?"

"Well Dave, yes, I have had a really good time with you these past weeks. And I've even put up with going to church every Sunday. But I like to dance, and I want you to take me, okay?"

"Allie . . ."

"Dave, let me put it this way for you. If you won't take me, I'll either go by myself or I'll find someone who will. Plain enough?" She was sure that given the way he felt about her he would do anything to keep her from going with another man. She was right.

"Okay, you win. But what about finding some place in Livingston that has live music? I'm much less likely to be noticed there. What do you say?"

"Fine. I'll check it out and let you know, how's that? In the meantime, why don't you pick me up around seven on Wednesday?"

"I don't think I should skip the Wednesday service, so how about I pick you up at ten instead? It will make for a pretty late night again, but neither of us has to get up early in the morning, so I guess it doesn't really matter, right? Are you okay with that?"

"Great. See you then." She leaned over and gave him one of those kisses that seemed to turn him to jelly right before her eyes. It was such fun to watch him.

She checked out the bars in Livingston and found one with consistently good live music and a small dance floor. The Murray sounded like it would do just fine.

Dave picked her up right at ten on Wednesday night. His eyes were glowing as they always did when he saw her, his love for her obvious. She met him at the door, but instead of exiting right away, she pulled him in and shut the door behind them.

"Come here, Dave. It's been too long. Kiss me."

He was only too willing to obey her command. Pulling her tightly to himself, he kissed her, a delicate, lingering, kiss. Not platonic, but not heated either. He was obviously controlling himself very well. Finally he pulled away.

"Ready?"

"Ready. Let's go."

"Where are we going, anyway? Back to Mixer's or did you find somewhere else?"

"Let's try the Murray in Livingston. It's only twenty miles over the pass, and I heard the food and the music were both good. Okay with you? It means you'll get home in the wee hours of the morning, but you won't be in a bar in Bozeman, which is what you said you wanted."

"Let's be on our way then, woman." He took her arm and escorted her to his pickup.

The Murray suited them both perfectly. The bar was not too large, and the atmosphere was like any other Montana bar, dark and smoky. It was easy to feel anonymous there. They found a table in the back of the room and sat for a while just taking it all in, Allie holding his hand the whole time.

"Time for a beer, Dave?"

"Sure. Be right back." He rose and left her to get a couple of beers.

When he came back she saw his face redden when he found a cowboy hitting on her. She smiled. This was just what she wanted—Dave incoherent with jealousy. She wanted him glued to her side, willing to do whatever it took to keep her to himself. She was smiling up at the good-looking cowboy, laughing throatily at his jokes, when Dave set the beers on the table. He came around behind Allie, and, draping his arm around her shoulder, he bent over and kissed her cheek. He then caught her chin and, turning her face, he kissed her full on the lips, a deep, possessive, hard kiss, before releasing her and giving his full attention to the cowboy.

"You can leave, now, friend. She's taken."

"You?"

"Yeah, me."

"But you're old enough . . ."

"I said leave. Now."

Allie came to Dave's rescue.

"He's right. He's with me, and I am definitely taken. Sorry. It was nice meeting you, though." She pulled Dave onto the chair next to her as the disappointed man left the table.

"I am, aren't I, Dave? Taken, I mean?"

"Definitely. You mean you haven't figured that out yet?"

"Well, I kind of thought that was the case. But just how taken am I, Dave? Where is this all going with us? Or are we just having fun together?"

Dave took a large swallow of his beer, then lowered his head before answering. "I'm not totally sure, Allie." He raised his head again, looking earnestly into those beautiful blue eyes. "You must have figured out by now that I'm in love with you. You have, haven't you? I wouldn't be here, in a bar, if I wasn't."

She smiled warmly at his obvious discomfort. "Yes, I was pretty sure of how you felt about me. But what's next for us?"

"I want to marry you, if you'll have me."

Allie was thrilled. She had him.

"Dave, I love you too, you know? But I don't know about being a pastor's wife."

"I think we can make it work, Allie. Not all pastor's wives are so involved with their husband's occupation. I know I don't make a lot of money, but we can live comfortably. I also understand all too well that I'm too old for you, but for some reason, it just doesn't seem to matter to me."

"Dave, I . . ."

"Will you think about it, please? Just think about it."

"Okay, I'll think about it. Hard. I do love you, Dave. I'm just not sure about the marriage thing. I don't know if I'm ready for that."

"Will you keep coming to church? Has that been too hard for you?"

"Yes, I'll keep coming, but just to Sunday morning services. I don't want to get too involved in church stuff, but for you, I'll come on Sunday mornings. Good enough for you?"

"Good enough. I love you, Allie." He took both of her small hands into his big ones. "I've never felt like this about anyone before in my life. Please say you'll keep me?" He was smiling bravely at her, hopefully.

She bent toward him and kissed him once more, a kiss full of passion and promise, and his response was all she had hoped it would be.

"Shall we dance, cowboy?"

He didn't answer, but took her hand and escorted her to the dance floor. He held her close as she leaned into him. They swayed to the music, lost in the rhythm and the moment. They stayed until the bar closed, drinking, dancing, and laughing. Allie did not smoke, but Dave smoked most of a pack before they left.

It was nearly three in the morning when they pulled up in front of her house. "Coffee before you head home, Dave?"

He did not hesitate. "Sure. Sounds good."

He walked her to the front door, his arm around her waist. Once inside, he sat on the couch while she made two cups of instant coffee.

Soon she returned, placed the cups on the end table, and sat next to him. Within seconds she made her move, and pulled him close, kissing him yet again.

She began stroking his hair, then his eyebrows as she drove him to oblivion. His desire for her was all too obvious. Suddenly he pulled away from her.

"Allie, I can't. I think I need to get going."

"Why?"

"It's not right. You and I both know it."

"But we love each other, Dave. We're talking about getting married. Stay. I want you to stay. Please?"

"Allie . . ."

"Shut up, Dave, and kiss me again."

He did as he was told. He did not go home that night.

Chapter 15

It was still dark when Dave finally came at least somewhat to his senses. Careful not to disturb Allie's slumber, he gently extricated himself from their embrace. He stood there for some time, watching her sleep, his emotions running more than wild.

What had he done? Dear God in heaven, what had he done? He had just spent the night with a woman young enough to be his daughter. Him. Pastor Dave Benson. It was so wrong. It was so right. She was so beautiful, so willing. He couldn't stop studying her in the darkness. Her skin glowed, pearlescent in the shadows. That glorious strawberry blonde hair swathed her face and neck. In her nakedness she was more than beautiful to him. There were no words; she was indescribable. He felt himself becoming aware and eager again, but reason finally manifested. He reached for the afghan and covered her gently. It was the last thing he wanted to do, but it was time.

He dressed slowly in the darkness, his eyes never far from her sleeping form. He found a cigarette and lighting it, inhaled deeply. His eyes closed in the feeling of fulfillment that sex and a good cigarette gave him. He might be a pastor, but Dave Benson was still a man.

He had finally given in, succumbed to his emotions and desires. Now what? She would have to marry him, that's what. She would just have to. He knew that one night with her would never be enough. He would be coming back for more, right or wrong. "*Somebody's knockin'.*" Definitely wrong, but it felt so very good!

Sitting in the big easy chair opposite the couch, he watched her, smoked, and fought with the devil inside of him. *God, what am I going to do? I know what I should do—I should walk out of her door and never come back. Never look back. Never see her again. I can't wait to dance with her again.*

Finally dawn began to break and he rose to leave. He wanted to stay with her and eat breakfast. He wanted to make love to her again.

He closed the front door softly behind him when he left. It was barely dawn when he pulled up to his front door. He entered his home slowly, his heart heavy. He wanted to just sit and think for the rest of his life, but it was daylight now, and he had things to do.

He showered, a long, hot shower. Funny how the books always talk about taking a cold shower, but that was the last thing on his mind. He wanted to shower, shave, have a good cigarette and a beer, and then he wanted to make love to Allie again. That's what he wanted. Instead, he took a shower, ate breakfast, and drank a cup of strong, black coffee. He did not let God enter his thoughts, only thoughts of Allie. Then he went to his study to work on Sunday's sermon. He was a hypocrite.

Later that afternoon his friend Gus called.

"Dave, can you meet me this afternoon? Do you have time?" His voice was hurried, desperate sounding.

"Sure, Gus. Where do you want me to meet you and what time?" They made plans and agreed to meet around two o'clock.

Dave was frantic. Did Gus know he had spent the night with Allie? Had he been seen sneaking home this morning? So what if he did know? Did it matter, really? It wouldn't if Allie would just marry him. He kept going back to that.

They met on a gravel road some miles out of Bozeman, where they could be totally alone. Dave's worry had only increased when Gus told him where he wanted to meet up. Was Gus going to confront him? How was he going to react? How much did Gus actually know beyond what Dave had already told him? It had to be bad or his friend wouldn't have insisted on meeting out in the country, away from prying eyes.

Gus was early, and Dave saw him pacing back and forth behind his pickup as he drove up. Parking behind Gus's vehicle, he cautiously exited and walked toward his friend.

"What's up, Gus? Something wrong?"

"Dave, what on earth are you doing?" His hands were shaking, he was so agitated.

"What exactly are you referring to, Gus? What do you mean, what am I doing?"

"You brought that woman to church, Dave. You actually brought her to church! How could you do that?"

"What are you talking about?"

"I saw her Sunday, Dave. Allie. She was at church. I saw her. Thank God Raven didn't. She can't be there, Dave, she can't. It doesn't matter how much you're smitten with her, she can't be in the same building with us!"

113

Dave slowly released the breath he didn't realize he had been holding. Gus didn't know he had spent the night with Allie—at least he didn't know yet.

"Gus, it's okay. She didn't come up to you or anything, did she?"

"No, I don't even know if she knows that I saw her there, but Dave, I won't have her anywhere around Raven or Catherine. I can't have that and you know it. You're going to have to tell her to stay away."

"I don't think I can do that, Gus. But you don't have to worry about anything. Why are you so upset, anyway?"

"Dave, what if she's wanting to get her baby back? What if she's changed her mind about letting us have her and she wants Catherine for herself?"

"Relax, Gus. She doesn't. She's only there because I asked her to come. She didn't want to come to church, but I told her if she wanted to date me she would have to come to church. No other reason than that I made her."

"How do you know that for sure? Just how do you know? Did she tell you?"

"No, and that's one reason I'm sure she has no plans to take Catherine away. She has made absolutely no mention whatsoever about her baby. She has never mentioned you or Raven, either. Never, not even once, so rest easy. I'm sure she has no desire to take Catherine away from you. If she did, I think I would have some idea."

"So why is she there? Why isn't she in some other church if she wants to go?"

"I told you, because I sort of made her come."

"Why would you do that?"

"Because it hasn't gotten any better for me, Gus. I'm so in love with the woman I can barely function. I want to marry her. I'd marry her next week if she'd have me. But I also know that I can't marry her and remain a pastor if she doesn't become a Christian. I don't know how else to get that accomplished besides having her in church regularly and hopefully the Holy Spirit will get ahold of her."

"Marry her?" Gus looked incredulous.

"Yup. I want to marry her. As soon as she'll have me."

Gus narrowed his eyes as he stared at his friend. "You're dating steady now?"

"Yes, we are."

"But . . ."

"But what, exactly? You have a problem with that?"

"Dave, how far has it gone? I was hoping that with time you'd come to your senses, you know? So how far?"

"I spent the night with her last night, if you really want to know. That's how far, I'm sorry to say."

"Okay, so you spent the night. That doesn't mean you . . ."

"Yup. It means exactly that. I had sex with her." He lowered his head, then raised it again to look Gus full in the eyes. "And I intend to do it again and again, as often as I can."

"Dave, you can't. The church will run you out of town if they find out, and you won't be able to hide it forever, you know that."

"I do know it. I haven't thought it all through yet. I don't know just what I'm going to do. Somehow I have to figure this all out."

"Oh, Dave!"

"But I do know that there's nothing on this earth that can make me give her up, so it won't matter, nothing you can say will deter me. I just don't have the strength to walk away from her. Sorry."

Gus lowered his head into his hands. "Dave, is there anything I can do? You're my best friend and my brother in Christ. There must be something I can do to help you?"

"I can't think of a single thing, Gus. I wish I could. I've gone too far, and there's no turning back for me, I'm afraid. But don't worry about Allie and Catherine. She's been really careful to come at the last minute and she sits in the very back. She leaves before anyone else. If she had any designs on Catherine I don't think she would try to be that inconspicuous. We haven't talked about it, but I suspect avoiding you is exactly why she is acting as she does at church."

"You really think so?"

"I do."

"I can tell you, Dave, that just as you are not willing to give up the woman you say you love so much, no matter what God would have to say about things, I'll put a bullet through anyone who tries to take my daughter away from me. I don't care who it might be. No one is taking Catherine away from us. Not now, not ever."

"I understand and I don't blame you. I pretty much feel the same way about Allie as you do about Catherine." He put his hand out to his friend.

"Are we still friends, Gus?"

"Still friends, for sure, Dave."

"Even with my fall from grace? Even with the fact that I'm sinning and I have no intention of stopping?

"Even so."

They hugged each other tightly, and parted ways, both grown men scared and unsettled.

Later that evening Dave drove to Allie's house unannounced. It was the first time he had come on his own like that, and he did wonder what his reception would be. But if she really did love him as she said she did, it wouldn't matter. His assumption was correct. Allie opened the door and instantly pulled him inside when she saw him.

She pulled him to herself, and, hugging him close, whispered into his ear how happy she was to see him and have him close to her again.

"You don't mind that I just showed up, then?"

"Am I acting like I mind?" She snuggled even closer into his waiting arms.

"I wasn't sure, just inviting myself, you know?"

"Dave, I told you that I loved you, and that means I'm thrilled to see you whenever I can. Frankly, I wish you would just move in here with me."

He pulled away from her then and sucked in his breath at her suggestion. It was something he had actually thought about if she firmly refused to marry him, but somewhere in the back of his mind he still wanted the whole thing to be legal and above board. He wanted a legal union, and the thought of her playing with him as she had with Doug repulsed him. He didn't want one-night stands and he didn't want to just live with her, he wanted her as his wife. But if she really refused to marry him . . .

"Allie, why don't we get married instead? What do you say?"

"Dave, I'm pretty sure I mentioned somewhere along the line that I have no intention of being a pastor's wife. Just not happening. But I do love you and I don't want us to separate, so why not just live together?"

"Allie, it's simply not right, I . . ."

"Hey, look at it this way. If we don't get along there won't be any messy divorce or anything. No stain of divorce on your pastor record. No fault, no foul, isn't that what they say?" She scowled at him. "How about dinner? Have you eaten yet?"

"I ate at home before I came, so I'm fine. Thanks anyway." He lied. His stomach had been in such knots over the whole situation he hadn't eaten anything all day. What he wanted wasn't food.

"Are you sure?"

"Yes, I'm sure."

"Then what do you want, Dave? What do you really want?

"Do you really have to ask, Allie? After last night do you have to ask?" His eyes bored ravenously into hers.

"No, I guess I don't. I confess last night wasn't enough for me either. I'm glad you came over tonight." She took his hand and led him down the hall to her bedroom, turning off the lights as they went.

Dave's mouth went as dry as a desert. He felt himself responding to her invitation in spite of his efforts to control himself. He wanted her.

They entered her bedroom and, closing the door behind them, she pulled him into her arms, kissing him the way he loved to be kissed. It was possessive and passionate. His brain held no room for any thoughts other than making love to Allie.

Tonight their lovemaking was slow, deliberate, and more than anything Dave had ever fantasized about. Last night had been wonderful, but they took more time tonight, put more thought into pleasing each other, each for their own reasons. He stayed until just before dawn again, leaving silently as he had done the night before.

At home the self-recrimination took hold of him once more. He chastised himself for his total moral depravity. *God, what have I done? What on earth am I doing?* He couldn't wait to go back again tonight.

As with most sins that overtake anyone, the first time is often the hardest. The guilt that weighs so heavily somehow lessens as the sin is repeated. It isn't long before little or no guilt remains, and reasons and explanations absolve us from our sins. Dave was rapidly losing all feelings of guilt. He loved Allie, and in his mind he rationalized that his love made it right in the end. While deep within himself, he knew this to be a lie, it became easier and easier to bury those guilty feelings and proceed with what his desires overcame. He started spending several nights a week at Allie's, always leaving before dawn.

He begged, he pleaded, he bargained, but all to no avail. Allie would not budge on the issue of marriage. She asked him for nothing, but gave all of herself except for that one thing. Constantly assuring him of her love for him, she drove him to ecstasy every time he made love to her, which he now did with total abandon. All thoughts of his sin were driven out of his head. There was nothing he wouldn't do to keeping sleeping with Allison Rose Morgan.

There were very few nights now that he didn't spend with Allie. His sermons were deteriorating. He passed off the Wednesday and Sunday evening services more and more frequently to his associate pastor. In his heart he had already left the church; all that remained now was to physically extricate himself.

Chapter 16

Allie was thrilled, to say the least, at how well her plan seemed to be working. It was obvious how in love with her Dave was. Not being a church-goer, she had no idea how far Dave had fallen when he started sleeping with her. In her world, that was a perfectly normal thing to be doing. While she wasn't actually what could be called an overly promiscuous girl, she had no hang-ups about sleeping with a man she really liked. She wasn't someone who had to have sex, but she enjoyed the activity and indulged when she was with someone she was fond of, and she was definitely very fond of Dave Benson. However, fond was as far as her feelings went for him.

Oh, he was drop-dead gorgeous, that was for sure. His looks generated open stares from women of all ages. He was probably the best dance partner she had ever had. Sex? She had been with her fair share of men, but she had never had a partner like Dave before. Why was he so good in bed? Was it age? Experience? Or just a natural talent? She didn't have any idea, but it did occur to her that if age was the main component, she was sorry she hadn't gone with some older men in the past. To simply say he was good in bed was a vast understatement. As a result, she waited eagerly for his late night visits, and was always genuinely happy to see him.

The only thing she wasn't happy about was his constant desire to get married. Allie liked Dave; she liked him a lot. But even though she constantly reassured him of her love for him, she still thought of him only as a very good friend and lover. The idea of marrying the man was never a serious one. She could not and would not ever marry a preacher—not happening.

What she would do, however, was enjoy him while she was with him, and use every available means to get her daughter back. Her only real hope was to keep Dave besotted with her so that in the future he would do anything for her, and that included going against his friends, Raven and Gus, to help her accomplish her goal. She smiled to herself as she thought more about her plan. As long as she could go to church and watch Catherine from a distance, when the time was right she knew she could get Dave to do as she wished. She only needed more time. Dave had to be utterly and completely powerless where she was concerned. By having sex with her several times a week now, she knew he was very nearly where she needed him to be in their relationship. She just wished he would shut up about marriage.

Several weeks into this new aspect of their relationship, it was obvious that they were both more than enjoying their rendezvous, and one night after passionate lovemaking, she brought up the subject again.

"Dave, why don't you just stay? Going back and forth to your house is kind of silly, don't you think? Wouldn't it be a lot easier to just stay here? Move in with me. I don't like it when you're gone."

"Allie, we've talked about this before. I'm a pastor. I can't be living with a woman I'm not married to, and you don't want to marry me, so that pretty well quenches that idea. Say yes and I'll be here for you." He pulled her close to him in the bed they were sharing. "Just say yes." He kissed her soundly.

"I told you I'm not ready to get married, Dave. You know that. But I love you and I want to be with you. I don't like this sneaking around any more than you do. We're sleeping together several times a week now anyway so what's the difference? Our feelings aren't going to change just because we don't have that little piece of paper, you know."

Fully sated, they lay basking in the afterglow of their passionate lovemaking, the darkness enveloping them, hiding their activity.

"Dave, just stay. Nobody cares if you do but you."

"No, not now, Allie. But I will stay until the wee hours like I always do."

The next morning he left early as had become his habit, leaving her sleeping soundly. Three days later he called.

"Allie?"

"Hi, lover, what's up?"

"I've been thinking, and I've come to a decision. Will you come over to my house for a few minutes? I won't keep you long, I promise."

"Sure, I guess I can do that. But what's going on? You never ask me over."

"Well, I am now. I'd come and get you but since you have a perfectly good car now, I guess you can drive yourself this one time."

"Okay, I'll be there shortly. But won't you tell me what's going on first?"

"Nope. See you soon, my sweet."

As she hung up the phone her brows furrowed in concern. What was going on? Surely he didn't want to break up with her, did he? She had only been to his house a couple of times in all the months she had known him, but now he was asking her to come over. Was he upset that she had refused to marry him yet again? It just didn't make any sense. She guessed she would find out soon enough, but she was still worried. Her plan was working so splendidly all she could think of was that the stupid man had better not do anything to ruin it!

Allie arrived at his house in less than an hour, and parking her car in front, nearly trotted up the sidewalk in her hurry to alleviate her concern. He met her at the door, a huge smile on his face.

"Okay, Dave, what's going on? And why do you have that silly grin on your face?" Her worry was slowly dissipating at his happy expression.

"Come in and sit down, Allie. I have something I want to say to you." He led the way into his living room, where she promptly sat on the couch. Dave sat in front of her on the coffee table, his face serious, his hands reaching for hers.

"Allie, I know you said you wouldn't marry me, at least not right now."

"Correct. Sometimes I wondered if you were actually listening to what I was saying, but I guess you really were."

"I understand, but, well . . ." He relinquished her hands and reached into his pants pocket, retrieving a small jeweler's box. Opening it slowly and carefully, he presented her with a small diamond eternity band.

"Dave, I told you . . ."

"Allie, listen to me before you say anything more, okay? Just hear me out for a minute."

She took a deep breath, then nodded her head in assent, petrified that he was about to ruin absolutely everything she had planned.

"I'm accepting your refusal, at least for now. But you know how I feel about you.

I've certainly told you often enough, and I think my sleeping with you should make it pretty clear, since you know I don't sleep around. Actually that's an understatement. I haven't slept with a woman since I became a pastor, and that was many, many years ago."

"If you're accepting my refusal then what on earth is this ring for? We're not getting engaged or anything, I told you." Her confusion was evident on her face.

"Will you wear this, for me? Will you be my woman, even if you won't marry me, Allie?"

"Dave, I don't think . . ."

"Please? I won't ask you for anything more if you'll just say yes to this one request. I'll even throw in one more carrot; say yes, agree to wear this ring, and I'll move in with you."

Her face lit up. He wasn't quitting on her. He wasn't going to ruin everything she was working for.

"You will? You'll really move in with me? When?"

"Will you let me put this on your finger, then?"

She held her hand out to him in response. "Put it where you want it, cowboy. I'm yours."

He carefully slid the ring onto the third finger of her left hand.

"Dave, I think that finger is supposed to be for engagement and wedding rings. Isn't this more of a friendship ring or something?"

"Not to me, it isn't. It shows the world that you're taken, even if you won't marry me. You're mine, Allie. You will belong to no other man as long as I'm around."

She didn't really care one way or the other which finger she wore the ring on; he had said he would move in with her.

"When will you move in, Dave?"

"How about right now? Would that be soon enough to suit you?"

"Now? Today?" She was beaming at him, thankful he had no idea why she really wanted him with her.

"Actually, that's why I asked you to drive over here. I put my pickup in the garage. I might be staying with you at least for a while, but I don't want to advertise the fact by having my vehicle parked right in front of your house for any length of time. I do have an image to protect, you know." His eyes were shining with his love and his decision.

"Wait here. I'll be right back." He rose to his feet and left the room only to return in moments with a small duffel bag. Dropping the bag when he entered the room, he walked over to Allie and gathered her into a possessive hug and kissed her soundly. He was committed now. "Let's go, shall we?"

He put his things into the trunk of her car and slid into the passenger seat, all the while looking furtively around him. He was obviously hoping no one saw him leave with her.

They pulled up in front of Allie's house and she killed the engine. They sat there for a moment, just looking at each other. Allie had never actually lived with a man before except for the time Aspen Windchase had stayed with her, but that had been a purely platonic relationship, and now that the fact was upon her, she found that she had some reservations. All the "what if's" she could think of flooded her mind. What if? But she had asked for this, and now she had, yet again, gotten her way; she determined to make the most of it. She would treat Dave Benson so well he would never leave her until she was ready to let him go. Never. And he would help her get Catherine once things were firmly settled into place. He was here, now. He was well and truly trapped.

They entered her house almost hesitantly. After all their passionate nights together, all their mutual proclamations of love, they were suddenly almost shy around each other.

Neither seemed to know just what to do first. It wasn't like the nights when Dave showed up for sex. They couldn't exactly just drop everything and rush to the bedroom like a couple of teenagers. It wouldn't seem right. Or would it? Who cared anyway?

Proper or not, normal or not, they fell onto each other as if they were ravenous, tearing at their clothes as they made their way down the hall. It was two hours later before they came out again. Exhausted, silly, holding hands, they walked to the kitchen for a badly needed cup of coffee.

"Allie, why are we dressed again?" He had a stupid, silly grin on his face.

"Well, I actually have no idea. Why are we dressed?"

"How about we drink this coffee and then take care of that?"

"Suits me just fine. How fast can you drink that coffee?"

"What do you say we forget about the coffee for now?"

His look was expectant, but unsure. She realized that he had no idea how she would respond to his frank desire. He looked very vulnerable. She reassured him with a wide smile as she reached for him again.

"The couch is closer, what do you say, Preach?"

The pattern was set. The days began to blur together as they spent all their time alone in Allie's house. She occasionally left to get groceries while Dave stayed at the house, apparently unwilling to be seen in public with her. They went to bed when they felt like it, made love whenever they wanted to, slept as late as they liked, and ate when they were hungry. Allie was thrilled. Each day they spent together cemented their relationship even further. Dave would in no way reject her when she asked for his help in getting Catherine.

After several days with no mention of church or his usual Sunday sermon, Allie finally asked him what he was doing about that.

"Dave, I love having you here, but you didn't bring anything with you but your clothes. What about your sermons? Don't you have to preach on Sunday, or did you ask your associate to take over?" They were lying in bed, tired yet again. They were both insatiable, it seemed.

"I told them I was taking a long vacation. I don't have to be back for three weeks. As far as anyone knows, I left town for a while. I don't think it would go over too well if they knew I was here." He reached over to stroke her smooth, naked skin. His eyes glowed as he gazed at her.

"Oh. Does that mean you're not staying with me permanently? I only get you for three weeks?" She pouted prettily, and then held her left hand up to gaze at the ring. It really was a beautiful, tasteful piece of jewelry. She almost wished she really did love the man. Life would probably be simpler in the end; easier to get her baby if she were married. But the fact remained that while she had vowed that Catherine was going to be in her life, a husband was not. If for no other reason, there was no way once she got Catherine back that she could stay anywhere near Bozeman. She may have to leave the state, and she knew full well that Dave would never leave his church. No, in the end he would stay and she would leave with her child. But for now, he was fun to have around, a great companion, and a very talented lover.

Allie did her level best to make herself essential to Dave's very being. He was such an honest, uncomplicated man that it wasn't hard. Since she really did like him; she didn't have to put on much of an act. She anticipated his every need and did her very best to fulfill all of them. If he was hungry, she made a fabulous homemade meal for him. She washed the few changes of clothes he had brought with him whenever it was necessary. She made sure he wanted for nothing sexually, and made herself available whenever he wanted her. They seldom got dressed from day to day; it didn't seem necessary.

She knew just by watching him carefully that he was as committed to her as he could ever be. His eyes followed her everywhere, seldom leaving her face or her body. He smiled continually. He held her hand whenever he had the chance. Love words were whispered softly into her ear whenever they were close. And yet with all of these demonstrations of his feelings, he never felt oppressive to her, and Allie enjoyed everything he did. She had full and complete control, and she enjoyed that power. He was totally hers.

Chapter 17

His three weeks of vacation were passing quickly. He would have to move home again and take up his pastoral duties once more. He didn't want to go.

He had stopped talking to God over two weeks ago. What was he supposed to say to Him? There was nothing he could say. He had spent agonizing hours and days praying for deliverance and freedom from the bondage he now found himself in with Allie, and all to no avail. He was aware of the moment he gave himself over entirely to his desires, but chose not to address the fact. He just stopped praying. *The rest of the world lives like this all the time, Lord. Is it really that wrong for me to live that way too? You created us male and female, you created that loving bond between us, so just how am I supposed to walk away from her? I can't. I just can't.*

But with all of his rationalizations, he knew exactly what he was doing, and his soul was now smeared with his sin. It wasn't just the sex with Allie, he realized. He found he wanted cigarettes more and more frequently. And alcohol. While he had never actually been an alcoholic, he had always enjoyed a good, stiff drink of whiskey. In the old days before he got saved, he spent most of his time in bars with other drifters and cowboys. Men just like him. And women, there were always as many women as he could possibly want. He knew women were attracted to his looks, and he had availed himself of the pleasures they offered whenever he wanted. Sex, alcohol, cigarettes—he had indulged in them all, but his only real addiction had been heroin. It was when the drugs had him at rock bottom that he had found his Lord and crawled his way up out of the pit and into the true light. He understood all too well that he was now back very nearly to the bottom of that pit again. He was smoking, and beer was no longer enough for him. Allie, bless her heart, bought him whatever he wanted, and whiskey was no exception. She gladly poured glass after glass for him, and, since in his case it only seemed to enhance his prowess, she was all too happy to oblige his desire for it.

She had stopped smoking and seldom drank now, but made no effort to hinder his indulgences. It had bothered him a little when she quit smoking and drinking, since that originally had been something they had happily shared at the bar. But it was okay with him if she wanted to quit.

After the first week he found himself asking her if she wanted to go dancing again one night. She had been thrilled that he wanted to go, and had willingly driven them both to the Murray in Livingston one evening. Dave had drunk more than usual, drinking whiskey rather than the usual beer, and had been overly attentive to his woman all night. His dancing had been so seductive that Allie had teased him about waiting until they got home before he tore her clothes off. He had just laughed at her, his hands roaming wherever they pleased in the darkness. When they finally made it back to Bozeman he had been insatiable. They had both loved that night.

Dave had some hard decisions to make, and he knew it. He was not willing to give Allie up. Nothing could persuade him to do that. He was also not willing to move out of her house. He loved her, he loved being with her, and the last thing he wanted to do was go back to being good old Pastor Dave Benson.

It never occurred to him that he might one day actually leave the church, but it seemed it had come to exactly that. It was Allie or Grace Bible Church and there was no contest; he would leave the church. He would find some way to support them; if nothing else, he could work as a general handyman. They would have to leave the area, though. When word got out about his "fall" there was no way he could face the humiliation he knew he would find in Bozeman. He would have to resign and leave everything behind if he was going to stay with Allie. He saw absolutely no alternative

One day he asked Allie to give him a ride back to his house.

"Why are you going home, Dave? You're not moving out or anything, are you? Please say you aren't!"

"No, don't worry. I have no intention of leaving you, my dear. I think it's time I got my pickup and a few other things. Maybe some more clothes, for one thing. I'm getting a little tired of wearing the same thing over and over. Would you mind too much if I parked my pickup in your garage? I still don't want to be too blatant about me being here. Sorry. I guess I should be proud enough of you to not care what people think, but I do. I can't help it.

"When do you want to go? I'll get dressed and take you whenever you're ready."

Two hours later she deposited him at his house, but when she started to get out of the car to join him, he asked her not to.

"Don't come in with me this time, okay? Just go on home and I'll be there later."

"You promise? You aren't going to chicken out on me now, are you?"

"I promise, but it might be a day or two. I have some things I have to do first. I'm not sure right now when I'm coming back, but I will, don't worry." He kissed her in a way she would not soon forget. She would be waiting for him.

Once alone in his house, he sat and thought. The house was quiet, only the ticking of the hall clock breaking the roaring silence. He sat alone in his house, with his thoughts and his God.

Somebody's knockin', Lord, and that knock is too loud for me to ignore. I have to go to her. I'm simply not strong enough to resist. We've talked about it for months now, you and I. I know you know the end from the beginning, and you know all my thoughts, my weaknesses. You know how much I love you, how I thought I would be serving you for the rest of my life. But Lord, you also know how much I love her, Allie. I honestly don't think I can live without her.

Oh God! How far have I fallen! How far from you and your grace! I know you haven't left me, it is I who have left you. We both know there is no way I can continue as a pastor for now and maybe never again. I don't know what lies ahead for me. Maybe she will change and become a Christian. Maybe . . . but I don't think I can wait for that to happen.

I can't live with her and remain a pastor, and I can't leave her. So I guess I leave the church. I'm sorry, Lord. So very, very, sorry. Forgive me, please. Cover me with your grace, and even though I don't deserve it and right now I can't even freely receive it, please keep me close. Hang on to me, Father, please don't let me fall too far, so far that I can't ever get back to you. Forgive me, Father. Forgive me. I pray in your Son's name, Jesus.

With that confession completed, he sank once again into the position of the cross, his face planted against the floor, arms outstretched. Tears flowed without ceasing for what seemed like hours. He had no sense of time. He was alone with God, his Lord, his salvation, but he was beaten. Done. Defeated. And the pathetic part of the whole thing was that it had all been done according to his own free will. No one had forced him into the situation he now found himself in. Hours passed, unheeded. He sobbed at his frailty.

Finally, later in the afternoon, he rose to his feet and called his good friend, Gus. "Gus, have you got time to see me again?"

"Sure, when do you want to meet up?" He heard the despair in his friend's voice. "Today or tomorrow, whenever is best for you is fine with me."

"Well, I am a little tied up today, so tomorrow would actually be better for me. How about tomorrow, anytime that works for you?"

"That will be fine. And Gus, can you just come to my house this time? You don't have to call first, I'll be here all day so just show up whenever it's convenient."

"Sure, will do." He hesitated. "Dave, are you okay?"

"No, but that's not important. We'll talk about it tomorrow, okay?"

"Sure. See you tomorrow."

Gus pulled up in front of Dave's parsonage the next day around mid-morning. Parking his pickup in front of the house, he got out, stood for a second, and then took a deep breath before walking up to the front door.

Dave called out to him to enter when he heard Gus's knock. "Come on back to my study, Gus."

Gus entered the study slowly, then walked over to his good friend and pastor, extending his hand as he did so. They shook hands heartily and wordlessly before Dave pulled Gus into a tight bear hug.

"Thanks for coming, Gus. You probably don't have any idea what it means to me that you are still my friend in spite of all you know about my life right now."

"Dave, I've got a few of those skeletons in my closet myself. None of us are perfect, remember? I think I've heard you preach that a lot over the years."

"Yeah, well, I hope you still feel that way when this conversation is over. Have a seat."

Gus sat and waited while his friend composed his thoughts. Dave was silent for a

time, his head bent, apparently deep in thought. Finally he opened the top drawer of his desk and pulled out an envelope.

"Here." He held it out to Gus, who took it hesitantly.
"What's this?"
"Open it."
Gus did as instructed ,and his eyes widened as he read.
"Dave, you can't be serious! This is a letter of resignation! No way! You're resigning?" His face had paled as he read.
"I don't have a choice, Gus. I have to resign. I'm hoping that you'll help me through this by giving it to the board for me. I confess I don't have the courage to do it myself."
"When?"
"It's effective immediately, at least on the last day of my vacation. It may not be right but I'm not giving up my salary just yet. But I'm not coming back after I leave here today. I'm taking only my clothes. I know it's asking an awful lot of you, but would you mind too much packing up my books and stuff and donating what you can or just throw it all out. I won't be needing anything in this house again."
"Dave, what exactly is going on here?"
"Just what it looks like, Gus. I'm leaving the church."
"But your books? Your papers? Why? What are you going to do?"
"Yes, everything. I told you, I won't be needing any of this again."
"Dave, take a break if you need to, a leave of absence or something. Take whatever time you need, but resignation? You can't resign; I'm not going to let you make that mistake."
"I'm living with Allie, now, and I have no intention of changing that living arrangement. I've asked her to marry me, but so far she's refusing. I even gave her a ring."
"She won't marry you?"
"Nope. Says she doesn't want to be a preacher's wife, and I know she means it. In the end, it's her or the church, and I don't know if I can live without that woman. So I guess it has to be the church." He sank back into the office chair, his head heavy in his hands. Tears glistened in his eyes when he looked up at his friend again.
"I'm so lost, Gus. So very, very lost. I can't even pray anymore."

"Dave, I'm sure this will pass. Give it time to play out, will you?"

"No. I can't do that. I don't want this to pass, Gus. I want to spend the rest of my life with Allie. And with how I'm living how, there's no way I can continue as pastor of this church."

"I get it. I know you can't still be preaching on Sunday mornings as long as you're living with Allie, but Dave, in time this will all seem like a bad memory to you. I'm sure of it."

"Gus, I can't. You know I'm right. I've sunk so low . . . I never in my wildest dreams thought this would ever happen to me. I'm back to drinking and smoking. I go to the bars in Livingston and hang out there with Allie, where we act like a couple of raunchy teenagers, drinking and dancing until the wee hours of the morning. I'm done, Gus. Thoroughly done."

"What about God, Dave?"

"What about Him?"

"You haven't given up on God, have you?"

"Oh, no, never that. I know I've hurt Him terribly, but I also know I am still His. No one and nothing can take my salvation away from me. I know that." He laughed sardonically. "I know it all better than anyone. I'm His, forever. I just can't live up to my promises right now. Maybe never again. I can't be what He expects of me, and I'm so very ashamed. You can't imagine how ashamed I am. I don't see any other way. I've thought about it over and over again. I've prayed. I've done the bargaining thing. You name it and I think I've tried it, but here I am. I don't know if I can ever be a pastor again. I guess in a way it depends on Allie. If she marries me, well, maybe. If she doesn't, that's it. You know it and I know it."

"So, what's happening right now?"

"I'm living with her, as I told you. I took three weeks' vacation, and I only have a few days left before I have to make any firm decisions as to my next step, other than this resignation letter."

"Does Allie know you're leaving the church?"

"No, I haven't told her yet. I probably won't until my three weeks are up. I'm sure she won't care much one way or the other about that, but I don't know how she'll feel about us moving away from here."

"You're going to leave Bozeman?"

"Don't you think that's for the best? How can I face anyone around here after what I've done? I can't. I don't have that much courage."

"How will you live? You've been a pastor for as long as I've known you. Dave, this whole thing is making me sick!"

"Oh, I don't know right offhand. I'm pretty handy, you know. I can fix most anything and I'm a pretty fair carpenter. I figure maybe I can just work as a general handyman somewhere. I have a good savings account, since I never really needed what the church was paying me. No family to support or anything. I'll be fine. As long as Allie stays with me, I'll be okay."

"Dave, I know this is a stupid question, but I'm going to ask it anyway."

"Go ahead, ask. What do you want to know that I haven't told you already?"

"I know you've prayed about this, and prayed hard. I guess I don't understand exactly why you haven't been able to get away from Allie and this whole situation. I believe in the power of prayer, and so do you. So what happened here? He delivered you from a heroin addiction, for heaven's sake, so why not Allie? I don't get it. Help me to understand, please." Gus leaned forward in his chair, hands clasped between his knees, his brows deeply furrowed.

"The best I can tell you is that while I wanted out of this situation, wanted deliverance, it's all really on the surface. I say I want out, but the truth is, I love Allie and I don't want to give her up. I have never felt this way before in my life, and the feeling is indescribable."

"I know what you're saying, Dave. I went through hell with Raven before we finally got married. So I do understand the 'feelings' aspect of this whole thing."

"The truth is I want my own way, deep down inside of myself. I want what is proper and acceptable, but apparently, I don't want it badly enough to let God take full control. I selfishly want to keep what I have. I guess in the end perhaps it isn't the fact that I'm not strong enough to walk away, it's because I really, truly don't want to. That's the crux of the whole thing." He sighed deeply in resignation. "You know, Gus, there's one good thing about this mess."

"What can possibly be good about all of this, Dave? I sure don't see anything positive here." He shook his head in the negative.

"I thought I understood how people could sink so low in their sin and rebellion, and I did in the normal sinful actions. Booze, cigarettes, drugs—you know I was addicted to heroin. Lust, pride, I knew them all. But this is totally different and harder to rationalize. A person in love to this extent keeps trying to figure out how it can be so wrong when it feels so right, as one of the country songs describes it. It's worse than heroin, I know that. No one can rightfully rationalize in his brain that heroin is anything but lethal. Love is a whole different ball game."

"Dave, you're sure? You're really, really sure? No other options here?"

"I'm sure. I'm leaving the church and leaving Bozeman in the near future. I'll probably have to leave the state in the end. Montana's a big state but I'm not sure it's big enough. Guess I'll find out." He rose to his feet, the discussion over as far as he was concerned.

"Will I see you again, Dave? Will you at least call me if and when you leave town?" He too rose to his feet, apparently accepting the fact that his friend was finished with explanations.

"Yes, I'll call you, but don't be waiting up for that call. It may be a while." He laughed. "I still have some time left before my resignation actually takes effect, so I expect it will be at least that long before you get any calls from me."

There was nothing left to say. Gus agreed to tie up all the loose ends for his friend, but there seemed to be nothing he could do to help his friend and now former pastor. They clasped each other tightly in their good-bye, then Gus, tears in his eyes, walked away. He shut the door to the study behind him.

Dave sank back into his office chair, head in his hands, tears flowing freely. He had now officially given up everything of importance in his life; his job, his church, his reputation, and his friends. There was nothing left now but Allie. Ah, Allie.

She was worth it all, wasn't she?

Chapter 18

He loaded up his pickup with everything he felt he couldn't or shouldn't leave behind. He took only his clothes, some favorite books, some papers, and his favorite, well-worn and well-marked Bible. He might be leaving the church but his Bible still held a high priority in his life. He wasn't actually leaving God or turning his back on Him, he just wasn't able to put Him first in his day-to-day life activities anymore. Allie had moved into that position.

Allie had given him a house key and he didn't bother to knock when he got to her front door. Unlocking it, he realized he was wearing a very silly grin for a man of his age. He couldn't help it. He was "home."

The house smelled like Allie. He inhaled deeply before calling out to her.

"Allie? You home?" He knew she was because her car was out front. He had parked his pickup right behind hers.

"Dave? You're home, finally! Welcome back my love!" She ran to him and enveloped him in a wonderful, tight hug.

That hug immediately wiped out the tension of the afternoon with Gus. It had been hard, very hard to tell his friend he was leaving. He loved Gus. He loved his church, but the years he had spent as pastor there were now only fond memories that he would cherish forever. He knew he would miss his old life, but now he had Allie and nothing else mattered anymore.

"Glad to see me, are you?" He was laughing at her eagerness.

"You know it, Preach. I was beginning to wonder if you had gotten cold feet or something and changed your mind about living with me." She punched him playfully in his shoulder.

He doubled over in mock pain at the pretend injury. "Oh, you're stronger than you look, girl!"

"Want me to kiss it all better for you, sweetheart? Not as tough as you look, huh?"

He unbuttoned his shirt until he was able to pull it over his shoulder, exposing the site of the injury.

"Here, you can kiss it all better now."

She did just that, kissing his exposed shoulder several times in quick succession before stepping back to gaze into his eyes.

"Better now?"

"All better, thank you."

"Let's see if I can make you feel better all over, shall we?"

"Just what do you have in mind?"

She didn't answer him but began to very slowly unbutton his shirt the rest of the way.

Her hands moved slower and slower as they moved downward. He wondered if she really understood exactly what she was doing to him, but stood immobile as she proceeded with her work.

When she had unbuttoned the shirt completely she gently pulled it over his shoulders, exposing his chest. That was his undoing. There was no gentleness in his movements as he grabbed her and, pulling her to him, began to love her.

Allie threw her head back and laughed out loud at him, then took his hand and led him down the hall to her bedroom. They didn't come out for hours.

Mindless after their lovemaking, Dave finally had the presence of mind to ask her if he could park his pickup in her garage.

"Sure, you can put it in there, I don't care, but isn't it easier to just park it out front?" "Easier, I guess, but Allie, I still don't want to advertise to the whole world that I'm staying here."

"Dave, you are such a prude! Who cares?"

"Well, my sweet, I care. Sorry. I'm still a preacher, you know?" He bit his tongue on that one; he hadn't told Allie he had resigned and wasn't sure when he would get around to that piece of information. He had no idea how she was going to take the fact that he was no longer employed. Oh well, he didn't have to mention it right away.

She cooked a wonderful supper for his homecoming celebration; rib steaks on the grill, fresh green salad, and ice cream for dessert. He didn't think he had ever been happier in his life.

After supper Dave parked his pickup in her garage and she helped him move his things into the house. He put most of it in the spare bedroom, out of the way and out of sight, not that Allie ever had visitors, and he certainly wouldn't be having any.

Sated and pleasantly tired from their exertions, they sat side by side on the couch in the living room.

"What can I get you, Dave? A beer? A cigarette?"

"I would love a smoke, my love, but have you got anything stronger than beer here?"

"Sure do. How about some nice Scotch whiskey?"

"Sounds great. Will you have some with me?"

"I'll stick with the beer, but I don't mind if you have whatever you want. Wait here and I'll be right back."

She returned shortly with a stiff drink and a lit cigarette for him, along with a beer for herself.

"I don't mind, really I don't, but do you think you might be able to stop smoking again? I know I'm the reason you started up, but it really is a pretty bad habit, and it tends to smell the house up. What do you say?"

"How about I quit next week? If you really mind I can just smoke outside and not in the house. Would that help?"

She laughed. "No, until you quit you can smoke in here. You're living here now, so treat this house like it's yours, okay? It is, actually. Yours I mean. We're a couple, now, so this house is just as much yours as mine."

"Why, thank you my love." He inhaled deeply and took a big swallow of the whiskey. The combination was putting him in the mood again. He turned his head to look at her. "Allie?"

"Yes?"

"What do you say?"

That look was back in his eyes. She pulled him to her. They passed the night on the couch.

The following week was spent as if they were on their honeymoon, at least that's what it felt like to Dave. He was totally consumed by Allie, even more than before, if that were possible. He followed her everywhere like a puppy, smiling, taking every opportunity to just touch her. He had come around to her way of thinking regarding marriage. Who needed it? He was just as married living with her as if he had taken vows in a church, and she continued to wear his ring. The only shadow was the fact that he was in hiding, but so far it hadn't really mattered to him.

After a few days, however, he started to get restless. Making love to his woman at all hours of the day and night was wonderful, but as the newness wore off he found he needed something else to occupy his time and his mind.

They started taking drives in the country in the afternoons, enjoying the scenery that only Montana could supply. Scenic drives through the mountain passes and abundant wildlife made for interesting and pleasurable days. Dance nights were fairly frequent, and Dave found himself looking forward to the bars as much as Allie seemed to.

They also started going to more movies. Where at first Dave would only go to G- rated movies, now he didn't care. He found he actually liked the R-rated ones, especially the ones with explicit sex and nudity. It turned him on and he liked that, especially since Allie didn't seem to mind, and was always ready for him.

While he had had his share of women in his younger, wilder days, sex then was nothing like it was with Allie. He never knew it could be so good. Sometimes he was almost sad that he had spent so many years alone. But then, alone was better than with just any woman. Allie was special.

On Sunday, Allie was up early, showered, and waiting for him in the kitchen, wearing only a robe.

"Good morning, love. Ready for coffee?"

"Always ready for coffee, Allie, just as I always seem to be ready for you. Come over here and let me have a good morning kiss?"

She did as he requested, and then sat next to him at the kitchen table.

"Shall we go to church this morning, Dave? You haven't been for the last two Sundays, and you must be missing it. I'll go with you—what do you say?"

He was speechless for a moment. "You want to go to church? What brought this on? I had to beg you to go before. What's up?"

"I just think we should go, that's all. Don't you want to go with me?"

He couldn't tell her that he no longer had a church to go to, that he had resigned and there was no way he could ever darken the door of Grace Bible Church again.

"No, actually, I don't want to go. I'm on vacation, remember? I think I want to make it a real vacation and skip church for now. Maybe when my time off is over. You don't really mind, do you?"

"No, of course I don't mind. Church was never my favorite thing, but I'm willing to go for you."

"Aw, that's so sweet of you. Thanks. But maybe in a couple of weeks."

"Okay. You can let me know when you're ready to return and want me to come."

He let the subject drop. He would have to tell her eventually, but other than the loss of his income, he assumed she would be happy to never have to go back to church because of him.

His vacation was over; he called his good friend, Gus, again. They agreed to meet at the Bacchus downtown on Tuesday afternoon.

Dave was waiting for Gus, having arrived some twenty minutes ahead of the agreed upon meeting time. He missed his friend, and while he was mad about Allie, he was finally starting to feel the emptiness that the lack of social friends was leaving him with.

"Gus! Thanks for coming, friend." He rose to his feet to greet his friend and they shook hands in greeting.

"Dave, I have to say you're looking pretty good for an old man. I hate to say it, but living with Allie must agree with you."

"Gus, I can't tell you. There are no words. I'm as in love with her as I ever was, actually more so as time passes. She's absolutely everything I ever wanted in a woman and more."

"You don't have to try to describe it all to me, Dave. I'm married to Raven, remember? You seem to forget that fact at times. I know Allie's a knock-out, but I've never met a more beautiful woman than my wife. And now that we have Catherine, I think she's gotten even more gorgeous, it that were possible."

"Well, you're right about one thing, Raven is truly a beautiful woman. Actually, I think she was the most stunning woman I'd ever seen before I met Allie, but she was already taken. What I don't understand is how a broken-down cowboy like yourself, with not much in the looks department, managed to lasso a woman like Raven. No offense, Gus."

"No offense taken. I marvel at that myself. God is just really, really good, isn't He?"

Dave was silent for a moment at that. The statement hit him right in the gut, and it wasn't a pleasant feeling. But Gus was right. God is in fact really, really good.

"Yes, Gus. God is good. Still and always." It was said softly.

"Did you have something special that you wanted to talk about, Dave? Or did you just miss this mug of mine?"

"Guess I just missed you." He paused. "Actually, I was kind of wondering how you got along with cleaning out the parsonage. That was a mean thing of me to do to you, I know. Sorry."

"It's okay. It only took me a couple of days. I got Pen to help, hope you don't mind. I went ahead and told him about your resignation."

"That's okay. It's not something I'll be able to keep a secret, after all. When I don't come back there won't be any hiding it."

"I haven't told Raven yet, and I asked Pen not to tell Maura. I figure there's time to tell them later, when we have to."

"Everyone will know within a week anyway. I'm trying to decide if I should get us moved out of Bozeman right away. We all know what's going to hit the fan when this town figures out we're living together. It would certainly be easier to leave before then, but I don't know what Allie will have to say about it."

"Have you told her that you resigned? Does she know?"

"Nope. I haven't told her yet. I can't imagine that she'll care one way or the other, but I didn't see any reason to tell her before I had to. Plenty of time." He sighed. He had thought that things would get easier once he quit the church, but the burden seemed to be growing heavier with each passing day, not lighter. He needed to confide in Gus.

"Gus, I have to unburden to someone, and as usual, you're it. Sorry."

"It's fine, go ahead. What's bothering you, besides the obvious?"

"Well, you know, I really thought that once I made up my mind to move in with Allie and settle this romance thing once and for all, well, I thought it would all get easier."

"It hasn't?"

"No, it sure hasn't. Oh, I love Allie, that hasn't changed any. But it's almost like something is missing, you know?"

"Like what?"

Concern was written all over Dave's face. Concern and confusion.

"I'm not sure. It's like hitting a flat on the piano in the midst of a song. That's about the best I can describe it. I love Allie, I really do, and the sex is unbelievable, if you must know."

"I have to confess that's one thing I really didn't need to know, but go ahead." Gus was smiling as he heard his pastor talking about sex. It was a little weird.

"Living with someone twenty-four hours a day, well, there's only so much you can talk about before you finally run out of things to say. So you eat and you drink and you smoke, and you go to bed, and when that's all over and done, you're still a little empty, it seems. I didn't think it would be this way, I guess."

"Do you think maybe it has something to do with the fact that you've essentially cut yourself off from all your acquaintances, and now also your job? Feel like maybe you're drifting a little? No rudder and no course, perhaps?"

"Yeah, I guess. Maybe when I get a steady job and settle in a new place I can get thing more squared away. When we move, I can start making new friends and maybe get some focus."

"I think that will help a lot. If you move, especially if it's a ways away from here where no one knows you were a pastor, I think you'll be able to hold your head up a little higher. No one needs to know you aren't married, either. People will just assume that you are."

"You're right, Gus. That will help. I'll broach the idea about moving in the next day or two to Allie, when the time seems right. Either way, I think moving is the only way to go."

They drank coffee, ate a sandwich, and visited some more the way men do. Finally Gus stood to leave. He had a lot of work to do at the stable.

"Sorry to leave you, Dave, but I really do have to get back to work."

"That's okay, Gus. I can't thank you enough for always being there for me. I don't know what I'd do without you, my friend."

"Always, Dave. Always. Anytime you need me, you just call and I'll be here. There's nothing you can do that will make me turn my back on you. I may not always approve of what you're doing, but

I won't quit on you. Now give me one of those good old-fashioned man hugs before I go, will you?"

They hugged fiercely, and Gus walked out ahead of Dave, who remained sitting in the booth alone for some time, his head lowered. Life was hard.

Chapter 19

He had only one day left before he was officially out of a job. He was going to have to tell Allie soon, and while he was concerned about this he actually had no idea why that was so. Allie certainly wouldn't care whether he remained a preacher or not, he reasoned. Maybe, just maybe, if he was no longer a pastor she would finally agree to marry him. She had repeatedly stated that his profession was the reason she wouldn't marry him, and if that was no longer a factor, why not? They could get married any time.

He wasn't too sure how she would respond to his need to move, but since she had essentially no friends in Bozeman other than himself, he couldn't see why that should be a problem for her. They had each other, and that was what mattered most.

Every morning when he first awoke he vowed that today would be the day he would tell her about his resignation. And every day he put it off. Instead he drank, smoked, took Allie dancing, and made love to her whenever possible. It was a wonderful vacation.

Then, suddenly, it was all over. His vacation ended; he had resigned, was officially unemployed and totally free of all responsibilities, and still, he didn't tell her.

On the following Saturday Allie brought up the subject of church once more.

"Are you preaching tomorrow, Dave? I'll plan on going with you if you are." They were sitting together on the couch, Dave reclining with his head in Allie's lap. She was slowly tousling his hair as she spoke.

"No, I'm not preaching tomorrow." He kept his eyes closed, partly out of pleasure at her touch and partly because he didn't want to face her.

"Well, should we go anyway?"

"No, let's just stay home tomorrow, what do you say?"

"I thought you wanted me to go to church? That was the deal we made, remember?"

"Yes, I remember. But I'm not going tomorrow, so you can relax for another week."

"Dave, I want to go to church in the morning. I really want to go, so let's go together."

He sat up at that. What was she talking about? She hated going to church and now she was nearly begging him to take her. What was up, anyway?

"Allie, I'm not going tomorrow. And if you must know I'm not going next week either."

"Are you giving up Sunday sermons and just taking the Wednesday evening prayer services then?" Her brow furrowed in puzzlement.

He rose to his feet and began to pace.

"I've got something to tell you, Allie. I think you'll be pleased, at least I hope you will."

"What is it, Dave? What's going on? And stop pacing, will you? You're acting like someone died, for heaven's sake!"

He stopped mid-stride and turned to face her.

"I've quit the church, Allie." There, it was out in the open. He waited for the grateful smile of encouragement that never came.

She didn't say anything for a moment. The silence was explosive as he waited for her to say something, anything. This was definitely not what he had been expecting.

Allie got to her feet at his announcement, then walked across the room and stopped with her back to him.

"Allie?"

There was no response.

"Allie, say something. Aren't you happy? Now we can get married and you won't have to be living with a preacher anymore. I've given that up, for you. It's what you wanted, isn't it?" He walked over to her, and, putting his arms around her, turned her to face him.

She pushed his arms away harshly. Her face was deathly pale, her eyes piercing as they bored through him mercilessly.

"You did what exactly? Did I hear you correctly? Tell me again what you just said."

"I said I quit the ministry. I resigned from Grace Bible Church."

"When is your resignation effective? Did you give them six months' notice, or a year, or what?"

"I took my vacation, and my resignation became effective upon the last day of that vacation."

She crossed her arms protectively, still glaring at him, livid with anger.

He reached for her again, not comprehending her reaction. While he hadn't known exactly what he expected from her, it certainly wasn't this.

"Allie, I thought you'd be happy about this, but obviously you aren't. I don't know why. What's wrong?"

"What's wrong? Why, nothing's wrong, Dave. Whatever gave you that impression?" She began laughing hysterically.

He reached out for her, wanting to take her in his arms and hold her, but she pushed him violently away.

"Don't touch me. Don't you touch me ever again, do you hear me?"

"Allie, please. I thought you'd be happy about this. Now we can get married. We love each other, Allie. What has my resignation got to do with anything?" He reached for her again but she stepped back away from him.

"I said don't touch me."

"Allie, it's okay, it's okay. The only thing that will change is that we'll probably have to leave Bozeman. Actually there's no probably about it. I can't stay in this town and live with you openly. I just can't do that, but we can go anywhere else you want to go."

"No."

"If you're worried about me being unemployed or not being able to take care of you, I'm pretty handy. I know I can get work. It's all going to work out fine, trust me."

"No."

"Look, why don't we just settle down here and you take all the time you need to think about this whole thing. I surprised you, I know. You weren't expecting this kind of news, I understand. But think about it, will you? I love you and I don't plan on going anywhere without you."

She walked away from him and went to her room, slamming the door behind her.

Dave was confounded, totally shocked at her reaction. What on earth was wrong with her? He really thought she'd be happy that he had resigned. She had never liked the fact that he was a minister, so she should be thrilled that he had quit. But in fact, just the opposite had taken place. She was beyond merely upset. Her reaction had been way over the top, to say the least.

He lit a cigarette and poured a stiff drink as he pondered his situation.

She had told him not to touch her. That couldn't be what she really wanted, no way. They were too good together; they loved each other. She didn't mean what she said. So what was she so angry about? No matter how hard he tried to rationalize what had just happened, he was at a total loss. It made no sense.

An hour later she came back out to the living room, dressed in a filmy nightgown.

She had washed her face, put some makeup on, and combed her hair. It was obvious that she wanted Dave to make love to her. Walking over to the couch where Dave sat savoring his third cigarette and his fourth stiff drink, she sat next to him, resting her head on his shoulder.

"Dave, love, I'm sorry. I don't know why I reacted that way. Forgive me?"

"You know I do, Allie. I love you. I'll always forgive you, whatever you do. You know that, don't you?"

"I hope so." She reached up and kissed him the way he loved to be kissed.

Her scent, with the perfume she had lightly applied, melded with the wonderful smell of the cigarette smoke and the taste of the whiskey. He put the cigarette out in the waiting ashtray and set his drink on the table. Pulling her into his arms, he returned her kiss, holding her so tight he was afraid he might actually smother her if he wasn't careful.

"Allie, I love you so much." He was mumbling into her hair as he caressed her. "Please, please don't ever tell me not to touch you again. I think I might die if I couldn't hold you, love you like this."

They made love on the couch, intensely and passionately. She had scared him earlier, and he desperately needed to feel wanted, needed, and loved by her again. She hadn't meant those things she said. It wasn't possible. She couldn't make love to him like this and then not want him to touch her. It just could not be.

When they were sated, they lay entwined on the narrow couch, pillow talk as usual flowing freely.

"Dave, is your resignation really final? It isn't, is it? I mean, you can still go back if you want to, can't you?" She was almost purring into his ear.

"Well, yes, I guess I could. But I don't intend to do that. I'd rather marry you, Allie."

"Let's not make any firm decisions tonight. Why don't you think about it for a few days. You might want to change your mind. I hope you will, anyway."

"Why, Allie? I thought you didn't like my being a minister? What's changed?"

"Nothing, Dave. Nothing's changed. I just want you to be happy, and I doubt that you'll be happy if you're not doing what you really love and feel called to do, and that's preaching. I can get used to it, don't worry."

"Allie, I want to marry you. I want to make the proverbial honest woman out of you."

"Let's talk about all of this another day. For now, just hold me." She snuggled closer into him, smiling to herself.

Over the course of the next few days Allie turned the heat up with her charm. She became Dave's "perfect woman" in any and every way it was possible. Dave wasn't sure what was going on, but he was enjoying it, whatever it was. He had thought that he couldn't possibly love Allie any more than he did, but her actions toward him only served to further cement his feelings for her. He never noticed that her behavior had become almost robotic. While they previously had occasional disagreements as any couple did, now there were none. She agreed completely with anything he said and was compliant with his every wish. What Dave was now living with was a situation that most men could only dream about. It was too perfect.

Finally, he had to bring up the subject of moving again. There was no way they could stay in Bozeman. Dave had guts, that was true, but not enough to allow him to face the ridicule that he knew was coming as soon as he was seen on the streets again. No, moving was not an option, it was a necessity, and it would have to happen soon.

One morning after breakfast, he took Allie's hand in his own and led her to the couch.

Pulling her down next to him, he gathered her close to his side and took a deep breath. His thumb found the ring on her left hand, and he began turning it gently on her finger.

"Allie, I mentioned it before and I know you didn't like the idea very much, but my love, we have to leave Bozeman. I can't stay in this town and live my life with any sort of peace. I will be judged, and judged severely, and while I don't like the idea of moving any more than you do, I can't live with that. Especially since I fully understand that I deserve that judgment. So, we have to move, and I'd like to do it this week. What do you think?"

"Absolutely no way in hell, Dave. I'm not going anywhere."

She tried to pull away from him but he held her close, refusing to let her go.

"Look, if you don't want to leave the state, maybe we could just go to Billings, or better yet, Great Falls. Great Falls is a little farther away and I don't think anyone will recognize me there. We can drive up tomorrow and look for a place to get settled." He gave her a light, reassuring squeeze.

"Dave, why don't you just get your preaching job back so we can stay here?"

"I will if you'll marry me. What do you say? Will you do it? Marry me? We're already essentially married anyway. We have everything but the license."

"I told you I'm not going to be a preacher's wife. Just can't do it. It's a permanent thing, you know, and I'm not up for that. I can't believe I'm actually living with a preacher, but marry one? Nope. Sorry."

"Allie, I have . . ."

"Dave, I thought you loved me! Did I miss something here?" She pouted, something that usually resulted in his capitulation.

"Allie you know very well that I love you desperately. I've given up everything for you, everything that was important to me. My self-respect, my job, in fact my life, for the most part. You know there's nothing I wouldn't do for you, but I can't stay here. We have to move."

"You absolutely, positively won't go back to Grace Bible? Is there nothing I can say that will change your mind?"

"Sorry, nothing will change my mind. It's you or the church, but not both, and I choose you. That should make you happy and I don't understand why you want me to go back there so badly. You don't like church, you've made that plain enough ever since I met you." He was starting to get a little angry at her attitude. He had done everything she had wanted and now this?

She pulled away and rose to her feet. Turning to face him she was silent for a moment and then she spoke.

"Get out."

"What? What did you just say?" Confusion and shock registered on his face. He couldn't believe what he was hearing. He must be misunderstanding what she was saying.

"I said get out. Gather up your things and get out of my house." The words were said flatly, devoid of emotion. Her eyes were glazed and unfocused.

"Allie, I love you. There must be some way we can work this all out. Just calm down, will you? Please?"

"Calm down? Calm down, you say? You tell me how much you love me and then you quit your job and tell me we have to move away? I told you already, no way in hell. No way on God's green earth. Leave!"

At her mention of God, his face finally paled. He had no idea what was going on, but God was finally back in the conversation, and he didn't like it. His conscience couldn't handle his lifestyle and God at the same time.

"Allie, tell me what's wrong, here. You can't just tell me to leave after all we've been to each other. What's the problem, anyway?" He stood up to face her, his movements forcing her to step back from him.

"What's wrong? Everything's wrong!" She began to laugh, softly at first and then it turned to hysteria. She lifted her left hand into the air, the ring in front of his face. Slowly, deliberately, she removed it from her finger and threw it across the room.

"Allie!"

"You fool, Dave. You absolute, idiotic fool. You really don't get it, do you?"

"Obviously, no, I sure don't. Spell it out for me, will you? I thought you loved me. You told me so often enough. You acted like you did." He lit a cigarette.

"Love? Dave, you're an old man. Oh, we were good friends, but it was obvious you wanted a lot more than friendship. Don't get me wrong, you've been a wonderful friend. You were better to me than anyone else ever in my life, aside from my parents, but love? No, sorry."

"Then what have we been doing all this time? Playing house for you was just that? Playing? Did you mean any of the things you said to me?"

Her face became rigid, as if cast in stone. Her eyes were glazed, mere slits in her stony, pale face. Words began to spew from her tense mouth, soft at first, but slowly rising in volume and harshness.

"I only did and said the things you wanted me to do and say. You wanted to make love to me so I did. And I confess, you're very good in bed. You're a great dancer. You have the looks. But the fact remains that you are an old man."

"Was it all just an act, then, for you?"

"You know, I took a good look at my life after my parents passed away, and what was it all for, anyway?"

"What are you talking about? My age never bothered you before, at least you said it didn't." His face became even more devoid of color, if that was possible.

"My baby, Dave. Catherine. What was the point? I gave her away because of my parents, not because I didn't want her. But they died. I should have kept my baby. I should have kept her!"

"But you did the right thing, Allie. You found wonderful parents for her. It was the right thing to do, and I'm sure you know that, deep inside. It all worked out for the best.

"For the best? For whose best, my friend? Certainly not for mine."

"So what has all of this got to do with me quitting the church and us moving away from Bozeman? I don't get it, sorry. Can you be a little more clear, here?"

"I want my baby back, Dave. I want Catherine. I had it all planned, and it would have worked if you hadn't quit the church. I had you so in love with me there was nothing you wouldn't do if I asked you. If only you had stayed at Grace Bible I would have become a regular attendee. I could have volunteered in the children's department and spent time with my daughter every week. And then I could have gotten Catherine back. With your help, since you're good friends with Raven and Gus, I could have gotten my baby back. Then we could have skipped town and been a happy family. I was never going to marry you, but I would have continued to live with you as long as I had Catherine with me." She was actually snarling now.

Dave walked to the kitchen to pour himself a stiff drink. Allie followed close behind him, vitriol spewing from her mouth with every step.

He swallowed the whiskey in three big gulps and then poured himself another. As he began to down the second drink, Allie finally became deathly quiet.

"Allie?" He made one last attempt to get through to her, to understand.

She slapped him hard across his face, then turned and walked heavily out of the house, leaving him alone in his imploding world.

Chapter 20

Allie backed her car slowly out of the garage and left the house, driving carefully, well below the speed limit, an automaton in every respect. She had no destination in mind, no plan, no future. Not now. She drove aimlessly, her mind ablaze with her thoughts.

How could Dave do that to her? She had planned everything out so very carefully and now this. Her plan depended on Dave remaining a pastor at the church. If they were together and he was the preacher, she could attend church regularly, and become one of "them." No one would think anything about it, and after a while she could work there in the children's program. Oh, she realized that the Whittackers weren't putting Catherine in the nursery just yet, but when she was older, she knew that would change. If she were a volunteer, she would get to spend time with her baby every week until at some point she and Dave would find the right time to run away with her.

She was pretty sure she could have pulled it off. She could have found some way to stay out of the Whittacker's sight; they would never suspect. It would all happen behind the scenes, so to speak. Spending time with Catherine at church would remove any shyness or fear her daughter might have, and when it was time to leave, she would go willingly with Allie. But she needed Dave to be there. She needed Dave to be so in love with her that he would do absolutely anything she asked of him, including taking Catherine and leaving town with them, together, as a family. He would help her get Catherine. But now?

He quit the church? He quit being a pastor just because she wouldn't marry him? Ridiculous! Just ridiculous. He had utterly refused to consider going back. She had tried her best, using everything she could think of to get him to return. She had catered to his every whim, agreed with him on virtually every subject, and made love to him whenever and wherever he wanted, but it obviously hadn't been enough.

And move away from Bozeman? Was the man crazy or something? She wanted Catherine back. There was no way she would ever move away from wherever her child was until Catherine was in her custody.

But Dave had ruined everything. All of it, her whole plan, and he didn't seem to care. In love with him? No, she was never in love with him, and she never would be, not now. He was one of those rare creatures, a truly good man, but he was old. He still had his looks, that was true, and he was very good in bed. He satisfied her in every way, but he was never going to be a man she would marry.

She had read the signs early on. She knew he was in love with her long before she suggested they start dating, and it wasn't long after that when she had him in her bed. At first her plan had been only a vague one, taking time to fully form. She enjoyed being with Dave. He was a great dancer and a good companion. She liked it that he had started drinking with her at the bars. It had been totally unexpected, but it was more fun to drink with someone than to drink alone. And there had been that unexpected bonus; with most men alcohol resulted in decreased libido and stamina, but with Dave it was just the opposite. They were good together.

But marry a preacher? Never! No way! Why on earth did he have to go and ruin everything? Why? Why? Why? She pounded the steering wheel in her frustration.

Did she really want him to move out? If she could convince him to remain in Bozeman, did she want him to remain living with her? She could see no point in that.

Damn! Now what do I do? How do I get Catherine back now?

The truth was staring her in the face. Without Dave, she was not going to get her daughter back. It simply couldn't be done. The only chance would be if she kidnapped her baby and ran, but she knew in her gut that she would be found at some point, and she would lose Catherine again. On top of that, she would probably end up in jail. No, without Dave all was truly lost.

She wondered if by any remote chance he could still be cajoled into getting his job back, but as soon as the idea formed in her mind, she recognized that it was too late. He had quit and made it very plain that his decision was final. *Christians had some of the strangest ideas. Living together was unacceptable? In this day and age? Who were they trying to kid, anyway?* It never occurred to her that true Christians had different moral values and principles. It was incomprehensible to her.

She drove to a park down along the Gallatin River, pulled into an empty campsite, and shut the engine off. She had to think.

It wasn't long before the tears began. The floodgates were open, and the torrent unstoppable. She cried without reason, not trying to understand what was happening. It didn't matter anymore. She had lost, and it was painfully final. What on earth was she going to do now? Did she really want Dave to move out? Did she really want to be alone?

How could she have him stay when every time she looked at him from now on she would see the face of her child instead of his? She would be seeing the daughter she would now never have. She couldn't do that. No, Dave would have to move out as she had told him to. If she wanted some company after he left she could always call Doug. He wasn't Dave, but he would be a good substitute. At least Doug would make no demands of any kind on her. He was a perfectly safe date for those times when she wanted one.

She didn't want to go back to the house, but she knew she would have to in order to see this whole thing through. Dave was probably not going to leave without a fight, a big one. He was now so in love with her that she was sure he wasn't going to leave easily. Well, it couldn't be helped. He still had to go whether he liked it or not.

She sat in the quiet park for over two hours, alternately crying and thinking, feeling sorry for herself. The finality of everything was taking a long time to become her new reality.

There was nothing to do but go home to Dave. She had to get the "ugly" over with, and the sooner the better.

The house was dark when she finally returned hours later. Turning on the lights as she entered, she finally saw Dave sitting at the kitchen table, a bottle of Crown Royal nearly empty in front of him. He was so drunk he could barely raise his head.

"You're back." It was a statement.

"Yes, and I see that you're still here. I told you to leave, remember?"

"You don't mean that, I know you don't." His words were so slurred they were nearly unintelligible. His color was high now, flushed from all the alcohol he had consumed in her absence.

"Yes, Dave, I actually do mean it, although I can see you're too drunk to leave right at the moment. You'll be lucky to make it down the hall to the spare bedroom." She left the kitchen and went to her room, slamming the door behind her.

She found a pack of cigarettes in the nightstand on Dave's side of the bed. Lighting one, she propped her pillows behind her and contemplated her present situation some more as she smoked.

Dave, her only good friend, had totally trashed her plan for the future. For their future, hers, Dave's, and Catherine's. She knew that without Dave she would never even get close to running away with her daughter. Now? Her world was totally shattered, finally, once and for all. She laughed out loud, hysterically. Dave wanted her to be more of a "goody two shoes" Christian? Why on earth would she want to do that? What had God ever done for her? Heaven? Hell? Did she care about either one way or the other? Life suddenly had no meaning for her. She saw absolutely no reason to get up in the morning.

Finishing the cigarette, she went to the kitchen for a stiff drink. Why stay sober? She might as well join Dave in his misery. She snorted. He probably still didn't get it.

He was still sitting at the table, nursing his latest drink. She didn't understand how he still had the strength to even lift the glass, he was so wasted. Retrieving a glass from the cupboard she took a seat opposite from him and filled it to the brim with the amber liquid.

They sat in silence, Dave's gaze fixed on his drink, Allie glaring at her friend, unblinking. She didn't have any idea what she expected of him at this point, so she finally rose from the chair and, carrying her drink, retreated once again to her bedroom. She sat there on her bed, drinking and smoking for what seemed like hours. Sometime later she heard Dave walking down the hall. His footsteps halted outside her door, where he stood motionless for some time before finally making his way down the hall to the spare bedroom. Good. At least he had enough sense not to come to her bed tonight. She actually smiled to herself as she contemplated his despair, hoping he was as miserable as he appeared. She wondered if perhaps there was still some small shred of hope that he might return to the church. Was it possible? Or had slapping him been the final blow?

She was willing to try absolutely anything if it would get Dave to change his mind. He was still in her house, and she knew that he still loved her. Knowing the man as she did, she was sure he would love her until he died. True love was like that, she knew, or at least she had heard it was like that. She had never loved a man that way and doubted that she ever would.

Remembering the past, Aspen Windchase came to mind. He had been a patient of hers in Billings a few years ago, and had even stayed with her for a time, although they were never a couple, much to Allie's chagrin. He had been in a coma, and when he awoke he was blind, but even with that handicap he had been so handsome he had nearly taken her breath away when she looked at him. And he was a good man, much like Dave. She had been pregnant at the time, and if only Pen would have loved and married her she would have had both a good man for a husband and Catherine now. She had tried her best to make him love her, but he had never "looked" at her that way. In the end he had left her, and she had given her baby up for adoption. He lived just outside of Bozeman with his family now, very near to his twin sister, Raven Whittacker, Catherine's adoptive mother. Life could be stranger than fiction at times.

And now? Now, as she reflected on her situation, she vaguely understood that she was no longer the person she had been only a few short months ago. She wasn't sure exactly how she had changed, in what specific ways, but she knew she was different. Before, if she had slapped Dave's face she would have been mortified at her action, but now? Now she honestly felt he had it coming, and had no regrets about what she had done. The world had become about her, and only her. Nothing mattered apart from her wishes, desires, and plans. The woman Dave had fallen in love with didn't exist anymore. While her external features remained unchanged, inside her soul nourished a darkness and desperation that she failed to recognize. The old Allie would have been sensitive to Dave's dilemma, but now she didn't care in the least if he was hurting or not. The old Allie had left, and the new one suited her just fine. She lit another cigarette.

There was no reason now not to indulge in any form of gratification that came her way. Cigarettes? She had thought to quit smoking when she got her baby back. But Catherine wasn't coming to live with her, so she might as well smoke all she wanted. Drink? Why not? Who cared and what difference would it make in this vast, dark world? The pleasures of the world bombarded her from all sides and she saw no reason not to indulge in all of them. She had enough money that she would never need to work again. Socialization? She could socialize all she wanted at the bars. She could do exactly as she pleased.

But Dave needed to move out. She was sure he would try to stay with her, but that didn't matter. She was none of his business anymore.

Finally, she decided that she wanted him to make love to her again. She knew it would hurt him, and she wanted to make him pay for ruining her plans. She put her cigarette out and went to take a shower before going to Dave. She smiled to herself, but it was actually more of a grimace. The old Allie had truly left.

Chapter 21

Dave, former pastor at Grace Bible Church, was a beaten man. Allison Rose Morgan, the woman he loved more than his life, the woman he had left the church for, had actually attacked him, slapping his face in her anger. Stunned, he sat there in silence as she stormed out of the house. He was numb; he felt nothing.

What on earth had just happened? He couldn't seem to fit the pieces together. They just didn't fit. He loved her, and she had returned his love. At least she had told him so often enough. She had even gone to church a few times. He had moved in with her, sleeping with her every night, making love to her, loving her in every way he knew how to love a woman. She was everything he had ever wanted and more. He had abandoned his principles, his vocation, his very life for Allie, and now she said she didn't want him anymore. She wanted him to leave. How could she ask him to do that? How could he possibly leave? How could he stay?

She wanted Catherine back? He remembered how Gus had reacted when he had seen Allie at church, warning Dave about Allie wanting her baby back. He remembered how he had assured Gus that taking Catherine away hadn't even occurred to Allie. She was simply in love with Dave and attended church to make him happy. How wrong he had been! If he was to actually believe everything she said, her plan all along had been grooming Dave to help her kidnap her daughter. Impossible! She had to be lying, she had to be!

But she had slapped him, hard. She had actually slapped him in her anger because he had left the church and wouldn't be going back. There was no room for misinterpreting her actions. She was serious. She wanted him gone.

He poured himself a drink, downed it, and then poured another, and yet another until he couldn't see well enough to pour any more. He was thoroughly drunk and thoroughly miserable, yet his mind seemed perfectly clear. His thoughts weren't random and incoherent; they were totally rational. The woman he was living with was definitely not the woman he had fallen in love with. And yet he still loved her.

When had things started to go wrong? He couldn't quite place it. When Joe died? When she started going to the bars to dance? When her parents died? It all seemed to blur together, and there was no one point where he could definitely say her transformation had begun. It didn't matter in the end, did it? He told himself that tomorrow she would be back to the old Allie, and they could think about starting their lives over in another town.

What was he thinking, anyway? Back to her old self? He wanted to believe that so badly! He wanted his dream back. But deep inside, he knew that Allie was now a different person. The once beautiful, soft hearted, loveable Allie was gone. The change had been slow and nearly imperceptible, but it was full-blown now. His thoughts came full circle once more. And still, he loved her.

He wanted so badly to talk to God about all of this, but he couldn't do it. His shame covered him from head to toe, a coarse and unforgiving garment that he pulled even closer to his body, entombing himself. Trapped and powerless, sinking ever deeper into desolation, and totally helpless to pull himself out.

He couldn't lose Allie, he just couldn't. There had to be some way to reach her, to make her see the facts. She had to understand that she was never going to get Catherine whether he tried to help her or not, which of course he would not do. He could never betray Gus and Raven like that, never. Besides, kidnapping was a serious charge, and he would be locked away for the rest of his life if they were caught. No, it should stay Allie and himself, the two of them, loving each other and living their lives together in peace and love.

Storybook fantasy. That's all it was, he realized. Would he be able to persuade her to change her mind and let him stay? Would she take him back? Would she love him as he loved her? He wanted so badly to believe it was possible, but his confidence was rocked. The fact remained that she had slapped him, and she had told him to leave. What on earth was he going to do? She wanted him gone, but he had nowhere to go.

Tomorrow. Tomorrow he would make a plan to get her back. There was simply no way he could accept her ultimatum that they were over and he had to leave. The thought of leaving her shot a pain through his chest that nearly knocked him to the floor.

He finally rose and walked down the hall, stopping just outside of her room, waiting, hoping. For what? He sighed softly and continued down the hall to the spare bedroom, where he would sleep alone for the first time since moving into this house with her.

Lying there in the darkness, his mind continued to race as he slowly sobered up. Questions, possible solutions, hopes, dreams—uncontrolled, they raced through his brain randomly, unceasingly. He finally drifted off to sleep hours later, exhausted.

She came to him sometime in the night, offering herself as she had so many nights before. Why had she come? She had told him to leave. Why? He never opened his eyes, but accepted her offering with gratitude and passion. He made love to her as if it was the first time, afraid all the while that it might be the last. He loved her with his body, giving himself completely, his emotions raw and evident in his passion.

When it was over, she rose from his bed and walked out of the room. Allie had not uttered one sound the whole time.

Somehow it was even worse after she left. What game was she playing now? She said she didn't love him, but she had just made love to him. She had told him to leave, but she had just come to his bed. What did she really want from him? He wanted another drink.

He also wanted . . . go away! No! He didn't want to give voice to what he wanted, even if it was silently going through his head, formlessly, but still it was there. What he wanted was a hit of heroin, and he wanted it badly. That old killer friend that he had managed to banish for so many years, heroin, was back with a vengeance.

He rolled over onto his stomach, pulling the pillow over the back of his head, trying to bury himself into nothingness, but there it was, as long ago in his past, no escape for him.

God! No, he couldn't call on Him. He had sunk way too low, and the shame, oh, the shame! He had preached God's grace unceasingly over the years, but now his mind told him it was beyond his reach.

But, she came to me tonight. She came to me and made love with me. Doesn't that mean that she has changed her mind? Doesn't that mean that she wants me to stay? The fact that she had come to him gave him hope once more. It shouldn't have.

The next morning Dave waited for her in the kitchen. She slept late and it was hours before she wandered in for a cup of coffee.

"Allie?"

"What?" She poured herself a mug of strong, black coffee and sat at the kitchen table to sip it.

"I think we need to talk. We need to talk this whole thing out."

"I don't see what we have to talk about, Dave. I told you everything yesterday."

"Look at me, Allie, will you?"

She raised her head and met his gaze full on, intense, riveting.

"I want Catherine. I needed you to help me get her. You quit the church so you can't help me now. You have no place in my life anymore, so you need to get out of it. You need to leave. That's all there is to say." She lowered her head again.

"You came to my bed last night. That has to mean something, I know it does. You can't mean everything you're saying. It doesn't make any sense."

"That was sex, Dave, pure and simple. I like sex, and you're very good in bed. End of story. I don't need you anymore. I can call Doug anytime for what I need."

"But you came to me!"

"You were convenient."

"Allie . . ."

"You can pack up your things and go today. I'll leave for a few hours, and I expect you to be packed and gone when I come home." She rose and began walking out of the room.

"Allie, I can't. I can't leave you. I love you, and I want to make a life, a future with you. Please!" He jumped to his feet, and catching up with her, grabbed her arm and turned her to face him.

"Allie, I'm not leaving you. I can't. I love you, you know that, and I can't just turn that switch on and off. I will love you forever. All you have to do is let me. Please, Allie."

She shook his hand from her arm, turned, and walked to her bedroom, slamming the door shut behind her.

He had no pride left, and followed her to her room. The door was slammed hard in his face, and he began pounding it with both fists.

"Allie! Open the door, Allie! We're not over, you and I, not by a long shot! Open the door, I said."

The door remained closed, solid and unyielding in his face. His fists and pleadings were useless.

An hour later she left the house.

He watched her leave, despair written all over his face. She couldn't mean it, it wasn't possible, not after all they had meant to each other. She loved him, she simply had to love him, somewhere deep inside of her. Maybe she just forgot for a while somehow. Maybe . . .

Maybe what? Maybe she would return home with outstretched arms, happy to see him? Maybe she didn't really mean what she had said?

He did no packing and made no effort to move out. He determined he would stick it out, take all of her abuse for however long it took for her to come to her senses. What kind of man would he be if he just gave up at the first sign of trouble? No, he would stay. However long it took, he would stay and see it through.

She was gone all day. He was worried to death about her, but there was nothing he could do. Confident she would return at some point, he sat, smoked, drank strong coffee, and waited. She finally walked into the house around eleven o'clock that evening. She wasn't alone; her old friend, Doug, was holding her hand as they walked in.

Dave looked up, stricken. His face drained of all color, and his breathing became rapid and shallow.

"Allie?" Why and what was he bothering to ask? It was all too obvious, the "what and why." Allie only went out with Doug for one reason. He was going to be sick.

"Oh, you're still here? I thought you were leaving." She kept her hand firmly clasped in Doug's.

"Dave Benson, isn't it? I met you at Mixer's once, I think." Doug obviously had no idea what he had just walked into.

Dave gave no answer, but just stared, totally beaten, all hope gone at last. Allie had finally made her point.

"Don't mind him, Doug. He was just here for a visit. He's leaving now, aren't you Dave? You can see yourself out." She smiled sweetly up into Doug's naïve face. "We're kind of busy right now." Not giving Dave even a cursory glance, she led Doug down the hall to her room.

He heard her bedroom door shut softly. Then laughter and muted voices exchanging, what? He went to the bathroom and threw up, then washed his face and, grabbing his jacket and pickup keys, left the house. As he walked to the garage he was sick again, retching violently over and over until exhaustion ended the spasms. There was nothing more he could do. Allie had given him her final answer and there was no going back. She was finished with him.

He sat in the pickup for some time, motionless, numb. He couldn't think and he couldn't seem to move. Two hours passed before he was able to back the vehicle out into the night. He had no idea where he was going, and began just driving slowly around Bozeman, keeping to back streets, lost in the vacuum that his mind had become.

He had gambled everything he had, and he had lost.

"Somebody's knockin'"

Chapter 22

At three in the morning he finally pulled up to Chase the Wind Stables; it was the only place he could think of to go. Climbing slowly out of the pickup, he staggered to the front door and began pounding it repeatedly, methodically. It was only a few minutes before the door was jerked open and the muzzle of a .357 revolver was staring him in the face.

"What . . . ?" The gun was hastily lowered as Gus saw who was standing there. "Dave? What on earth are you doing here at this hour?"

"Gus, I, can I come in?" The words were mumbled, barely coherent.

"Sure, Dave, come on in, but . . ."

Dave staggered past him into the hallway. He could barely stand and appeared totally drunk although he was stone cold sober. Seeing a chair, he sank heavily onto it, his head immediately becoming buried in his big hands.

Gus walked over to him, and, resting a hand on Dave's shoulder, waited for him to speak and explain why he was here in the middle of the night. Dave's shoulders began to shake and it wasn't long before the tears came. They sat together like that for some time, until the tears started to ebb and Dave was able to talk.

"Dave, are you drunk?"

"Sorry, but no. I'm totally sober."

"Then what's going on? Can you tell me?"

"Gus, she kicked me out."

"She what?" Gus's shock at this statement was evident. "What do you mean, she kicked you out?"

"Just what I said. We're over, Gus. She doesn't want me anymore. Told me to leave, just like that."

"And you left? Why didn't you stay and try to talk this all out? You two have been together for some time now, and there has to be a way to straighten this mess out. I'm frankly a little surprised that you up and left like that just because she told you to leave. That's not like you, my friend." He shook his head in disbelief. "How about we go sit in the tack room and talk over a cup of coffee? Sound like a good idea?"

"You should go back to bed, Gus. I can wait here if you don't mind and we can talk in the morning. How's that?"

"As if I'm going to be able to go back to sleep after all this! No, let's go do our talking right now. Wait for me in the tack room while I go tell Raven what's going on."

"Can you just tell her it's me so she doesn't worry, and save the rest for tomorrow?"

"Sure. I'll be right back. Make yourself comfortable." Gus left him to go to his wife, his head shaking as he walked down the hall to his room.

Dave was waiting in the tack room where he had visited with his friend so many times over the years. He wanted to start the coffee while he waited, but couldn't manage to find the strength.

Gus returned, made the coffee, and they waited in silence while it perked. Finally it was ready and, pouring two mugs, Gus handed one to his friend and took the other himself, settling onto a chair opposite Dave. He waited until Dave was ready to talk. The silence seemed to drag on forever, but finally, Dave took a deep breath and began.

"I told you, she kicked me out."

"Yes, but why on earth did she tell you to go? It makes no sense, Dave."

"Turns out you were right, Gus. You were right all along."

"What do you mean, I was right? Right about what? I don't remember saying anything negative about you two being together. You're grown-ups, and I figure you sure didn't need me telling either of you what you should and should not be doing." His brows furrowed in his puzzlement.

"She wanted Catherine, Gus. That's all she ever wanted, as it turns out."

"Catherine?" Gus's face became set and rigid. "Over my dead body, Dave. Over my dead body!"

"I know that, Gus, and I told her that." He shook his head in his despair.

"Okay, okay, let's slow down here and back up a little. How did this all come about—how did you find out? Did she actually come out and tell you she wanted Catherine? And what did that have to do with you? I don't get it."

"I'm not totally sure when it all started with her, Gus, but she's changed. She changed slowly from that sweet, beautiful woman into someone I don't even know anymore. When I told her I had quit the church she pretty much 'lost it.' She even slapped me at one point. That's when it all came out, how she was using me in the hope that I would help her kidnap Catherine and run away with her somewhere. She told me how she plotted to make me fall in love with her to the point that I would do anything for her, but I needed to stay at the church to make it all happen."

Shock and disbelief showed on Gus's face. He was visibly shaken at this revelation. "Dave, you wouldn't . . ."

"Never, Gus. I would never betray you like that." *I might betray my God but I would never betray you, my friend.*

"Okay, so you refused to go back to the church? She didn't love you enough to stay with you?"

"I don't think she ever really loved me at all. She used me, in every way she could. I apparently was a fun companion. Gus, I took the woman to bars, I danced with her, drank with her, smoked with her. Slept with her." His eyes closed in shame as he remembered.

"Well, even if you wouldn't help her get Catherine, I don't really see why you're here. What was that 'straw that broke the camel's back'?"

Dave raised his tear-stained face to Gus, pain written on every line, clouding those brilliant blue eyes.

"She brought another man to the house last night."

"What? A man? And you were there?"

"I'd actually met him before, at one of the bars, before we were a couple. But yes, they walked in together, holding hands. She told me I could find my own way out as she led him down the hall to her bedroom. I heard them . . . I . . ."

"That's okay, Dave, you don't have to say anymore. I get the picture. I'm so very sorry, my friend, so sorry. I don't know what to say." He shook his head in emphasis. "So, I hate to even ask, but what are you going to do now?"

"I don't know. I'm so numb I can't think very straight. The only place I could think of to go was here. Sorry."

"That's good, here is where you need to be, with friends. Why don't you stay with us until you're ready to move on? Raven won't mind, I know."

"I don't know, I hate to do that to you two. I'm not someone you want or need to have around when I'm like this. Gus, I'm no good to anybody now. I can't even pray! How can I talk to God when I've betrayed Him like this?"

"Dave, you know He's there for you whenever you're ready. You've preached it often enough, remember?"

"The words came easy from the pulpit, Gus. It's not so easy when it gets personal." He shook his head, eyes downcast.

"Well, we don't have to make any big decisions tonight, Dave. You just plan on staying here as long as you need to. You can use Pen's old room. It's been empty for a long time so it's no trouble."

"What about Raven? She might have something to say about all of this."

"Raven won't mind at all. I know my wife and I'm positive she wouldn't want it any other way. She'll be upset if you show up like this and then leave. Just stay with us."

Dave didn't respond, but nodded his head in assent. He had nowhere else to go anyway.

"If you've finished your coffee, why don't I walk you back to Pen's room and get you settled?"

"Sure. Okay. I'm done." He rose to his feet and walked with his friend back to his new room.

Gus made sure Dave had everything he needed, and then turned to leave.

"You didn't bring anything with you? No suitcase or overnight bag? Change of clothes? Anything?"

"Nope. I just walked out of the house with my jacket and left. Sorry. Didn't even bring a toothbrush and I have to confess I could sure use one right about now. Happen to have a spare I could bum off you?"

"Sure. There's everything you could want or need in that bathroom, and it's a private one at that, so whatever mess you make in there won't bother anyone but you. But you don't even have a change of clothes with you?"

"No. I told you, nothing but the jacket."

"Well, we'll worry about that in the morning. Oh, on second thought, I guess it will be later than morning. We're pretty much there already; it's already nearly five, my friend."

"Gosh, I'm sorry, Gus. I ruined your night and you didn't get much sleep thanks to me."

"Don't worry about it, Dave. You just do whatever you want do to and we'll give you a call when breakfast is ready, how about that?"

"No, no breakfast for me. I couldn't swallow a thing right now. The coffee was good enough. I think I'm going to go to bed and try to sleep. I'll poke my head out when I'm up and around, okay?"

"Fine with me. I'll let Raven know so she won't worry too much. You just rest as much as you want. If you need anything, let me know. Oh, I can borrow some clothes for you from Pen tomorrow, since I think you two are about the same size. Okay with you? Until we get your own stuff, whenever that is."

"Fine. I hate to bother everyone like this, though."

"It's no bother, you know that. You'd do the same for me, I know."

"One more thing, Gus."

Gus raised his brows in question.

"Could you maybe not tell Raven and Pen everything that went on with Allie and me tonight? We can talk about it all later?"

"Sure thing. Don't worry. They won't ask and I won't tell. I leave all of that up to you whenever you're ready. Sleep well, friend." He turned and left Dave alone in the room, shutting the door softly behind him. He stood for a moment in silence just outside the room, shaking his head slowly from side to side, his shoulders slumped, before he turned and walked back to his room and Raven.

Dave didn't bother to undress but flung himself onto the bed, lying on his back, arms outstretched. Lying there in the darkness, he tried to reflect and think rationally, but it was impossible. Fragments of thoughts and sentences rapid-fired through his brain in no semblance of order. He tried to focus, to think, but it was no use. Exhaustion finally overtook him and he slipped into a fitful sleep. It wasn't long before his restless slumber morphed into a sleep so deep he laid as one in a coma.

Morning came and went and he didn't stir. Afternoon slipped by and he did not awaken. The world was spinning, moments slipping away, and still he slept on dreamlessly, a blessed, dreamless sleep. An escape from the torture of the reality he would now face when he awoke.

Chapter 23

He came awake with a start. Where was he? Where was Allie? Suddenly his head felt like it was about to explode and his hands went to his forehead in an effort to quell the pain. He hadn't drunk before coming to Chase the Wind Stables, but he felt like he had the mother of all hangovers. He felt terrible, and that was an understatement. And the questions?

Suddenly it came to him: he was at Gus's and Allie was not with him.

It all came back with a rush. Allie had told him to leave. Allie had brought Doug home with her. Allie didn't want him anymore. No one wanted him anymore. He was completely, totally empty inside. All that he had been was gone, or so it felt. He wanted to pray, to connect with his Lord, but he couldn't do even that. Rational thought was beyond him.

But he wanted something; what did he want? Allie? Well of course he wanted his love, but she didn't want him. Coffee? Cigarettes? No, what he really wanted was a hit of heroin. He ached for it as he had years ago. But no, he couldn't go there, he couldn't. He wouldn't go there—at least not as long as he was staying with Gus and Raven. There. He had opened the door to a possibility he had formerly ruled out completely. He shook his head.

Lord, help me! That old longing is back that I thought I had banished forever! Dear God in heaven!

He slammed his fist onto the bed by his side. What was he thinking? Heroin? Again? And he had the audacity to ask God to help him? It was his own sinful desires that had gotten him into this mess to begin with. He felt he had no right, no right at all to ask God to help him yet again.

He wanted a drink, and he wanted one very badly. He wanted to lose himself in an alcohol-induced stupor far away from the world. But he would have to go out to get it himself. The only alcohol Gus and Raven had around here was what was in some horse liniment they kept on hand for the occasional equine injury. He would have to get himself together somehow and go to town to get what he needed.

And his things. He would have to get his things from Allie's. How on earth was he going to do that? He couldn't ask Gus to get them for him. That would be asking too much of his friend. Besides, now that Gus knew that Allie had planned to kidnap his daughter, it would be unthinkable to have the two of them in the same room together. No, he would have to suck it up and do it himself. Not that there was much for him to gather up at her house. He had taken only a few changes of clothes and books. But there was his Bible. He wanted his Bible more than he wanted anything else, although he had no idea why that was so. He felt so far from God at the moment; why would he want his Bible? He certainly wouldn't be reading it anytime soon, he was sure of that. It would seem like a sacrilege of some sort after all that he had done, and yet . . . he wanted it. Leaving it would be like leaving a part of himself. No, he would have to go today and face Allie one more time.

He found himself thinking about that meeting. Maybe she had thought things over by now and didn't really want him to leave. Maybe she really did feel about him the same way he felt about her. Maybe she wanted him to stay after all. Maybe . . .

But she had brought Doug home with her, right in front of him, rubbing his face in her betrayal. Could he ever forgive her for that? No! No way! And yet, he still loved her, and deep within himself, he knew he would forgive Allison Morgan absolutely anything. If only she would want him again. If only she would love him as he loved her.

He sighed and went into the bathroom to take a hot shower. He was going to see her again; he would at least be clean. If he had any hope of reconciliation he had to be at his best, and underneath everything he was thinking lurked the faintest hope that somehow, some way, he could win her back.

As Gus had promised, he found everything he needed in Pen's old bathroom. He emerged an hour later clean-shaven, his hair glistening and wavy from the hot shower. Even in his agony he remained a very handsome man.

Gus hadn't disturbed him so he had to put on the clothes he had worn the day before. They reeked of cigarette smoke but he didn't notice. Smokers were seldom aware of the odor they gave off, or how their homes or clothing smelled.

It was nearly noon when he finally emerged and went to find his friend. He checked out the kitchen, then the tack room, and finally the arena where he found the couple working with two of their current "clients." He heard them laughing companionably before he saw them.

Leaning over the rail, he watched them unobserved for some time, jealousy piercing him sharply. Raven and Gus were still so in love even after several years of marriage; their eyes shone as they looked at each other, laughing and joking as they rode.

Finally, Raven noticed her pastor and quickly guided the colt over to him.

"You're up. Good. Gus said I wasn't to wake you so I didn't, but you must be hungry. Let me finish this lesson up and I'll fix you something yummy and filling, what do you say?" She smiled broadly at him, her vibrant blue eyes flashing, giving no hint that anything was out of the ordinary. Raven was an exceptional woman in many ways.

"Thanks for letting me sleep. I didn't realize I was that tired, but as for food, I'm really not very hungry."

"Impossible! You're a man and men are always hungry." Raven laughed at him.

"No, really, I'm not. I guess I could use a cup of coffee, but no food, thanks anyway." He nodded at Gus who had just ridden over to join them.

"Dave, you're not going to pass up my wife's cooking, are you?"

"Sorry, but I really don't think I can eat anything right now. I'll just go make myself a cup of instant coffee and be on my way."

Gus eyed him narrowly. "You sure? You haven't eaten in a long time, so maybe . . ."

"No, a cup of coffee is all I need for now. It's okay if I come back here for a few days, though, right?"

"Of course. Stay as long as you want. I'd offer to go get your things for you, but, well, I think you understand why that wouldn't be a very good idea."

"Yeah. I get it." He lowered his gaze to the sandy floor, and then quickly looked up again.

"But where's Catherine? Who's watching her while you two are training horses?"

"Oh, she spends most of her days with her cousins at Pen and Maura's house. The kids have a great time together and Maura really enjoys having her." She looked hard at Dave, her curiosity evident but her good manners keeping her silent.

"It's okay. Gus, you can go ahead and fill Raven in on everything you think is relevant while I'm gone. Guess I can't hide things forever, especially if I'm staying with you folks for a while. I'll see you both later this afternoon."

Gus nodded, tipping his hat to his friend, as Dave turned and walked away.

He went to the kitchen and made himself a cup of instant coffee, taking it back to his room. He sat there for some time, gathering up the courage he needed to go back to the home he had shared with Allie. He didn't know whether he hoped she was there or that she was gone somewhere.

An hour later he finally rose to his feet and slowly walked out to his pickup. It was time to make the final break.

His heart sank as he pulled up to her house and saw her new car parked outside. She was home. Was she alone? He walked ever so slowly up to the front door and knocked. She had kicked him out and while he still had a key, he knew he was no longer welcome to just walk in as he had done in weeks past. He knocked again. Finally, the door opened.

"Oh, it's you. Come in, Dave." She turned and led the way into the living room.

He followed her warily into the room where they had made love so many times. The memories crashed over and through him as he stood there in the center of the room, unable to move.

"Allie, I . . ."

"You what, Dave? I'm assuming you came for your things?"

"Yes."

"Well, go ahead, gather up whatever you're going to take with you." She stood in front of him, her arms crossed over her chest, her silky strawberry blonde hair framing her delicate face.

Intoxicating. She was still totally intoxicating to him. He wanted her just as much as he ever had. All thoughts of her infidelity left him, and he saw her as he had always seen her. In that moment he had a flash of understanding as he recalled the story of Hosea in the Old Testament and all that the prophet had gone through with his wife. As Hosea loved his wife even after her infidelity, Dave loved Allie, still. Involuntarily he reached for her.

She started to pull away, but then relaxed and let him pull her to himself. He buried his head in her hair, inhaling the scent that was uniquely hers.

"Allie. I love you. You don't really want me to go, say you don't. Please."

"Dave, I told you how I feel and what I want. I don't love you. I'm not sure I ever did. I told you that already. And yes, I still want you to move out. I don't need you anymore. I'm sorry." But she did not pull away.

"Let me stay, please." He began planting light kisses on her hair. Then he slowly brushed her hair aside and gently kissed her neck. "Allie, let me." He was totally lost yet again in spite of everything.

"Yes, Dave. Yes. Go ahead. Make love to me. You're very, very, good at it, you know." She melted into him.

They made love there on the couch, and it was good. They were always good together.

Dave was exuberant. Allie was letting him love her. She had forgiven him. She must have changed her mind, or else why would she let him . . . ? He took his time, tasting, touching, loving. He poured his heart out in his actions one more time, and when they were finished, she let him hold and caress her.

She was going to let him stay, he was sure of it. After what had just happened between them, there was no way she was still going to tell him it was all over. No way on God's green earth. Impossible.

But he was wrong.

"You can leave whenever you get your things together. I left a couple of boxes in the spare bedroom for you to use. You can let yourself out." Gathering up her clothing, she pushed herself away from him and walked away to her room. The door made a soft sound as it latched shut.

Nothing had changed. Allie had just had sex with him one more time and it seemed to mean nothing to her. Nothing at all. For him the experience was immeasurable and indescribable. It was beyond wonderful and fulfilling. He had given everything as he always did with her, and it meant nothing. Tears trickled slowly from his clenched eyelids as he lay there, empty and alone. Again.

It took him several minutes before he was able to get up and put his clothes back on. In a daze, he stumbled down the hall to the spare bedroom, and, finding the boxes she had mentioned, he tossed all of his things into them, and then carried them out to his pickup, one by one. His well-worn Bible graced the top of the wadded-up clothing in the last box.

His final trip into the house was to gather up all the cigarettes, beer, and alcohol he could find. They filled one more box. Silently, he left Allie's house for the last time.

Before going back up to the stable, he decided to take a detour to Billings. The drive took nearly two hours, but he wanted to stock up on some things, and there was no way he was going to risk being seen in a liquor store in Bozeman or Livingston. He did allow himself to wonder why it mattered if anyone saw him now; he had left the church and fallen about as far as anyone could fall. What did it matter anymore? For some reason he didn't understand, it still did.

It was nearly seven o'clock that evening before he arrived back at the stable. He let his hosts know that he was back and would they please not disturb him. He would see them in the morning.

He carried the boxes into his room, completing the task with the two he had filled with his purchases in Billings. He had enough liquor to enable him to stay drunk for at least two weeks, which is what he fully intended to do. *"She had blue eyes and blue jeans . . ."*

He drank that night until he passed out, which is exactly what he had planned when he left Allie for the last time. His headache the next morning only served to let him know he was still alive, and still in the hell of his own making. He was up early, however, and made it to the kitchen in time for breakfast. He would have preferred to skip all meals and just drink himself literally to death, but he knew he couldn't do that at Gus's home. It wouldn't be fair to the Whittackers, and somewhere deep inside of himself the fact that a little girl lived there also was a definite deterrent.

He selected the chair furthest from where Raven and Gus usually sat and lowered his weary body slowly onto it. Catherine was sitting in her high chair, her golden head shining in the sunlight that filtered through the kitchen window. She really was a beautiful child. Raven and Gus were very lucky parents. The little girl stared at him, never having seen him before.

His head required a little tenderness this morning; no jarring allowed. He sat quietly, his head down, wishing he could just be alone.

"Good morning! Here's your coffee, which we all know you can't function without any more than we can." She carefully set a mug in front of Dave. Raven was all smiles and warmth for her new guest. Turning to her daughter, she introduced Dave to her.

"Catherine, this is our friend Dave. He's going to stay with us for a while, so be on your best behavior, okay?" She kissed Catherine on her forehead, and then turned to start frying the bacon for her men.

"Sleep all right? Is the bed comfortable?" Gus questioned.

"It's fine. I slept okay." Dave kept his eyes lowered. He couldn't look his friend in the eye.

Gus watched him shrewdly. He was sure that Dave had drunk heavily the night before. It was very obvious that he wasn't feeling too well this morning.

"You okay, Dave?" Gus asked softly, so softly that Dave barely heard the question.

"No. No, I'm not okay. But we can talk later if that's all right with you?" He didn't want to discuss any of this in front of Raven. This was "man talk."

"Sure. Why don't you help me feed the horses after we finish breakfast and we can talk while we get some chores done? Are you up for it?"

"Okay."

Dave did not speak again during the meal. Raven looked over at him quizzically every now and then, but when she saw Gus nod his head in the negative, she did not look at their guest again.

When the meal was finished, Dave and Gus rose in unison to leave the table. "Dave's going to help me feed, Raven, so I'll see you later in the arena. I'd help you with the dishes, but Dave and I need to have a little chat." He walked over to give his wife a light kiss on her cheek before motioning to Dave to follow him as he headed for the stall area.

Dave had been the proverbial "jack of all trades" before becoming a pastor, and feeding horses was done mechanically. They began talking as they worked.

"So, Dave, how are you really doing? I know you drank last night. Did it help?"

"Drinking never helps, Gus, you and I both know that. But right now it seems to be the only way I can deal with this. At least when I drink enough I can pass out and have a little peace."

"But then you wake up, right?"

"Yup. Then I wake up and it starts all over again. Gus, I don't know how I'm going to make it through this, I really don't. It hurts so bad!" He choked in his misery.

"Well, the worst is over as far as I can tell. You got your things, so you don't have any reason to see her again, do you?"

"Gus, we made love again when I went there yesterday. Well I guess I should clarify that statement. I made love. Allie had sex."

"So, doesn't that mean there's still hope?"

Dave laughed roughly. "When we were finished she told me to get my things and leave. Implied was the 'don't ever come back' part."

Gus stopped dead in his tracks. "You two, well, you . . . and then she told you to leave?"

"She sure did. Gus, I swallowed whatever pride I had left and begged. I said all the right things, I . . . she still told me to leave."

Gus shook his head.

"What I really don't understand is why she let me make love to her, and acted like everything was going to work out, and then when it's over she tells me to leave again. Said she didn't love me and never had." His voice caught, and in his pain he turned and slammed his fist into the barn wall, startling the horse in the closest stall.

Slowly and deliberately, Gus placed the feed bucket he had been carrying on the floor, then walked over to his friend and placed an arm around his shoulder in an effort to comfort him in some way.

Dave's shoulders began to shake, and he dropped to his knees as the sobbing overwhelmed him. Gus dropped with him, and turning Dave into himself, held him as he cried. Words were unnecessary.

They stayed that way, locked in the embrace, for a long time until Dave's tears finally subsided.

"Sorry, Gus. I didn't want to drag you into this, I really didn't. But what on earth am I going to do?"

"Well, for starters, you're going to bunk here with Raven and me for as long as you need to. Just promise you won't go to sleep with a lit cigarette and burn the place down."

Dave raised his head and stared at him. Gus knew he was smoking too?

Gus laughed at the puzzled look on Dave's face. "What, you thought I couldn't smell the cigarette smoke on you? Your clothes reek of smoke, my friend. Frankly I'd be a lot happier if you would smoke outside rather than in the room, if that's not too much to ask."

"Okay. Deal. I won't smoke in the room anymore."

"Thanks. I appreciate it."

"How much does Raven know? What did you tell her?"

"I told her the truth. That Allie kicked you out but you still love the woman and are pretty broken up about the whole thing."

"What did she say about me staying here? I'll find someplace else to go if my being here will upset her, or you for that matter."

"No. She loves you too, Dave, and she feels really bad for you, so don't worry about staying here for as long as you need to. She understands, you know. Her past wasn't so squeaky clean either, but it's all new since she became a Christian." He paused. "God's still there, you know. Have you been praying?"

"I can't, Gus. What I've done . . . I'm so ashamed. God is so far away right now I just don't feel like I can go to Him. Not like I am. I've fallen so very far! And I knew better, I knew better all along but I did it all anyway." He shook his head. "No, I don't talk to God these days."

"He didn't leave, Dave, you did. He's still there; you know that. Just talk to Him like you talk to me. He'll hear you and He understands. You've preached that for years so why can't you take your own advice?"

"Maybe someday but not now. I'm too ashamed. Allie still consumes me, Gus, even after everything that has happened, she's still all I can think about. I love her, my friend. I probably always will."

Gus sighed. "Well, take your time. If you need me, I'm here. If you want and need some physical work to fill your time, you let me know. There's always plenty to do around a barn as you well know."

"Thanks, Gus. Right now I just want to hole up in that room. Maybe later."

"All right. You let me know when you're ready."
"Gus?"
"Yeah?"
"Did you tell Raven about Allie planning to kidnap Catherine and run away with her? Does she know about that plan and my part in it?"

"The part you didn't participate in? No, I didn't tell her anything about any of that. All she knows is that Allie broke up with you and you don't really know why. I won't tell her about Allie wanting her baby back. Raven doesn't need to know any of that."

"Okay, that's good, I think. And don't worry about Allie trying anything. She knew she didn't have a chance without me to help her, so while I don't have any idea what she'll be doing next, I'm positive she's given up all hope of ever getting Catherine back. You can rest easy. Catherine's safe."

"Shall we get these horses fed, then? I've got to work with these colts or I won't be able to pay the bills." He laughed good-naturedly.

"One more thing?"

"What now? I thought we covered everything?" Gus looked puzzled yet again.

"Well, I'm really too embarrassed to be eating with you two. I can't have Raven cooking for me like that. Do you think she'd mind if I just fixed myself a sandwich or fried an egg or two when you're working the colts? I promise not to leave the kitchen a mess for her and she won't even know I've been in there."

"She won't be happy about not cooking for you, I'm sure about that. But I'll talk to her and explain as best I can. She'll worry about you not eating right, but she won't mind if that's what you really want to do. It will be fine, so just go ahead and fix yourself whatever you want whenever you want it. I'll square it all with Raven."

"Thanks. I'll stay out of the way so you folks will forget I'm even here."

"No chance of that, Dave. I know you're here, and I know you're hurting. Just remember that I'm here for you, whenever you need me. And I'm praying for you." He patted his friend on the back. "See you later. I have to get to work."

Dave watched his friend enter the next stall, then turned and walked back to his room.

Closing the door behind him, he poured himself a drink. Finishing the drink while still standing up, he set the glass on the counter by the bathroom sink and took the bottle back to the bedside table. It was still morning. He would be drunk again by noon.

Chapter 24

By noon he was indeed very drunk. His mind was finally slowing down along with his speech. He was miserable, but he liked the stupor the booze instilled in him; he liked it very much. Finally, his mind dulled, he drifted off to sleep.

Several hours later he was nearly sober. Wanting a cigarette again, he kept his promise and went outside to smoke. He was all alone as he leaned against the barn, puffing his cigarette, taking in the view of the Bridger Mountains. They were so close it seemed they were only a stone's throw away. But the beauty of Montana was wasted on him today. His thoughts kept racing to Allie, over and over again. It was Allie, Allie who didn't want him anymore.

He lit another cigarette, inhaled deeply, and let the nicotine fill his lungs. A good cigarette was hard to beat. He wondered distantly why he had quit smoking all those years ago since they were so enjoyable. Oh, right, he had gotten born again and become a pastor. Wincing at the memory, he stubbed the butt out and put it into his pants pocket. He was considerate enough to not leave evidence of his bad habit lying around for his hosts to pick up.

Back in his room again, he realized that he was quite hungry, but not as hungry as he was thirsty. Food could wait. He found his bottle and began to lose himself in it again. It didn't take long before he passed out once more.

The pattern of his new life was established. Drinking and smoking, he passed through the hours of the days oblivious to the world outside of his room. He did not see Raven or Gus and he didn't care. He took his belt up another notch as the weight began to fall from his frame. Food was the last thing on his mind. The faint lines that etched his face deepened and his color faded, becoming pallid and sallow. His eyes lost their sparkle and appeared vacant. The days dragged on, one after another, and the pattern he had set for them did not vary.

Occasionally he realized that he did indeed have to eat at least a little, and when he knew the kitchen would be vacant, he made his way there and put together a sandwich, so at least he wasn't starving to death, even though he looked as if he might be. These occasional forays to the kitchen always left just enough evidence that he was still alive and eating, so Gus and Raven would have no need to come to the room to check on him. He didn't want to see anyone. He didn't want to wake up each morning either, but he did. Life just didn't seem fair.

One afternoon he stumbled his way to the kitchen to make himself a peanut butter sandwich expecting the kitchen to be vacant. Lurching, drunk as usual, it took him a few seconds to realize that he was not alone. On the floor in front of him was a little girl; Catherine was crawling around all by herself.

Spying the newcomer in her world, she suddenly stopped crawling and sat upright, staring at the big man. He stared back, apparently in shock.

And then Catherine smiled at him—a huge, happy, baby smile. Her eyes were sparkling, her baby cheeks round, full, and very rosy with her recent efforts. Giggling, she reached her arms up, wiggling her tiny fingers in an obvious request for Dave to pick her up.

Instinctively, Dave reached down for her before he caught himself as he stumbled. He was too drunk and unsteady to pick the toddler up. He cursed under his breath, and then went to sit on a chair.

Just then Raven came running into the room.

"Catherine! There you are! What are you doing in here, girl?" Smiling in relief, she bent down and scooped her daughter up into her arms, swinging her around as she did so before holding her tightly to her chest. Suddenly she noticed the big man sitting at the table.

"Oh, Dave, I didn't realize you were here. Sorry. Catherine up and crawled away when I turned my head for a few minutes, and suddenly she was just gone. The little stinker! Anyway, what can I get you while I'm here? Hungry for anything in particular?"

"No, thanks. I'm fine."

"You're probably wondering why Catherine's here today instead of at Maura's. Maura has a bad cold so Catherine had to stay with her boring old momma today." She nuzzled her daughter's golden curls.

"Oh." Tears glistened in Dave's eyes and he said nothing more.

Seeming to understand that Dave was embarrassed, Raven spared him and, telling him she would see him later, turned and left the kitchen with a now-squirming Catherine.

The tears were no longer just shimmering in Dave's eyes; now they began to course down his cheeks. His humiliation was complete. Raven, his best friend's wife, had just seen him drunk. He was too unsteady to even pick up a smiling baby. What must she think of him? It wasn't like she wouldn't realize his condition since Raven had drunk heavily in her past also.

But it came to him with a great sadness that he would either have to sober up or move out. He could not stay around an innocent baby and remain drunk all the time. Who knew what could happen? He couldn't do that for his friends' sakes.

He stumbled back to his room and had another drink. So, what was it going to be? Quit drinking or move? What kind of choice was that, anyway? How could he do either one? The trouble was, he wanted to stay with Gus and he wanted to keep drinking. He didn't want to leave and he didn't want to stay sober. What did he want?

Well, at the top of the list was still Allie. However, he found that heroin had moved up ahead of the alcohol and the cigarettes. He wanted the escape that heroin had provided him in the past, and he wanted it very badly.

But where could he go if he didn't stay here with Gus? Maybe if he kept the bedroom door locked and made sure not to be seen, he could continue. Maybe Raven hadn't realized how drunk he was when she saw him. Maybe even if she did know, she wouldn't tell Gus. Maybe. Maybe pigs would fly.

Gus came to visit him later that evening. He was surprised to hear Gus knocking on his door, even though he halfway expected it.

"Can I come in?"

"Sure, Gus, come on in." He heard Gus turn the knob on the door and then realized he had locked it.

"Wait a minute, let me get the door."

Unlocking it, Dave led the way into his room. They both took seats before beginning the conversation.

"You probably know why I'm here, Dave. I'm sorry, but we have to talk about things." Gus kept his gaze downcast, obviously in distress at having to confront his friend.

"Yeah, I know. And I'm sorry, Gus, I'm really sorry. I won't let it happen again, I promise."

"Just how drunk were you, Dave? Just a little or a lot more?"

"What did she tell you?"

"Just answer the question. What she told me doesn't matter; I want to hear it from you."

"Well, I was pretty drunk, I think."

"And just how drunk was 'pretty drunk'?"

Dave looked away from his friend, too embarrassed to face him. "Too drunk to pick her up, which is what we both wanted. Sorry."

"Sorry isn't going to cut it, Dave, and I think you know that." Gus sighed deeply.

"Yeah, I know."

"So? What's the plan? You're going to have to sober up and get back to living, Dave. You can't go on like this, and you know that."

Dave looked back to his friend at this. "I can't? Frankly I don't see any reason why not? I'm perfectly content living in a fog. I'm probably as happy as I think I'm ever going to be again in this life."

"Dave, as much as I love you, as much as I think the world of you, and as much as I want to help you through this mess your life has become, I can't have you drinking around my daughter."

"I know. It won't happen again, I promise."

"How can you promise it won't unless you're ready to stop drinking? That's the only way you can be sure and you know it. Besides, you're been here for nearly two weeks and we both know you can only live this way for so long. It's time to get back to living, my friend."

"Give me just a little more time, okay? I'll come around soon, I promise. If not, I'll leave."

"One more week, Dave. One more week, and then this has got to stop. You know I love you like a brother and it hurts me more than you can imagine to see you like this. You've seen both me and Pen through some really hard times, and now it seems to be your turn. But at some point you're going to have to help yourself. We can't do it for you."

He reached over to put his arm around Dave. "Dave, you have to snap out of this. Somehow, some way, you have to. Start with prayer. Start with God. There's nothing He can't and won't forgive, and you know that. Start now."

"Maybe tomorrow. Maybe the day after that. Maybe next week, I don't know. All I know is I hurt so bad right now that I can't think. All I want to do is escape however I can. And God? Yeah, I know He's there. I'm a pastor, remember?" He shook head slowly. "Well, at least I was, once. Not anymore."

"Dave, listen to yourself, man!"

"Gus, my head knows there's nothing I can do that God won't forgive, but my heart is so seared with guilt and shame that forgiveness seems totally impossible right now. Maybe never. So for now, I need that escape the booze is giving me. Sorry."

"One week, Dave. One week from today. If I can help you in any way, please let me know. I'm willing to do whatever I can."

"Yeah, I know. Thanks. For now, though, I think I want another drink. See you later." He rose and motioned for Gus to leave. He needed to be alone again with his misery.

The next afternoon Gus brought Aspen with him to try to get through to Dave. Dave had helped Pen recover from his drug addiction a couple of years ago, and no one knew better the depths of despair that a man could sink to than Aspen Windchase. Pen had awakened from a coma to find himself blind and unable to remember even his name. Despair had resulted in a prescription drug addiction, and Dave had spent weeks with him helping him through his withdrawal and recovery. A strong Christian, Gus hoped that Pen would somehow be able to get through that steel wall Dave seemed to have built around himself.

Dave was surprised to see Pen with Gus when he opened the door. Somehow he never expected Gus to share his situation with anyone else. He should have known; the three of them had been close friends for years.

Pen held his hand out to Dave. "Dave, good to see you again, even if it is like this."

Dave was drunk, as he remained all day, every day. He reeked of alcohol and cigarettes, taking a shower now only every few days. He hadn't shaved in nearly a week and he looked and smelled like a derelict. The pastor had disappeared.

"Well, come on in, friends. Nice to see you. Find yourselves a seat." He swept his arm to encompass his small room, then took a seat on the edge of the bed and waited. He was drunk but he knew what was coming and he wanted none of it.

"Before you both get started, let me put a stop to it all right now. I already pretty much went over this with Gus yesterday so there's no need to hash it all over again."

Pen and Gus exchanged worried looks before turning back to Dave. Pen spoke first. "Dave, we only want to help, you know that. It looks like you're in pretty bad shape, my friend."

"Yeah, I guess I am, and I'm happy being that way, so you can save it."

"Dave, I . . ."

"Look, we both know you of all people understand where I'm at now. But you're forgetting or missing one little part of this."

"What's that?"

"You had a reason to get away from your addiction. You had Maura and your sister, Raven, and Gus. I've got no one."

"Wrong and you know it. You have us, remember?"

"Sorry boys, but neither one of you have long silky hair and a sexy voice. Neither one of you can hold me at night and make me feel like a king among men. Friends just aren't the same as the woman I love. I have no future without Allie, and she doesn't want me. Therefore, the way I see it, I have no future. So, I might as well smoke and drink. What's the use?"

"Dave, let us . . ."

"No. Don't you understand? I don't want to stop. I like being constantly drunk. I like it just fine, so you can both leave now. Just go and leave me alone. Please."

Tears glistened in Dave's eyes. His friends acknowledged them between themselves, and then rose to leave.

"Okay, Dave. You win, for now. But remember, you have to start coming around in one week. I've warned you, and as much as I love you and want to help you, one more week is all I'm giving you." Gus's voice was firm.

The men left the room, and Dave poured himself another drink. Closing his eyes, he laid back on the bed and let himself drift off into nothingness once more. Tears coursed down his cheeks unheeded as he acknowledged that when he awoke, he would be right back in this hell that had become his life.

For the next six days he remained lost in the alcohol induced fog he had come to love. He made himself a sandwich when he was famished and certain that no one would be in the kitchen, but otherwise drank continuously until he passed out. When he awoke, he repeated the scenario. Each day became a blur, and he would have lost track of all time if it were not for the calendar hanging on the wall in the bathroom. He retained enough presence of mind to cross each day off as it passed.

He awoke around eleven o'clock one evening. Shaking his head to try to clear the fog a little, he stumbled into the shower and began to clean himself up. Clean shaven once more, he dressed carefully in clean clothes and then stripped the bed of the filthy sheets. He pulled the boxes he had moved in with from the closet and, throwing his things into them, took them out to his pickup. The last thing remaining in the room was that old, nearly worn-out Bible of his. He stared at it for a moment, and then walked out of the room, leaving it on the bedside table.

He settled himself in the driver's seat and started the engine, but then just sat there, letting the engine idle. Why wasn't he leaving? After several minutes, he shut the engine off. Without conscious thought, he went back to his room and, picking up the Bible, held it to his chest as he took it with him back to the vehicle. He started the engine again, put it into gear, and drove quietly away from Chase the Wind Stables and his friends. It was exactly one week to the day from Gus's ultimatum.

Chapter 25

The next morning Gus noticed right away that Dave's pickup was no longer parked in the yard. His heart literally skipped a beat as he walked as quickly as his game leg would let him back to Dave's room. He knocked even while he acknowledged the futility of the gesture. He knew his friend had left before he even swung the unlocked door open.

The room, as he expected, was empty. Dave had taken everything he had brought with him when he left. He had stripped the bed, and the dirty sheets were neatly piled in a corner. On the bedside table was a one hundred dollar bill. Payment. Gus nearly swore at this; as if he would take payment from his friend and former pastor for helping him when he was at his lowest. Stupid man!

He went to the kitchen and found Raven starting breakfast. "Raven, Dave's gone."

Raven spun around, her shock at this announcement obvious on her face. "What do you mean, he's gone? Why would he leave without saying anything? Where did he go?"

"I don't know, I mean I have no idea where he went. He didn't say anything to me yesterday about going anywhere, and I just assumed he was planning to stay with us until he could get himself pulled together." Gus began wringing his hands in his concern. Dave was in no condition to go anywhere.

"Did you say something to him, Gus? Did you say something to upset him in some way, even if you didn't mean to?"

"Well, after he and Catherine met the way they did in the kitchen, I did tell him he was going to have to somehow, some way, pull himself together if he wanted to stay here with us. I told him I couldn't risk having him around Catherine when he was drunk, which is pretty much all the time now." He sighed deeply. "I told him I would give him a week to sober up, and if he didn't, he was going to have to leave. Guess he took the leaving option."

"Gus, you didn't! How could you give the man that kind of a choice?"

"Raven, remember the choice I gave you before we got married? It's that old 'tough love' thing. Even though I loved you more than my life, I couldn't stay with you and allow you to escape your reality; I had to leave. If I hadn't left you would never have grown into the woman you are today."

"Yeah, I remember. It hurt like hell, believe me. But you came back to me, Gus. You came back. Will Dave?"

"Well, I sure hope so, although I don't really know. But I am convinced that we couldn't just enable him to drown his sorrows here every day for the rest of his life. At some point he has to sober up and get himself together again. So yes, I did give him that ultimatum, but honestly, I really thought he'd give in and let us help him sober up and get on with his life."

"Well, looks like you thought wrong. So now what are we going to do? He can't be out there all by himself in the shape he's in. How on earth will he get by?"

"I know. We have to find him, somehow." His brows furrowed in his distress. "Maybe I should go talk to Allie. What do you think?"

"Over my dead body! You absolutely will NOT talk to Allie." She glared at her husband.

"But maybe he went back to see her? What if he's at her house right now? If he's not there, at least maybe she would know where he went. What else can we do? We can't leave him out there alone. He'll never make it out alive at the rate he's been going. We have to do something! Have you got a better idea?"

Raven paused, thinking. "Well, you could start by driving by her place and see if his pickup is parked out front. How's that for a beginning?"

"Fine, except he used to park in her garage. He could be there and we wouldn't know. But I guess it wouldn't hurt to drive by just in case. I'll go right after breakfast."

"Okay. At least it's a place to start. But you absolutely must not approach Allie, Gus. It would be different if we didn't have Catherine, but we do, and we can't risk getting involved with that woman on any level. Frankly, I used to like the girl, but after what she's done to Dave, well, it's going to take a lot of time and prayer for me to get over the bad thoughts and feelings I have for her right now. Sorry."

Gus ate quickly, and after giving Raven a quick kiss on the cheek, he headed to Allie's house. Dave's pickup was nowhere in sight. He frowned, wanting desperately to march up to her front door and ask her about Dave, and not only what she knew about his whereabouts, but to confront her about how she had treated his friend. But he kept himself in check, keeping the promise he had made to his wife. He exceeded the speed limit driving back to the stable. He found Raven tacking up a colt.

"His pickup wasn't anywhere around Allie's place. I drove around several blocks to be sure, but there's no sign of it. Now what do we do?"

"I don't know, Gus. Maybe we should just let him go. What do you think?"

"Nope. Can't do that." He shook his head in the negative. "Why don't I go talk to Pen and see if he has any ideas? Maybe Dave talked to him before he left." His face brightened at the thought. "Do you suppose he went to Pen's place?"

"I doubt it. I think he's just gone, but I think talking to Pen is a great idea. Maybe between the two of you you'll come up with something."

"Do you mind if I go over there now? I know I need to get working with these colts, but my mind won't be on them as long as Dave is missing. Sorry."

Raven smiled. "You go right ahead. Our friend comes first. See you later."

Gus left and drove the short distance over to Pen's home. Aspen was shocked to hear that Dave had left sometime during the night and had no idea where he had gone.

"So what do we do, Pen? I think somebody has to have it out with Allie, don't you? Even if she doesn't know where he is, she might have at least some ideas about where to start looking. And frankly, I really want to give that woman a good piece of my mind. Sorry. Can't help it."

"I agree with you on all points, but I think Raven's right in that you for sure shouldn't confront her. Let's think on this a little. How about coffee while we do our thinking?"

"Sounds good. Coffee always sounds good!"

"Why don't we let Maura in on this new development? She might have some ideas. What do you think?"

"Can't hurt."

"I'll go get her."

Maura joined them at the kitchen table, their two children tagging along behind her. Gus filled her in on everything, and they started exchanging ideas between the three of them as they drank.

"Boys, I think I should be the one to go see Allie. She knows me, but I'm not a threat to her in any way. The only history we have together is mostly a work history, but you two, well, I agree that someone needs to go see her, and I think I'm the best candidate. What do you think?"

They exchanged glances between them, and then the men nodded their assent in unison.

"You're right. Gus and Raven have her daughter, and I lived with her for a while after I left the hospital." Pen shook his head, remembering. "She tried so hard to convince me that I was Catherine's father so I would marry her, but I just couldn't confess to something I didn't believe was true. So in the end, yes, Maura, you are the best choice." He looked over at his wife. "Are you sure you're up to it though? I doubt it will be a pleasant visit for either of you."

"Don't worry, I can handle Allie. If nothing else, I'm older than she is, which should count for something. Respect for your elders and all of that." She smiled at the men. "I'll go right away. You'll watch the kids, Pen?"

"Of course. And take as much time as you need."

"Okay, boys. See you later. Pray for me!" She rose to her feet and waving goodbye, left on her new mission.

An hour later she had pulled up in front of Allison Morgan's home. Taking a deep breath, she gathered her courage and walked bravely up to Allie's front door and, after knocking, waited patiently.

Allie's shock at seeing her former friend was evident, but the shock soon gave way to a warm smile.

"Maura, nice to see you. Come on in. What brings you here?" Allie was all smiles as she led Maura into the living rom.

"Allie, I'll get right to the point. Is Dave here with you, and if not, have you seen him?"

"What? Dave here? No, I kicked him out. I thought you knew that, all of you up around the stable." She flicked her hair with one hand as she turned away from Maura. Her eyes hardened. "I should have known this wasn't just a nice social visit."

"Allie, what on earth happened with you two? The last I heard, you were in love and Dave was living here with you. He even left the church to be with you and now you've broken up with him?"

"That's a fact. Why, what's it to you?"

"Allie, don't you know how much that man loves you? You're all he can see or think about. Don't you have any feelings for him at all after all this time?"

"Shall I be blunt with you, Maura?"

"Please do. Blunt and honest is just fine. But tell me, what on earth is going on with you?"

"I liked Dave, I really did. But I didn't love him. Oh, I thought for a while that maybe I was a little in love with him, but come on, Maura, he's old enough to be my father!"

"His age didn't seem to bother you, and besides, lots of men marry younger women. You seemed happy together. What went wrong?"

"I didn't want to get married. Not to him, anyway." She spun around, leaving her back to Maura. "What I really wanted was Catherine, and the only way I had any hope of getting her was if Dave helped me. When he quit the church that was the death knell for us. I didn't need him anymore."

"What did you say?" Maura's face turned ashen in an instant.

"I said I wanted my baby back, and I needed Dave to do it. Happy now?"

Maura recovered quickly. "Is that what you wanted from the beginning? I don't believe you. Sorry, but I don't quite believe that. Try again."

"Oh, in the beginning he was my best friend. I was content that Catherine had a good home, and I had a good time with Dave. But then, well, I don't know what happened or when it all changed, really. But it did. The longer I was around Dave the more I wanted Catherine."

Maura listened quietly as she continued.

"Hey, Dave was fun, he's awfully good looking, and he's really good in bed, if you must know. But he left the church. And he kept trying to get me to become 'more' of a Christian, I guess you could say. Well, I don't need any more church stuff. I'm fine the way I am. So, I guess I don't need Dave any longer. Plain enough for you?"

Maura sank onto the couch, her knees weak. "Allie, what happened to you? The Allie I knew was a sweet, likable, good-hearted girl. Everyone liked you, but now? You're cold now, Allie. So cold."

"Yup. You're right. I guess I am cold, aren't I? Well, I don't know exactly what happened. Call it life if you want. My life is all messed up and there's no way I can straighten it out. I've lost everything that was ever really important to me, and I'll never get any of it back." She turned on Maura, her eyes slits of anger.

"If that stupid husband of yours had just accepted that he was the father of my baby and married me like I wanted, none of this would have happened." Her arms swept the room in her anger. "None of this. But no, he was too high and mighty to stay with poor old Allie. But it turns out that you were good enough for him, weren't you? So now you have everything, and I have . . nothing. I admit it, I'm bitter as hell. So what? What's it to you?"

"Dave's my friend, Allie. We won't talk about Pen; that subject is off the table for you."

Allie snorted.

"Allie, is there any chance at all that you'll take Dave back? Can't you give him even a little hope?" Maura was pleading now.

"No. No way. I'm done with him. He was a good friend, and he satisfied me in many ways, but no longer. I have new friends now, and they satisfy me too. I don't need Dave Benson clinging to me anymore."

Maura shook her head in disbelief at the coldness now radiating from the once-lovely, kind girl before her. She sighed deeply, and then began again.

"Allie, Dave's missing."

"So? What do you want from me? He's a grown man; I'm sure he can take care of himself."

"No, I don't think he is able to take care of himself right now, so we're all worried about him. Allie, he's been drinking non-stop ever since he left here. He's not well. We need to find him. Do you have any idea, any idea at all where he might have gone?"

"Nope. I have no idea and I really don't care where he is. He's not here and that's all I care about."

They were both quiet for a few moments. Finally Maura spoke.

"What are you going to do now, Allie? You're not working. You have no family here. You made Dave leave. What's next for you?"

"Why do you want to know? What do you care?" Allie riveted her cold eyes on Maura.

"Well, believe it or not, I do care about you. I'd like to see you be happy again. I'd like to see the old Allie come back into the world. I confess that I don't really like the new one very much."

"Well, I'm thinking about moving back to Mandan. I don't have any family left, but I do have some good friends from high school. I haven't decided for sure yet, but that's what I've been thinking."

"Sounds like a pretty good idea to me."

"I know, you just want me gone from this area, far away from Raven and Gus and Catherine. Don't pretend you care about me." She frowned.

"No, actually, I really do care about you. I would like to see you happy again. Life is too short to be spent in anger and bitterness. In the end, it isn't worth it. Think about it, Allie, and be happy." She rose to her feet. "I'll be leaving now. Sorry if I disturbed you, but think about your future. I'm sincere in my good wishes for you."

At the door, she turned back to Allie once more before exiting. "If you hear from Dave, will you let me know? Please?"

"Okay."

"Thank you. Take care."

Allie watched her former friend walk out of her life. *Yes, I think that I should go back to Mandan. In fact, that is exactly what I am going to do. Thanks for coming, Maura. You actually helped me make up my mind.*

She left for North Dakota the following week, taking all of her possessions with her. She would not be returning to Bozeman. There was nothing for her anywhere in Montana.

Chapter 26

Pastor Dave Benson's final descent had begun. Leaving Chase the Wind Stables had stripped him of his last support, his friends. He hadn't wanted to leave, but in his heart he realized that as long as he was drinking that heavily he couldn't stay there, and he had no intention of ceasing that activity. And the cigarettes. Gus had asked him to smoke outside, which was a reasonable request, but he didn't want to inconvenience himself to that extent. He preferred to stay in his room with his whiskey and smoke there, something he understood was a dangerous practice. It would be all too easy to fall asleep with a lit cigarette in his hand, and what then? He could burn the stable down. People could get hurt. No, it was better that he left. But now what? Where was he going to go?

He drove down by the Gallatin River and spent the rest of the night in his pickup. Nights in Montana are always cold, and that night was no exception. He slept only fitfully until he took the keys out of the ignition and stowed them in the glove box. Then he pulled a bottle out from under the seat and drank until he no longer felt the cold. The sun was nearly halfway through its daily course before he woke up and lit another cigarette.

Sober once again, he tried to plan his next move. He was going to need some cash; that much he knew. Well, he had plenty of that saved up; he could survive for quite a while on his savings if he didn't plan on eating too much, and using most of it for his current vices.

He got out of the vehicle, stretched, then got back in and drove to Bozeman where he took much of his savings out of the bank in one hundred dollar bills. From there he drove to Billings where he spent the next three nights in various bars, drinking until closing time and sleeping in his pickup until the bars opened again. He drank, he smoked, and he slept, trying his best to erase all thoughts of Allie and his downfall from his mind. It was impossible, but the numbness brought on by the whiskey certainly helped. He lived for anonymity and his next drink.

Living out of his pickup left him unable to wash up or shave regularly. Soon he was nearly unrecognizable. Dirty, unshaven, and stinking from unwashed body odor, it wasn't long before he was unwelcome even in the bars. The second time he was asked to leave, the rejection penetrated deep enough for him to realize he needed to clean himself up, at least for a few days. He parked his vehicle a couple of blocks from the local Rescue Mission, and then presented himself as a homeless person in need of assistance, which in fact he was.

He was able to stay at the Mission for a week, during which time he bathed and shaved, and was once again presentable. However, there was no drinking allowed, and he didn't want to live that way. Also, he had to listen to some preaching, and he was unable to sit through that more than once. The former preacher had fallen too far.

He checked out of the Mission one day, thanking the staff for their kindness and assuring them that he was a changed man, and then drove around until darkness veiled his approach to a bar he hadn't yet patronized.

Clean-shaven, with some new clothes he had purchased, he looked as handsome as ever, though worn. He drank, he smoked, and then unexpectedly found himself checking out some of the women hanging out at the bar. It wasn't long before one of them sauntered over to his table and sat down with him.

"Mind if I join you for a while?" Her voice was sultry, and her clothing was molded to her body. Makeup had been applied heavily, but she smelled good, and while not terribly attractive, she wasn't too hard on the eyes either.

"Sure. Suit yourself." He eyed her closely, a war beginning within him. He knew it. He felt it.

"You here by yourself?" She was looking around in case he was with someone, although she thought he had come in alone.

"Yup. All alone. You?" He didn't really care, but it was polite to ask.

"Yeah, me too."

She was a hooker, there was no doubt about it. Dave had been around enough of them in his past that he was not easily fooled. The war within him was short.

"Let's not waste time, shall we? You have a place close?" Dave got right to the point.

"Buy me a drink or two first, honey?" She leaned in close to him exposing her impressive cleavage. It wasn't wasted on him.

"Sure. What are you drinking?"

They drank and smoked for a while, and then the woman took his hand and led him outside and down the block, stopping at a door that she carefully unlocked for them. They went up a steep flight of stairs where she kept a small apartment.

Her name was Dianna, or so she said. Her apartment was dark and sparsely furnished, but it was clean, not that he cared much one way or the other. He had come with her for one purpose, and only that one purpose. While he hadn't put much thought into why he had followed her, now that he was here, he began to wonder. Why? What was he doing? *I love only Allie, so why would I want to sleep with another woman?* He didn't know and he didn't care. Sex would make him feel better, he knew. It always did, and if it wasn't with Allie, well, so what?

"Have anything to drink here, Dianna, is it?" He would love another drink and one more smoke before getting down to business.

She hesitated for a moment, and then "Yeah, I got some beer around here somewhere. But haven't you had enough already?"

"I never have enough, if you want to know. I want another smoke, too. Do you mind?"

She retrieved two cold beers from the small refrigerator and put one in front of her guest while popping the top of the other one for herself. Her eyes widened as she watched Dave down the can in one long continuous drought, and then light up a cigarette.

"Now I'm ready. Let's get to it, shall we?" Dave was all business now. While not impolite, he wasn't wasting any time either.

When it was over, he slept, warm and exhausted. He was awakened within half an hour.

"Wake up, sugar. Time is money and I need to get back to work. I need the bed, you know?"

He rolled over onto his back and slowly opened one eye, fixing it on the woman. "Dianna, was that your name? What would you say to my staying here for a few days? I've been sleeping in my pickup and it gets pretty cold at night. How about it?"

"Uh, look, let me be plain. I have to make a living, you understand? If you stay here I have no customers. So, sorry, but no."

"I'll pay you. How much do you want to let me stay here for a week?" He laughed. "I can pay what a cheap motel would cost me but not the Ritz or anything, so don't be too greedy, okay?"

She quoted him a figure that was not out of reason, and he nodded his acceptance.

"One more thing, though, honey. That's for the use of the apartment only, and it doesn't include my fees. I can't be losing income because I have a permanent guest, you know? And you'll have to pay in advance. Can't have you skipping out on the deal."

"How much for everything, including your 'services'?" He turned on the charm and smiled provocatively at her. "Give me a reduced rate since I'm a safe customer and you won't have to worry about being attacked or anything. What do you say? Your guaranteed safety for a week should be worth something to you."

She thought it over for a few minutes, and then agreed. "Okay. One week. You can stay here for one week. But I'm not supplying any meals for you. Deal?"

"Deal. I'll leave in a week. Just don't be making any demands on me, agreed?" "You pay me in advance and we'll get along just fine."

They settled into a routine. Dave paid her what she asked, and on the second day he gave her money and asked her to buy him plenty of beer and cigarettes, along with a little food. She did the shopping and he stayed in the apartment drinking, smoking, and availing himself of her body whenever she was willing. At first she kept her services limited to once a day, but her guest was so proficient and good-looking, she relaxed her standards and became willing whenever he felt the need, which became more and more frequent. He had no limits anymore, and he didn't care.

The week was nearly up, and they were lying on the bed enjoying cigarettes and beer. He wanted to sleep, but tonight she wanted to talk.

"Dave, where are you from, anyway? You never talk about yourself and I'm curious."

"I didn't pay for counseling, Dianna. Leave it."

"Aw, come on. Tell me a little about yourself, please?"

"I'm from all over, I guess. Most recently from around Bozeman. Been gone from there for some time now." He took another swig of the beer but kept his arm around her. She was nowhere close to Allie, but she was warm and willing, and that was now enough.

"What did you do in Bozeman? Ranch work?"

He laughed, but was just drunk and relaxed enough to tell her his previous profession. She was the first person since he had left Gus's place to take enough interest in him to ask. "No ranch hand. Pastor."

She sat straight up in bed at that one. "What? You're saying you're a preacher? And you're here? With me, a . . . ?"

He pulled her back into his embrace. "Ex-preacher. Not a pastor anymore. I'm here with you, aren't I? Paying for your services? That should tell you I'm no preacher anymore."

"What happened, if I may ask? Had to be something big, unless you weren't too committed in the first place."

"Yes, to me it was big, and no, you can't ask. Well, you can ask but I have no intention of telling."

She looked at him slyly. "A woman."

"I told you, I'm not telling."

"I'm right, I know it. A woman. What happened? Did you get her pregnant? What?"

"I'm not playing this game with you." Angry, he rose from the bed and left her while he went to get another beer. "Leave it alone."

"Okay, okay, I get it. You don't want to talk about it, but maybe I can help somehow, if you'll let me." She smiled up at him.

He turned his back on her as he dressed quickly, then grabbed his beer and walked out of the apartment. There were two days left of his one-week agreement.

He didn't return until he was too cold to stay outside any longer. She hadn't left and the door was unlocked.

"You're back." It was a statement. She was dressed again and had obviously been waiting for him. "I was worried about you. You okay?"

"I'm fine, just a little chilled. Why don't you come over here and warm me up?" More beer, more cigarettes, more sex. Dave was exactly where he wanted to be. The next morning, Dianna approached him again.

"Dave, our agreement is up tomorrow, I know, but how about staying on with me? I could reduce your rate a little if that would help?"

"Why?"

"Well, to be frank, I kind of like having your around. You're nice and a real gentleman, and I like that. So how about it? Stay on with me?"

"I don't think so." He showed no emotion, since he felt none. She didn't really matter to him one way or the other. She was pleasant to be around, she was clean, and she was agreeable in bed, not that he asked for much. The fact was that he gave more than he asked for, but he felt no compulsion to stay with her.

"Why not? We're good together, aren't we?"

"We're fine, but I have no real reason to stay."

"Too expensive?"

"That's not it."

"How about I just charge you for the use of the apartment and not anything extra for, you know?"

"Frankly I can get the extra anytime I want it for free, so that's not the problem. I just don't feel like staying. Sorry. I won't be supporting you so I guess you'll have to go back to work."

The look on her face said it all. His comment stung, but she was, in fact, a working girl. She lowered her eyes but said nothing more.

He stayed one more day, and then while she was out buying some necessities, he gathered the few clothes he had with him and whatever beer was in the fridge, and then walked out of the door.

Dianna returned later to a cold, empty apartment. She put her purchases on the kitchen table, then sat down and cried for over an hour.

Chapter 27

Settled once more in his pickup, he gassed up and then headed south toward the Crow Reservation. Somewhere near Crow Agency he noticed a large rustic sign with bold hand-lettering along the highway that read, "***Jesus is Lord on the Crow Reservation.***" He read it in passing and scowled. *I am indeed Lord here, Dave. Welcome.* He shook his head and pulled the pickup over to the side of the road. Where had that come from? *Welcome? I don't think so. I'm too far gone, Lord, and you know it. I don't think there's any going back now.* He lowered his head, and then sat quietly for some time. He tried to pray, but nothing would come.

Lord, I'm so sorry. You know how sorry I am. How could I ever ask you to forgive me, to take me back? Impossible. He wasn't praying, he was just talking to himself, getting nowhere, his head spinning in circles. He started his vehicle up again and began the search for an out-of-the-way bar in which to spend the night.

It wasn't hard to find; he drove a few blocks off the main drag and there it was. He parked behind the building and sauntered in the back door. Once more the smells were welcoming him. He breathed the stale, smoky air deeply into his lungs. It was almost like coming home, in a way.

It didn't take long for a lonely woman to approach him, and while she was attractive and pleasant, tonight he wasn't in the mood for anything other than whiskey and cigarettes. Except—there was one more thing that he found himself craving. It crept up on him slowly, stealthily. Heroin. The whisky, cigarettes, and women were no longer enough. He wanted his old nemesis back, and while somewhere deep within himself he recognized the danger, he no longer had the desire or the will to keep himself from it. He did not ask around for any, but he knew that eventually it would come for him, unbidden, and he was ready. His life was over. He had lost everything, including his very identity, and he no longer cared. Nothing mattered to him anymore. He understood very well that he had done this to himself, and had no one else to blame. Every now and then Allie intruded into his thoughts, and he wanted very much to blame her, but he knew that was not fair. His failures were his own. He felt totally abandoned and alone. God? He wanted His comfort but his despair and shame would not allow him to seek God out again. He had convinced himself that he was beyond God's redemption, and he would receive his just rewards. *"The wages of sin is death."* It was in the Bible, and the Bible was true.

> *"I heard about her, but I never dreamed*
> *She'd have blue eyes and blue jeans."*

It came back to Allie, the woman he had loved beyond reason. The woman who had totally deceived him. The woman who had led to his downfall.

He surprised himself. Later that night a young woman approached him. The usual ensued: drinks, cigarettes, small talk, and then the offer of the bedroom. He started to refuse but acquiesced in the end. Why not? He certainly had the time and he was definitely able, and even if he thought he wasn't interested, he knew that was not really a factor. He went with her to a small room that she kept in the back of the bar. But this time was different. This time she offered him what he was craving the most, and the fight within him was fierce.

Somewhere, somehow, he found the strength to turn her down. He wondered, afterward, where he had gotten the strength to refuse the hit. God? He doubted that very much. He was too far gone, and God certainly wasn't anywhere around for him. No, it had somehow come from deep inside, the realization that heroin was something he simply could not return to. He kept thinking that he couldn't fall any farther than he already had, but he knew that one hit of heroin would truly be the last step on the downward spiral. Later, he found that he was proud of himself for resisting the temptation. *"Pride goeth before destruction."* That was also in the Bible somewhere, but right then he couldn't remember exactly where.

The months passed and nothing changed for him. Occasionally the thought passed through his mind that he ought to call Gus and let him know he was okay. Well, not exactly okay but at least still alive, but he never bothered to actually make the call. He had convinced himself that not a soul in the world really cared one way or the other whether he was alive or not.

A year passed, and his funds finally started to deplete. He needed to work to support his drinking, smoking, and prostitute habits, but he was in no condition to keep a steady job anywhere. Who was going to hire a drunk? What kind of work could he possibly do when he was inebriated most of his waking hours? Oh, he still had enough money to last him quite a while, but the reality was that in the end he was going to run out. He needed to find something that would at least pay for his lodging.

He started asking in the bars he was frequenting. He would fit right in there. It took a few weeks, but he finally found one that was willing to exchange a cot in a back room for "janitorial services." He was cleaning the filthy bathrooms, scrubbing the toilets, in exchange for a place to sleep. The bartender threw in some free drinks and snacks; he had it made.

A few weeks passed and it was obvious to the rest of the regular patrons that Dave was a permanent fixture of sorts. The women were taking notice, and finally one lonely soul asked the bartender if he was "available," and if so, what was the going price for his services?

"I don't know what he charges. Why don't you come back tomorrow after I have a chance to talk things over with him and I'll have an answer for you then."

At first Dave was appalled at the suggestion that he perform for money.

"Look, you're paying women to have sex with them for your enjoyment. Why not get paid for doing the same thing? You get your fun, they get theirs, and you have an income instead of always shelling it out. Makes perfect sense to me. You already have that room in the back, so you won't have to rent out a room or anything. You give me ten percent of your take and I'll throw in all your meals for free in exchange. What do you say? You're really not out anything but your time, and you seem to have plenty of that."

"I'll think about it, how's that?"

"I need to know by tomorrow, since I promised the lady who desires your services an answer by then. Hey, it's not every man that is so good-looking the women are ready to pay him for what they want."

So Dave became a male prostitute. It was that easy. He always used protection, and with his good manners and looks, he had as many customers as he wanted as the word spread. In fact, he wanted no customers at all, but the money was good, he was popular, and he now got his meals for free along with his bed.

He told himself that he didn't care. He told himself every day that he deserved exactly what he was getting. He had asked for all of it all on his own, and he had no one else to blame. It didn't matter anymore how far down he went; he was too far away for God to ever find him again. There was no going back. *"The wages of sin is death."* Still.

As the corruption spread in his soul, his despair grew. He was totally unaware of the actual depths of his depravity and the price he was slowly paying. Oh, he knew it was all sinful and very, very wrong, but somehow he was personally distant from the reality of his situation. It was all happening to someone else, not him. He was emotionally detached.

Physically, he had everything he needed and wanted. Food, shelter, sex, drinks, cigarettes; he had it all and enough money to really enjoy it. He had everything but heroin.

One woman became a regular customer of his. She was in her forties, he thought, always very clean and polite. She was well dressed, appeared rather affluent, and wore a large diamond wedding set. He had asked her once if her husband had any idea what she was doing at night, but she just smiled and told him it was none of his business. He asked no further questions. It was obvious that she had developed more than a little fondness for Dave, and she began offering various "tips" for his excellent service. At first it was extra money, then occasionally she brought him homemade baked goods. Twice she brought him a new shirt, still in the plastic.

And then one evening, after services were properly "rendered," she dressed slowly and then lowered her face to his to take one more kiss from him.

"I'm leaving you a special gift tonight, sugar. A very special gift. Hope you enjoy it. I'll see you again maybe tomorrow night and you can tell me how you liked it, okay?" She smiled knowingly as she left his room, closing the door softly behind her.

He lay naked in the darkness for some time before finally turning on the light to see what she had left him this time. On the little table next to the cot was a small, pristine, paper bag, folded at the top to conceal the contents. He opened it slowly, wondering what special "goodie" she had brought him.

He nearly dropped the bag when he saw what was inside. It was a syringe, filled with a cloudy liquid, and a thin rubber tourniquet. Heroin. A gift for a fallen pastor. His gut churned with the turmoil the sight of that syringe brought him. He wanted it so badly he began to literally salivate in anticipation. *I can't. I just can't.* But even as the words spun through his brain, he found himself reaching for the items.

He reclined on the cot, his back against the wall, the syringe in one hand and the tourniquet in the other. Tears seeped unheeded as he stared at what he held in his hands.

Reason entered his mind just long enough for him to realize that some caution was needed. He rose from the cot, went to the door, and quietly turned the lock. This was something to be done in private, and he couldn't risk being discovered.

Walking back to his cot, he positioned the lamp closer to him; he needed to see his veins clearly. Resting once more with his back against the wall, he held out his left arm, staring at it before applying the tourniquet. Scars from his previous years of addiction shimmered in small, shiny welts along the vein tracks in his arm. Old friends.

Tourniquet in place, he inhaled deeply with supreme satisfaction, located his target, and then began to insert the needle.

The needle would not go in. He tried once more. The needle bent but would not penetrate his skin. Again, and yet again. His frustration mounted with each failure.

Was the scar tissue the problem? He switched the tourniquet to his right upper arm, pumped his fist, and waited for a vein to rise; it didn't take long. He was a little clumsy with his left hand, but try as he might, the needle would not penetrate his skin. Finally, he gave up, ripping the tourniquet off and throwing both it and the syringe across the room where they bounced off the opposite wall. What? He nearly screamed out loud in his anger and tears of frustration welled up in his eyes.

When his tears had dried and he had calmed somewhat, he dressed and went out to the bar where he sat dejectedly on a stool. The bartender knew him well and soon there was a tumbler of whiskey in front of him. He gulped it down and asked for another.

A couple of women approached him, their eyes questioning.

"Go away, girls. Not tonight."

"Aw, come on, we need you, honey."

"I said, not tonight."

"How about we . . . ?"

Dave slammed his fist violently on the bar's surface. "Another day, another time. Not now. Leave me alone."

The girls walked away, mumbling as they went. Dave had never turned them down before.

He sat there for some time, nursing his second drink, alone and lonely.

"Are you lost, friend?"

Dave turned to look at the man suddenly sitting next to him. There had been no one else at the bar when he sat down, and he certainly hadn't noticed anyone coming over. He wasn't usually rude to anyone, but tonight was different. He wanted to be drunk and alone. He wanted that hit of heroin so bad he could taste it, and his frustration at his inability to inject it knew no bounds.

"What's it to you?"

"You look lost. Maybe I can help."

"I don't think so. No one can help. Leave me alone." He took another swallow.

"I can help. Why don't you let me?"

Dave turned to look at him then, ready to knock the man off his stool in his growing anger. His glare met the blackest eyes he had ever seen. Dark, shining eyes full of compassion. He was Crow, obviously from the reservation. With long hair tied back into a ponytail, a threadbare denim work jacket, and roughened, wrinkled hands, he was very old. His face was deeply lined, etched with craters that hinted at the years and hardships he had seen in his time.

"What do you want?"

"I just want to talk to you. I can help."

"Thanks, but no one can help me now."

"God can, if you let him." It was spoken softly.

"Mister, you don't know what you're talking about. I left God a long time ago." Tears glistened in his eyes, adding to his frustration.

"He hasn't left you, son."

At that, Dave got up and walked back to his room. He didn't need an old man telling him, Dave Benson, former pastor, about God. God would never take him back and use him again after all he had done. He had betrayed his savior, and he would have to pay the penalty.

Entering the small room again, he picked up the items he had thrown on the floor, deciding to try it one more time, and again, the needle bent but would not pierce his skin. *Why won't it go in? It used to be so easy for me, like breathing, and now?*

He pondered his dilemma. A needle that bent? Finally, a distant memory came back to him. Allie had told him that when she was pregnant, before giving birth, when the nurse tried to start an IV, the needle had bent. It had finally gone in, but the nurse had laughed and told her that pregnant women often had very tough skin and the needles bent often. Well, he sure wasn't pregnant, but at least there was nothing supernatural about the whole thing. He wasn't the first one that couldn't get the job done.

An hour later he went back out to the bar. There were several men seated there now, but the old Indian was gone. Curious, he asked Pete, the bartender about the man.

"Pete, remember that old man that sat next to me when I was out here earlier? I'm just wondering if you happen to know him?"

"What man are you talking about, Dave? I don't remember seeing you talking to anyone. You were all alone out here, just you and your whiskey."

"No, there was an old Indian that sat next to me. He had a ponytail and was wearing a jean jacket. Lots of lines in his face. Remember?"

"I think the booze finally got to you, man. There was no one sitting next to you. Sorry."

Dave stared at Pete in bewilderment. There had in fact been an Indian sitting next to him at the bar. He knew it. He had been as real as he himself was. Shaking his head, he looked around for another customer. It wasn't long before he was escorting another woman back to his room. He was smiling courteously once more.

Chapter 28

It was nearly a week before his heroin benefactor returned. He was happy to see her, hoping she might leave him another "tip." Alone together in his dingy room, they sat on the cot for a few moments before removing their clothing.

"Did you enjoy my gift last time, Dave? I brought it special for you."

He wasn't quite sure how to respond. Should he feign ignorance? Protest that he didn't use drugs? Say that he had no idea what was in that syringe?

"What gave you the idea that I would like your gift?"

"The tracks on your arms, silly. Anybody could tell you use. Didn't you like it?" She smiled sweetly at him.

"Loved it, if you must know. Great tip. I do have a request though."

"What's that, two hits instead of just one?" She laughed out loud. "It's not cheap, you know, and I'm already paying you plenty."

"Well, if you plan to tip me again, how about powder next time. I know it's not quite as good as the liquid, but it's easier for me to use. What do you say?"

"Treat me right tonight?"

"Don't I always?" He smiled broadly at her. "How about I show you an extra special time tonight, and if I deliver, you come back sooner?"

"Let's make a deal. You satisfy me next time for free, and I'll bring you what you've requested. Sound fair?"

"Very. Let me make a special impression on you, my dear." He lowered her onto her back and proceeded to make good on his promise.

She returned in three days; his eyes lit up when he saw her as he anticipated the gift she would be bringing him. A needle might not go in, but as long as he was breathing, he could certainly snort a hit just fine.

She was dressed especially nice this evening and had obviously taken extra care in her appearance.

He met her as she walked in, and, taking her arm, escorted her directly to his room. "Well, did you bring it?" Expectation shone in his eyes.

Laughing, she pushed his chest until he was forced to sit on the cot. "Eager, aren't you! Yes, I brought you some. Powder, just like you wanted. But first, you must do for me what you do best, like we agreed, okay?"

"Come here, woman, and let me get down to business. I promise to make tonight very memorable for you." And he did.

After she left, he opened the paper bag, and there it was in a plastic pouch; heroin in powder form. He felt giddy with anticipation, salivating once again with pleasure at the release he knew was coming.

Pouring some carefully on a piece of the paper bag, he rolled a dollar bill up into a small tube and lowered his face to the powder. Just as he inhaled deeply, a small breath of air scattered the fine powder everywhere.

"What the . . . " There was no fan in the room and he had been holding his breath as he prepared to inhale. He tapped some more powder on the piece of brown paper and tried again. And again, a soft swish of air from somewhere blew the powder out of his reach.

Angry now, he tried one more time, and once more a small burst of air from out of nowhere blew his prize away. There was no more heroin.

He pounded his fist on the table in frustration, and just as he had done the other day when the syringe failed him, he went out to the bar for a stiff drink. This time he looked carefully around him before he sat. There were two cowboys sitting together at the far end of the bar, but aside from them, he was alone. Pete brought him the usual.

He was on his fourth drink, gulping from a tumbler instead of a shot glass, when he heard the voice again.

"You are still lost, my friend." It was him again, the old Indian, wearing the same outfit as the last time.

"Nothing has changed, if you must know. But I'm a little drunk and I'm not even sure at this point that you are real."

Laughter, soft and deep. "Oh, I'm very real, have no doubt."

"What's your name then?"

"Alex. Alex Two Bears, and yes, I live here on the Reservation, and I am indeed very old."

"How old is old?"

"Not for you to know, my friend. The important thing is that I am here to help you find your way back. That's all that matters."

"Forget it. I don't need to go anywhere. And I'm not lost." He turned back to his drink, the Indian beside him forgotten. When he finally rose to leave, the man was gone.

He staggered slowly back to his small, dark room, eager to pass out on the cot once more. He reached for the lamp to turn off the offensive light when he saw it; his old, worn Bible was lying right there on the small table next to his cot. *How did that get here?* He shoved it to the rear of the table, turned out the light, and rolled over onto his side. He would pack it away in the morning. He was alone again.

Dave started going out for walks in the early morning hours just after the bar closed and shortly before dawn. The fresh air felt good in a way he couldn't explain, and he enjoyed his solitary walks in the Montana darkness, when everyone else was cozy, warm, and sleeping. He was alone, and he liked that. After Christmas the Northern Lights floated above him, undulating in their colorful dance across the sky. He would stop and watch them as long as he could stand the cold, and then move on. He walked when it was cold and clear, as well as when it snowed and walking was difficult. It was all the same to him; life was difficult, something to be endured.

January rolled around, and winter held the Big Sky Country in a firm, unrelenting grasp. Twenty degrees below zero was not uncommon, and the wind often blew, howling like something demented. He was already cold from his constant torment, so the frigid temperature made no difference to him. It was all the same.

A strong storm had blown up just before closing time, but Dave was looking forward to his nightly walk anyway. He had worked hard cleaning the bathrooms during the day and "working" during the evening. The bar had closed, work was done for the night, and he craved some of that fresh, cold, Montana winter air. Donning the heaviest coat he owned, he wrapped his neck and head with a wool scarf, lit a cigarette, and headed out the back door for a short, invigorating walk. The temperature hovered around zero, snow falling heavily with the wind picking up by the minute, bringing a ruddy blush to his cheeks and rendering his lips stiff. The snowplows wouldn't be out for a few hours yet and he was alone, braving the harsh weather. The snow was soon over a foot deep, covering the ground unevenly.

Through the wind-driven snow he saw a white mound directly in his path. It appeared to be a body buried nearly completely in the swirling whiteness. He moved as fast as he was able in the deep snow, hoping the person was still alive.

Brushing the snow off as fast as he could, he saw it was a man, wrapped snugly in a large blanket. He gathered him up close to his body, terrified at the possibilities before him. Brushing the snow from the man's face, he recognized the old Indian from the bar.

"Mister! Are you okay? Answer me, say something?"

The man's cold lips could barely articulate words, but he groaned.

"Come on, get up. You have to get up and get going or you're going to freeze to death out here, and from the looks of you, it won't be long." He helped the old man to his feet and held him close to keep him upright.

"Where do you live, I'll take you home. Speak to me!" He had walked quite a distance from the bar; hopefully the man lived fairly close by. Dave could feel the cold emanating from the old man's frame.

A gloved hand came up and pointed across the street.

"Over there?"

The old Indian nodded in assent as Dave held him as tightly as he could, slowly trudging through the snow across the street to a shabby dwelling that looked as if the weight of the new snow would surely topple it before morning. It was a building that should have been condemned.

"This it?"

The man nodded, and Dave, finding the door unlocked, staggered into the hut with his burden. Depositing the man on a threadbare couch, he went back to shut the door, and then collapsed onto the floor in exhaustion. Drunk, cold, tired, hungry, and still alone even with this old man who had tried to befriend him, Dave was as lost as he had ever been. He passed out in seconds.

He awoke two hours later. Looking around, he found he was alone in the darkened room. A lamp gave off a soft glow in an adjacent room, and he heard Alex Two Bears moving around in there. He sat up, soaking up the warmth that enveloped him. The room was shabby and sparsely furnished with a worn couch and two wooden chairs. He stayed on the floor, wanting badly to go back to sleep. Pulling a small flask from his pocket, he drank deeply until he felt the alcohol spreading throughout his body, warming his veins. It left him lethargic and very relaxed.

"You're awake, I see."

Dave looked up at him with bleary eyes. "I guess you could call it that."

"Thanks for bringing me home. I could have died out there in that cold."

"You're welcome, but what on earth was an old man like you doing out in that weather?"

"Taking a walk, just like yourself, my friend."

"How do you know I was taking a walk when I found you?"

"What else would you be doing after midnight in the snow?"

"Fine. So what were you doing huddled on the ground like that? I nearly killed myself getting you back here."

"Oh, I slipped and fell and then I was just too cold to get up. But I wasn't worried. I knew you would be coming for me."

Dave looked at him sharply with narrowed eyes. "Just what do you mean by that?" Something was going on here that he didn't like. Was this some sort of "Indian magic" that he had heard about over the years? Was he dreaming? Too much booze? He closed his eyes.

"What do you want from me?"

"I want nothing from you, nothing at all."

"Then why? What?"

"How about I make us both a nice cup of hot chocolate. It's perfect weather for hot chocolate." He didn't wait for an answer but turned his back and ambled slowly from the room, leaving Dave alone in the shadows.

He knew I'd be coming along? That's what he said. How could he possibly know I'd be out in that snow? He shook his head in bewilderment. He must have heard the old man wrong. There was no way the Indian could have known he'd be walking at that time of the night, or that he'd be walking in his direction, for that matter. No, he could not have known.

Alex returned shortly with the two mugs of hot chocolate. Steam from the hot liquid rose in welcome for the weary men. Dave remained sitting on the floor while Alex took the couch.

"Thanks, Alex. This does look good."

"You're welcome. Nothing like hot chocolate on a night like this." He smiled warmly at his guest. "Why don't you sit in one of these chairs?" He motioned with his free hand to the two wooden chairs that decorated the room.

"Thanks anyway, but the floor's fine with me. Hope you don't mind if I . . ." Dave didn't finish the sentence, but pulled the flask from his pocket again and poured a hefty amount into the hot drink.

"No, I don't mind. But I think you do."

"If I minded I wouldn't pour it in, now, would I?"

They sat and drank in silence for some time. Finally Alex spoke. "Dave, when are you coming back?"

"What? What are you talking about? Come back where? I don't have any place to go back to." He scowled and then looked squarely into Alex Two Bears' black, liquid eyes. "You say you knew I would be coming for you tonight, and if you knew that then you must know that I have nowhere else to go. No place I need or even want to be, for that matter." He lowered his head and took another sip.

"Back to your Father, Dave."

Dave's head snapped up at that declaration. "My father's been dead for years. I have no father to go back to."

"Not your earthly father, Dave, your real one."

"Just what do you think you know about me? I'll tell you what you know—nothing! You don't know the first thing about me except that I'm living in that bar." Angry at the old man's presumptions, he rose to his feet and began pacing.

"You're wrong, Dave. I know all about you."

"Yeah? Like what, exactly? What is it that you think you know?" He swallowed the last of the hot chocolate in two quick gulps and continued pacing.

"I know you're a pastor and you have left the church and your calling."

Dave stopped in his tracks. *Did I say too much one night when I was drunk? I can't remember? I don't think I did, though. No, I'm sure I didn't. So how?*

"What makes you say something like that? You don't know anything about me, old man. Nothing at all."

"I know you think your sin is greater than God's grace; that as a pastor your sins are somehow greater than anyone else's. Pride?"

Dave snorted in disgust at this. "Hardly. Not pride, that's for sure. What? You think there's something to be proud of that my sins are so great?" He laughed out loud.

"Don't you think you've run long enough and hard enough?"

Dave looked at him intently. Something was happening, and he couldn't quite grasp it. "I'll never be able to run far enough. Never. You seem to know everything about me so you must understand that about me too."

"You've run far enough, young man. It's time to stop, to stand, and to surrender once gain."

"I can't. I've wandered too far." Somehow, in some way, Dave understood that this old Indian did indeed know all about him, and with that realization he felt a freedom he hadn't felt in a very long time. There was no need to hide anything since Alex seemed to know all about him already. He stared into nothingness, alone with his guilt. "I've fallen too far, and there's no going back. I can't."

"Dave, didn't you see that sign along the highway when you drove into town that first day?"

"What sign? There are lots of signs along the road." He looked puzzled.

"That old weather-beaten sign that says, '*Jesus is Lord on the Crow Reservation.*' That hand-lettered sign that sort of stands alone." Alex's voice remained calm, unhurried, almost a monotone. Soothing, comforting, and yet authoritative.

Dave thought for a moment. "Yeah, I remember seeing that sign. So what?"

"Jesus is Lord. You believe that to be true, still, after everything you've been through, don't you?"

"Of course I do. I never stopped believing in God or His Son. Never. I just can't come back, not after everything I've done. I'm not worthy to be forgiven, and I can't forgive myself. Let's start there."

"And just exactly what have you done that is vile enough to make God leave you, at least in your mind?" His face was expressionless, a mask, yet his eyes were riveting.

"I thought you said you knew everything about me. You tell me."

"Dave, He never left you; you left Him. You didn't have to do that."

Dave turned and pounded his fist into the dirty wall. "You don't understand, old man! I betrayed him! Over and over again, I betrayed Him!"

"So? He didn't leave you."

"I left because I'm too ashamed. I can't face Him in my shame. How can I? I was a pastor, for heaven's sake!"

"Yes, exactly. For heaven's sake, Dave. He's waiting for you, you know. You can't run forever; He won't let you."

"My shame and my guilt . . ." Tears glistened in Dave's eyes as the torment within him raged.

"Dave, is there a sin you can think of that Christ didn't die for? Any single sin? Any combination of sins and betrayals?"

Silence permeated the shadowed room and Dave fought with himself.

"I was a pastor, Alex. A pastor, don't you understand? How can He possibly ever forgive my sins as a pastor? I was supposed to be an example, a leader, a counselor. But in fact I'm nothing but a hypocrite. A lousy, stinking hypocrite."

"You preached it for years, forgiveness of sin and grace. Why can't you believe it for yourself? Are you somehow less in the Father's eyes than anyone else? What makes you think it applies to everyone but you?"

"I told you, I was a pastor! How can He forgive that?"

"Romans 8:28 ring a bell with you? *'And we know that all things work together for good to them that love God, to them who are the called according to His purpose.'*"

"And just how can everything I've done possibly work for my good? I might have been called, once, but look at me now. That doesn't sound too true of me at the moment, now does it." It was a statement, not a question. He shook his head in rejection.

Alex lowered his voice dramatically. "Then what about Romans 8: 38 and 39? Remember those two verses? You preached them often enough over the years. *'For I am persuaded that neither death, nor life, nor angels, nor principalities, nor powers, nor things present, nor things to come, nor height, nor depth, nor any other creature, shall be able to separate us from the love of God, which in is Christ Jesus our Lord.'* Do you really think these verses are true for everyone but you?"

"Everyone but me. I told you, I've fallen too far." He shook his head as his tears began to fall.

"Do you still love Him, Dave?"

"Oh, yes! He's my Lord and my Savior! But I'm not worthy!"

"You love Him, and you believe Him. You're repentant, and that's all that's required.

He has plans for you, Dave. Big plans. You are still called and loved. Just let Him be your Father once more." He rose to his feet. "I'll be back in a moment. Just rest, okay?"

Dave waved at the Indian, too choked with emotion to talk.

He sat on the floor, alone in the room, silence like a soft cloak enveloping him, as he cried noiselessly. Finally he looked up and around at his surroundings. As his gaze roamed the room, suddenly he uttered an audible gasp.

Why hadn't he seen it before? It was obvious and stood out in stark contrast to the dull walls. Rising to his feet, he walked over to the painting, crudely framed and hung on the bare wall. It was only a cheap print, but its message came across to the former pastor with a blunt and powerful force.

It was the well-known picture of Christ standing at the door of a house, his fist raised in a knocking gesture. *"Behold, I stand at the door and knock; if any man hear my voice, and open the door, I will come in to him, and will sup with him, and he with me."*

He sank to his knees in front of the picture, reality finally dawning and washing over him as the Spirit filled him as if for the first time. *If any man—that verse really does say "any man." Jesus saves everyone who repents and calls on Him, even fallen pastors. Even Dave Benson.* That song came back that had haunted him for so many months, only this time new words comprised the lines.

*"Somebody's knockin', should I let Him in?
Oh, it's King Jesus, would you look at Him?
I've heard about Him but I never dreamed
He'd come lookin' just for me!"*

"Father!" Dave shouted the word, and then fell prostrate on his face as he had in the past, as he finally allowed God's love to wash over him and cleanse him once more. He sobbed for what seemed an eternity before exhaustion overcame him and he slept.

Sometime the next morning Dave awoke to find himself on the dusty floor in a ramshackle building. He was alone in the room, which was empty of any trappings or furniture. An empty, vacant building that had once been a home to someone.

He rose slowly to his feet, rubbing his hands against the cold that was seeping through his frame. Where was he? How had he gotten here? Oh, right. The snowstorm and the old Indian. But where was Alex Two Bears? He looked around the room. There was no couch and no chairs, only that cheap print on the wall of the picture of Christ knocking at the door.

"Alex?" There was no answer. He was truly alone.

But something was different. He was different. It took him a moment, but then he smiled. Yes, he definitely was, in fact, very different.

He stood there for a moment, lost in thought as warmth, no longer coming from a bottle, washed through his body. He felt almost euphoric, as if he might be actually glowing. Suddenly he remembered the heroin he was unable to inject or inhale. God's intervention was the only explanation for his salvation from that old nemesis.

Thank you, Father, thank you! He bowed his head and prayed for some time, silently, communing with his Savior and Lord. Then he turned and walked into the forlorn room that had once been a kitchen, and, pulling the flask from his pocket, he slowly poured the contents down the drain. Smiling for the first time in months, he walked out of the ramshackle hovel and started back toward the bar that had been his home for so long.

The sun was out with the dawn of a new day; it glistened on the fresh snow, sparkling as only fresh snow can. It was beautiful. For the first time since leaving Allie, Dave was able to see beauty around him. He stopped for a moment and marveled at his surroundings. He had missed so much! The air was clean and fragrant to his starving senses. He breathed deeply and suddenly realized he had no thought of a cigarette. The craving was gone.

He twirled around in the snow, and, scooping up hands filled with fluffy white crystals, threw his prize flakes up into the air, laughing as he did so. Freedom. He had forgotten how wonderful freedom was, and he knew he was truly free at last. He stopped, staring up at the brilliant blue of that big Montana sky. "Father, you are so good!" He was shouting, and he didn't care if anyone heard him or not.

Back at the bar he asked to borrow the phone. He dialed the number he still retained in his memory, and waited patiently. It rang five times before he heard a voice on the other end.

"Hello? Chase the Wind Stables."

"Gus? It's me, Dave." The silence on the other end was palpable. He smiled.

"Dave? Where? How . . ."

"I'm fine, Gus, I'm really fine." He couldn't help himself and laughed out loud. "Would it be okay with you if I came back?" He was unable to see the tears that glistened in his friend's eyes at this request.

"Please come! Dave, are you really all right?"

"I'm back, Gus. I'm truly back. I'll see you in a few days."

He wasn't sure what God had planned for him now. He could never go back to Grace Bible Church, he knew that, but that wasn't the only place on God's earth that he could be of use. He had a story to tell, and there was no lack of people to tell it to. He would start right here in this bar, with its patrons and his now-former customers. There were a lot of lost souls here, just as he himself had been, and they needed to hear the Good News too. Jesus truly does save anyone, no matter how lost; he was living proof.

A week later he packed his few belongings and headed back to Bozeman and his friends. His Bible rested prominently on the seat beside him. Three people had been saved in the bar before he left the Reservation; three lost souls now found. As he drove north he once again passed that rustic hand-lettered sign proclaiming "***Jesus is Lord on the Crow Reservation***," and he found himself humming the tune to the song that had plagued him for so long, the new words ringing in his head:

> *"Somebody's knockin', should I let Him in?*
> *Oh, it's King Jesus, would you look at Him?*
> *I've heard about Him but I never dreamed*
> *He'd come lookin' just for me!"*

"Somebody's Knockin"

Someone removed the original hand-lettered sign mentioned in this book several years ago. The new, full color sign shown below replaced it in 2013.

"The Crow tribal government sponsored a large billboard sign proclaiming 'Jesus Christ Is Lord on the Crow Nation' in late December . . . 2013 called, 'The Crow Tribal Legislature to honor God for his great blessings upon the Crow Tribe and to proclaim Jesus Christ as Lord of the Crow Indian Reservation.'" (indiancountrymedianetwork.com)

About the Author

"Somebody's Knockin'" is Catherine's fourth novel set in the Big Sky Country of Montana.

Also by Catherine Boyd is the Windchase Family Saga trilogy. *"Flight of the Crow,"* first in the series, is followed by *"Raven's Redemption,"* and finally *"Aspen's Ascent."*

Catherine holds a BS degree in Agricultural Production, Animal Science as well as an Associate degree in Nursing. She spent thirty-five years living and ranching in Montana.

After her divorce she worked in the area as a general ranch hand and then as a sheepherder near Bridger, MT. After becoming a Registered Nurse, she worked in small rural hospitals and nursing homes.

Made in the USA
Middletown, DE
10 January 2020